Earth Angel

Judie Stein

authorHOUSE®

AuthorHouse™
1663 Liberty Drive, Suite 200
Bloomington, IN 47403
www.authorhouse.com
Phone: 1-800-839-8640

First published by AuthorHouse 3/13/2009

ISBN: 978-1-4343-8668-7 (sc)
ISBN: 978-1-4343-8666-3 (hc)

Library of Congress Control Number: 2008903980

Printed in the United States of America
Bloomington, Indiana

This book is printed on acid-free paper.

ACKNOWLEDGEMENTS

My #1 thanks to my husband, IRA FRIEDMAN.

I bow to Writer/Producer/Director, DAVID WICKES, whose help and guidance made EARTH ANGEL a reality.

Heartfelt thanks to URIELA OBST SAGIV for her encouragement and editing.

Thanks to the compliments of Hollywood Uber Maestros, RON MEYER and DANIEL MELNICK, courage was given to take EARTH ANGEL out of the freezer and into the world,

Hugs and dances around ANNA-MAIRE BUSS of BUSSROOT who made the words of EARTH ANGEL come alive with her design.

MOST THANKS to the ANGELS who gave me this story to write.

"THE ONLY REAL TIME IS THAT OF THE OBSERVER, WHO CARRIES WITH HIM HIS OWN SPACE AND TIME."

ALBERT EINSTEIN

CHAPTER ONE

They stopped the forced feeding three months ago. She still hasn't had any food or water.

How does she survive?"

"Says she can convert light into energy and store it in her body - like a plant."

"You've got to be kidding."

"No, I'm not."

Detective James Parker sat in the passenger side of a gray unmarked police car flipping through files on his lap. He tried swallowing the excitement in his voice, but he wasn't succeeding.

His partner Sergeant Richard Boyle glowered at him. In the department for over thirty years, Boyle was close to retiring and pissed to be stuck with an ambitious rookie who was studying for a law degree and taking this case too seriously. This enthusiasm was making Boyle's thin patience, thinner.

"A precedent was set," Parker continued haltingly. "Her lawyer, James Scanlon - know who he is?"

Boyle glowered.

"Big time!" Parker continued, ignoring Boyle's reaction. "Scanlon brought in evidence that people can exist without food, citing an Indian woman who had not eaten for 55 years, another in Canada who started fasting in 1923..."

"They must have been skinny," Boyle laughed, patting his ample stomach bulging over the buckle of a cowboy belt, engraved, C.O.P..

Parker pulled a file out. "The background on this case is interesting. The state Supreme Court overturned a lower Court decision to continue intravenous feeding against the patient's will. It's all here in the transcript. Wanna read it?" Parker held the paper out to Boyle who waved it away.

"Whataya nuts? I'm driving. You read it."

Parker cleared his throat. "The Supreme Court ruling in the case of Jenny Webster, declared unanimously that she has a 'fundamental right' to refuse food or drink."

"Ha!" Boyle snorted, "rights..."

Parker went on. "After due deliberation, Judge Robert Gray wrote that for self-determination to have any meaning, it cannot be subject to the scrutiny of anyone else's conscience or sensibilities. It is the individual who must live or die with the course of treatment chosen or rejected, not the state."

"Yeah?" asked Boyle, skeptical.

Parker raised his eyebrows and smiled. "She's been in that hospital without eating for three months." He paused, waiting. Again Boyle didn't react, so he continued. "According to the reports she's healthy as a horse."

Boyle frowned. "I don't believe it."

"But its here. A matter of record."

"It's bullshit. The whole thing's a put on. Someone's slipping her something. Can't you see it? You've got a lot to learn!"

2

Boyle gunned the gas pedal of the late model Chevrolet, swerving around a corner and barely missing a young woman pushing a baby stroller. Parker didn't seem to notice as he searched to get his bearings. The car slammed to a stop in front of a two-story apartment that hadn't seen a paintbrush in more than ten years. On a dusty lawn in front, a gaggle of rumpled old people sat on aluminum folding chairs, gossiping in the pale sunlight. Parker checked the address against a document in his hand. He hadn't expected Jenny Webster's apartment to be in a place like this.

Feeling conspicuous as he climbed out of the sedan, Parker felt six pairs of curious eyes turning to stare as a gust of wind revealed the gun holstered beneath his jacket. Boyle nodded to the group as Parker marched stiffly past them, his eyes straight ahead, his neck prickling with the old people's stares. Across the street two young boys, their pale skinny legs bruised and scratched, kicked fiercely at each other as they played soccer on the sidewalk.

Boyle opened the front door using a passkey. The elderly audience gazed knowingly. They knew who those men were. Cops. They shifted in their plastic webbing, watching the action like it was a television screen.

An old woman with skin like crumpled tissue paper pushed her loose teeth back against her gums with a practiced finger and hissed to a fat woman in the next chair. "It's about that girl on the second floor."

"She hasn't been here for awhile," the plump woman agreed.

"Right."

Boyle puffed his way up the stairs to the second floor and followed Parker down the peeling corridor to apartment 2A. "I can't believe this fasting business," he wheezed as he fumbled through his master keys. "She's got to be getting something, pills, water - someone's passing her something."

"Not according to the hospital," said Parker, wrinkling his nose against the sour cooking smells that permeated the hallway.

"Hospitals," snorted Boyle. "What the hell do they know? I knew a guy once - cat burglar. Climbed out of a hospital window every night for two weeks.   Hid his loot in the Director's office."   He chuckled. "One night the guy broke his leg trying to climb back in. I read him his rights while they set the bone."

A child screamed in the apartment across the hall. A woman's shrill voice yelled back. There was a sound of breaking crockery.

"Nice neighbors," observed Parker as Boyle jammed a key into the lock. The door opened.

"Jesus H. Christ," breathed Boyle.

"What is it?" asked Parker.

Boyle didn't answer but walked straight in. The apartment was sumptuous. Elegant furniture beautifully placed on polished hardwood floors glinted in shafts of pale sunlight filtered by oriental window screens. There were potted ferns and palms casting geometric shadows on the glossy white walls, and a white marble Parsons table used as a desk with a sleek lap top computer placed precisely in the center. Brushed aluminum trays held papers, floor to ceiling bookshelves covered one wall, and a mass of elegantly framed lithographs covered another.

"Why in the hell would she live in a neighborhood like this?" Parker whispered. Chills ran down his spine as he looked at the exquisite room. He had never seen anything like it except in magazines. He wondered at the dichotomy; extreme elegance in working class rent control. There was a paradox here, a huge contradiction.

"Cheap rent," said Boyle, as if reading Parker's mind. "She makes decent, but not great money at the News. Maybe the furnishings were gifts from her boyfriend - her late boyfriend."

Parker shook his head. It didn't fit.

Boyle picked up a book from the coffee table and frowned. "Take a look at this," he said handing it to Parker. The title read "Tantric Art; a Guide to Ecstasy". "Some kind of porn. Keep it as evidence."

Parker started to say something, thought better of it, and put the book in a plastic bag he unfolded from his briefcase.

There was a slight thump from the bedroom. Parker put down the briefcase and moved toward the bedroom door.

"Where are you going?" asked Boyle irritably.

Parker didn't answer. The bedroom was like the rest of the apartment - stylishly furnished with a thick piled carpet and a king sized bed. Parker looked up, fascinated by the folds of a huge and delicate canopy that hung from the ceiling like a softly billowing tent.

"Nice place for an orgy." Boyle was standing beside him. "Can you imagine what that cost?" he said, shaking his head at the opulence of it all. "I could have put my kid through college with what's in this place." Boyle turned on his heel, making for the kitchen.

Parker wandered to the window and squinted through the blind. Down in the street, a bag lady was pushing a shopping cart piled high with debris gathered from heaven knows where. Parker turned and surveyed the room again. As with the rest of the apartment, everything was perfectly placed. Silk pajamas lay on a pillow, folded as if for a shop window display. On the opposite pillow sat a porcelain doll, smiling vacantly in a state of permanent welcome. Suddenly he frowned. His eyes had fixed upon a small water glass that was lying on the carpet close to the night table. Could this have caused the noise, which had drawn him into the room? Parker almost laughed at himself for thinking it. There was no breeze in here, and all the windows were closed. The noise had probably come from next door.

"Seen enough?" yelled Boyle from the living room. "Time for lunch."

Parker turned to see Boyle entering the bedroom with a crystal jar of almonds in his hand.

"Lunch?" he echoed.

"Yeah lunch, that stuff you eat off plates when you're hungry. What are you staring at?" asked Boyle, lifting the jar to his lips and shaking almonds into his mouth.

"Isn't that against regulations?"

"Perks of the job." Boyle chuckled. "She won't miss them. She's going to be in Clifton for awhile, and then prison."

Parker watched as his partner munched. "Clifton's an expensive sanitarium isn't it?"

"So," shrugged Boyle, "her boyfriend paid for it. Maybe it was the hospital bills that killed him.

"You know," said Parker. " I really don't understand this. How can we charge a woman with murder when she was locked away in a hospital room thirty miles from where her boyfriend died? It doesn't make sense."

"Look," said Boyle. "The D.A. thinks she did it, her fingerprints were there, and we have to find out how."

"It's crazy," said Parker. The charge can't stick."

"I don't know how she did it," said Boyle, "but she did, believe me."

"But how?" Parker's brow furrowed with exasperation. "She never left the sanitarium."

"Oh for Christ sakes," growled Boyle, finishing the almonds. "Don't you get it yet? Its an alibi."

"Some alibi! She was locked in a hospital room."

"Okay, so it's the greatest alibi ever - but, I've got a nose for these things. She did it and she's not going to get away with it."

"With what? They're not even sure how he died..."

"She sets up the alibi by asking the hospital attendant to call the police..."

"That's no reason to pin a murder rap on her."

"So, you tell me, how did she know this Jenkins guy was going to die?" challenged Boyle. "Do you think she was clairvoyant or something?"

Parker stared at the carpet.

"Come on, you're out of your depth. You need to eat. Food's good for the brain." Boyle turned back into the living room and opened Parker's brief case, methodically he tipped the contents of the aluminum trays into the case and began to close it.

"Wait," said Parker, crossing to the computer and picked it up. "If it's evidence you're after, it's here."

"Right," said Boyle, with a defiant look. "I was going to do that."

Parker stared back at him and snapped his case shut.

"We passed a place on the corner," said Boyle moving toward the front door. "Italian food. Cheap."

Parker glanced around the room for the last time, and then slowly followed Boyle out of the apartment. When the front door had clicked shut, only the soft ticking of the bedroom clock disturbed the silence. Then, a slight shadow flitted across the bedroom wall. Someone was moving beyond the half opened door. A woman's hand was picking up the fallen glass and replacing it neatly beside the lamp on the night table.

CHAPTER TWO

"Jenny," the gray-haired man said softly, "Jenny, please."

Sunlight was filtering through the barred window of the small visitor's room, painting a primitive mask of dark and light stripes across the face of the man sitting there. Opposite him sat a slim young woman, her straight blonde hair cut short, her hands folded primly in her lap like a nun awaiting benediction.

"Jenny," he said again, "will you please talk to me?"

She stayed silent. She used to call him Uncle James as a child, but now she could think of him only as a noun, "her attorney".

"Jenny, we're been here almost two hours," he was saying. "How can I help if you won't say anything?"

He got up and moved to the window, trying to control the exasperation he felt. He had known Jenny Webster since she was a baby. Her father had been one of his best friends. He had watched her grow into an intelligent adult and a fine journalist - yet here she was, in a sanitarium about to be indicted by the Grand Jury for murder and she was pulling the silent act.

"Jenny," he turned to her, "I'm going to say it again, what you've told me and the authorities is preposterous."

She didn't answer. It wasn't necessary. He had already made up his mind what to think.

"Can't you see why we're all concerned?" The moment he uttered the word "concerned" he knew it was a mistake. Too formal, too pompous. He shook his head self-deprecatingly. "Guess I'm sounding like a lawyer," he sighed.

She started to smile, and using that as an opening he took a few paces forward and squatted stiffly beside her chair. "Jenny, you have to trust me," his voice cracked.

Slowly she turned her head. "Please," he was saying, "please let me help you." The potted flower on the coffee table had caught her attention. It was wilting, bending, probably from the tension the attorney was creating. She tried to comfort it, send it soothing vibrations, but the flower didn't respond. It stayed bowed and unmoving.

He stiffly pulled himself up and went over to a small writing table. He sat at it and drummed his fingers on the leather top. "I don't know how much more we can do today. I'm not getting through to you. Can you understand my dilemma?"

Why should she answer him? She had already told him everything he should know. He just didn't want to accept it. When the Voices wanted to communicate with him, they would come through and talk. The hair on the nape of her neck tickled. The part she had shaven off was growing back. She had wanted to shave it again, this time all over, but the nurse had taken her razor away. Jenny had tried to explain that she needed a smooth head to receive transmissions, but the nurse had laughed.

Jenny smoothed back the hair at the top of her head, hoping she could stay receptive. She couldn't see the attorney very clearly, only the black and white stripes of light that passed through and over him.

He pushed his chair back abruptly. "Look Jenny, you could not have been with Tim when he died. He was in the mountains and you were in this hospital miles apart. There was no way you could have been in two places at the same time. You had a dream, and by improbable odds, it came true. That's it. Now stop telling that story."

She looked longingly out the window. The sun was starting to set.

"Tell me, Jenny..." His voice rose with impatience. "Did you think you saw Tim die when you were sleeping?"

She closed her eyes. He hadn't believed a word she had said.

He cleared his throat. "I know you didn't kill him."

Her hands gripped the sides of the chair. She had been there to oversee, to help Tim through to the other side. She had told him that many times. Why did he choose not to believe her?

He leaned closer, his elbows on his knees, his hands folded in front of him, pleading. "You saw him in a dream, like a movie in your head."

She merely stared, driving him off the chair and to the window. The reflected light wiped out his features. All she could see was the darkened outline of a human head, like the silhouette picture she used to have as a child. She had loved that picture - three dimensional with black felt figures pasted on top. She would lie in bed at night watching for hours the figures running up and down their black-felt stairway. The man turned to her. She could no longer see his face, only his swollen arthritic hands.

"According to the doctors you're suffering extreme trauma from the rape. I wish I could have gotten you to sign yourself out. Now, they're getting a court order to keep you here while the Grand Jury is investigating. I wish you hadn't ignored me. It could be too late."

She closed her eyes and inhaled deeply. He had not absorbed anything, and was resisting the possibility there might be a reality other than the one in which he was living.

His voice had a tinge of exasperation. "You want to play crazy. I'm beginning to think you are crazy for staying in this place and throwing your life away." He crumbled a paper.

Jenny shivered.

Scanlon softened. "I understand you may need some help, but you don't have to be locked away. There are better, more private ways of dealing with these fantasies of yours than being shut in here." His voice sounded hoarse. "If you keep up this crazy act, you're going to be lost." His voice broke; he took a deep breath to steady himself.

She didn't want to explain her beliefs to him again. The Voices weren't taking over and if she had to do it herself she'd get too emotional. He hadn't believed anything she had said about the conspiracy either. He did not want to understand.

"All right Jenny!" He startled her as he sat down beside her. "If you're going to continue your little game, I don't want any part of it." His narrowed eyes peered over his glasses at her.

Maybe she should try to explain once more. An inner jolt shook her, warning her to be silent.

The attorney slouched in his chair and swung it side to side. "They're putting together a competency hearing." He sounded weary. "If you are declared incompetent you may have to stay in the hospital for a very long time." He sighed.

Jenny tightened. He dismissed her belief that one could never be locked away, because one could always soar away in spirit.

"You can be flip," he was saying more loudly, "because you know underneath it all you can have your freedom. But once the Court sends in their own State appointed doctors for evaluation, they may declare you 'non compos mentis' and then it's a whole other matter."

She shuddered. He leaned closer. She wanted to draw away but she was frozen.

"If that happens there will be people deciding your fate who are not as gentle or considerate as we have been, and you won't be able to stay here. This is top of the line. I hope you never see the inside of a state mental hospital."

She had seen the inside of a state mental hospital. It was horrific. She stayed riveted.

He smiled with the discomfort of one who rarely smiles. "I've known you a long time. When your father made me Executor of his will, I took the trust seriously and vowed I'd care for you as if you were my daughter." His voice softened. "Jenny, I can help you."

She looked away. His words were compelling.

"You may have stepped beyond the comfortable boundaries of what society calls sanity, but I believe that one person's insanity is another person's reality. Who is to say where we should draw the line? I don't have that answer. But the State thinks it does." He rose and came uncomfortably close to her. She shrank away. He kept talking. "I do know sure as hell you didn't kill Tim. You're hurting yourself by saying the things you do. You're also hurting others who care."

She looked at the floor. If anyone wants to be hurt they're doing it to themselves. She only wanted to be herself, not another person's version. If people "cared", they'd open their eyes and give her respect, and not try to force her into a pre-fabricated mold.

He shook his head sadly. "Look..."

She had the power to leave. A piece of paper that said she could or could not do something meant nothing. She was free. She could leave her body.

He was looking increasingly sadder.

She smiled at his fear of insanity. Some of the "craziest" people in the hospital were her best friends. And they were the least crazy of any people she'd ever met. A lot less crazy than this man sitting next to her whose wife goes from one cosmetic surgery to another, whose daughter lives for trendy clothes and night clubs, and whose son deals drugs from the family estate's guest house.

Scanlon kept talking. "The minute you lose your legal rights, it could be disaster. Also, I think you better start eating something."

She straightened her back. She had told him about the Yogis who stay closed in caves for years without food. Although he had first resisted, when she threatened to get another lawyer, he used her information and got the court order to reverse the intravenous feeding. She smiled. He probably had thought she would not last this long.

He grabbed his cold cup of coffee and drained it. "You're a talented young woman. This is a waste. I ask you to save yourself and your answer is to smile and stare. All that talk about voices, your Guides, leaving your body, and now this fasting business. I'm glad to see you're getting nourishment from somewhere."

She felt her body tighten.

Scanlon started to speak again, but she could only see his lips. They were moving but no sound was coming from them. She felt his concern. It touched her. Were the Guides trying to teach her something? Did she have to go back to the world to test her new knowledge? What if she forgot it once she returned?

An inner vibration began rattling her. Thoughts were spinning. The hospital is easy. It's filled with kindred souls. Why does she have to go back to the chaos of society? Is it really it the circle of fate, the law of life that makes one repeat past mistakes and experiences?

She closed her eyes. The planet called Earth was beneath her. She could see skyscrapers, cars, factories, pollution, circling in a perfect blue and white sphere, spinning nearly uncontrollably in the openness of deep space.

She was at the edge of a treadmill now, leading toward the planet. She did not want to get back on it. She was terrified if she didn't, she would fall into an endless void. She never wanted to be helpless or ignorant again. CHANGE! CHOICES. What if they plunged her into the darkness of past mistakes, of sleeping wakefulness?

The chair was turning. The walls spinning. The floor pulling her down from her chair.

Big strong arms lifted her off the floor onto the sofa. She tried to pull away. She didn't want to be touched, didn't want the feel of someone else's skin against hers. Something strong was under her nose. Ammonia. Why did the Guides have him touch her? What were they preparing her for? Why was Tim gone? Why wasn't he here to protect her? What is this lesson? Graduation from here must be very far away.

She still had not mastered the hole in her heart that was Tim. It wouldn't close off the terrible feeling when she realized he was no longer with her. She was alone. She would forgot she could re-create him, draw a visual picture of such intensity that he could be made whole once again.

That she could step over the threshold of reality and enter the world beyond, the world where Tim still existed, where they could once again hold each other for what felt like many lifetimes. They came together more fully at those times than before he "died".

But she tended to forget that quite often now, falling instead into the despair of emptiness she labeled, Tim.

A fat black Mont Blanc pen moved across a yellow legal pad, grating into the paper, etching into her nerves. She had become very sensitive, experiencing things super physically, the simple action of pen against paper setting her nerves on edge. The attorney looked at her, assessing her. She let their eyes meet. He was relieved, and then upset to see she wasn't cringing. She was exhibiting great power. But of what kind?

He put on his veil of professionalism. "I'll try to come see you in the morning. If I can't I'll call. I told you, I leave for London tomorrow." He shifted, straightened, and weighed his words. "This talk about being in two places at the same time and higher powers is not good. You lose credibility."

"That's what the detectives said," Jenny whispered.

He was thrilled she spoke; yet shocked at her words.   "What?"

"The detectives said it doesn't make sense."

"What detectives?"

"The ones in my apartment."

"When?"

"While I've been here with you."

He leaned forward, intense.   She shrank away.   His energy was too strong, it was upsetting.

"How do you know that?"   His tone was grim.

"One of them almost caught me when I bumped into the night table."

He stared at her.   "What?" he asked again.

"The water glass fell to the floor."   A smile nearly entered her lips.

"I don't believe this."   He pulled his face into shadow.   His secretary had called just a short time before he landed to tell him a search warrant had been issued for Jenny's apartment.   No one else knew about it.   Certainly not Jenny.

"Who told you they were there?   Did I mention anything to you about a search warrant?

"About detectives Boyle and Parker?"

He froze, scrolling through his mind how she could possibly have this information.   He was uncomfortable with this strange feeling of confusion.   He was used to dealing with more clarity than this

"Did you read my mind?" he tried joking.   If she had, it would have had to be in his unconscious.   He had not given the warrant a thought once it was out of his hands.

"You're imagining these things." It almost was a question. She didn't answer.

Scanlon wrote something on his legal pad then peered over his glasses. "You were not in your apartment this afternoon," he declared, acting as judge and jury. "Your apartment is in Los Angeles." He was talking to her patronizgly treating her like a child or an alien. "You've been in this room for the last two hours. Maybe you've been daydreaming, you certainly haven't been communicating, but your body has been here."

The smile once again played at her lips. "That's right. My flesh, I do leave physical shapes around."

"Jenny," he slammed his hands on the desk, making her jump. He didn't seem to notice. "How can I believe what you've just said? How can I? I've been with you for over two hours and you tell me you weren't here. How could you be elsewhere? I see you. I'm not hallucinating. Should I videotape future meetings to prove you don't go anywhere? It's your imagination, and if you continue to talk like this you'll be committed."

She brushed some hair away from her eyes.

"One day you'll find yourself with your fantasies gone and locked behind bars with a bunch of crazy people and with no way of getting out." He stood up, shuddering.

"May I go back to my garden now? The flowers miss me. I haven't spent any time with them this afternoon and I'd like to tuck them in for the night."

"You can be with your flowers when we're through." He took a deep breath, it sounded shaky. "You're making this difficult. You have to trust me."

Sidelight coming through the window touched off the gray in his hair and outlined him in white. It was a sign from the Guides - she could trust. She settled back into the hard upright chair, started to cross her legs, and then decided not.

He sat down, breaking the light halo. "The D.A. has put one of his best detectives on the case, Sergeant Boyle. If they build a case the Grand Jury will indict you." He took out his handkerchief and wiped his damp brow. "Nobody believes or understands what you're saying. They think you masterminded Tim's death." His lips were turning even paler. "We have to prove your innocence. That's how it works."

She didn't respond.

He sighed. "Have a good time with your flowers." He waved his hand. "Give them my love."

She smiled at him and left. He watched her walk into the garden, her hair blowing around her face gently, and sit next to a bed of white daisies. A soft breeze moved them toward her as if they were saying hello. A chill ran up Scanlon's spine as he watched the girl and the flowers bend toward each other in what looked like a greeting.

He had tried reading up on some of the things Jenny talked about when he took her case. It was true that a high Lama or Yogi in India and Tibet had been reported doing some of the things she had said. But the reality of that with a young woman in Twentieth century America was highly unlikely. In all probability the high-strung demanding life she had led simply catapulted her into a nervous collapse. She was sensitive, intelligent and motivated. If he had to work day and night, he was going to make sure Jenny Webster was not indicted for murder or committed for insanity.

He sat back in the chair and closed his eyes. Suddenly a small light started to glow in the middle of his forehead. He caught his breath and opened his eyes.

Jenny was standing in the midst of the white daisies, smiling at him as she gently stroked the petal of a flower. She winked and smoothed tendrils of hair from her face, then turned and walked away.

She looked back, smiled again and waved. He didn't wave back, but watched as she walked up the path. Shaking his head, he packed up his briefcase to leave.

CHAPTER THREE

Jenny continued up the path past the women's wing of the hospital. She turned left in front of the Central building, turning her head to avoid the sight of the bars, trying to shut out the sounds of the shrieks and screams escaping through them. She hurried toward the tree shaded path leading to the cottage where she had recently been moved.

"You should leave, you should leave..." pattered a singsong in her head. She tried to block the mocking chatter as it hurried alongside her.

Turning the corner she slowed as she came to her new lodging, the institution's version of a halfway house. Here, twelve female patients lived. They had their own hours and permission to walk the grounds unattended during daylight hours. Some even had small pets like cats and birds. Penelope, a former housemate had kept Mortimer, a large rat she found outside the kitchen door. Penelope had been trying to teach Mortimer to sit up and beg. She was starting to have a little success. Leaving Mortimer alone for a moment she ran to get him a treat. An attendant, not knowing Mortimer was a pet, saw him only as a rat and chased him down the corridor, unmindful of Penelope's screams to stop. He cornered Mortimer in a broom closet and quickly ended his life. Traumatized, Penelope had to go back to the main house, and get injected with tranquilizers and wrapped in icy wet sheets. Jenny never saw her again.

Jenny didn't have a pet. She had once had an argument with

Carolyn, another housemate, over Ra, the large yellow Tabby, now lying on top of the balustrade, sunning himself as she climbed the stairs. He yawned as she paused to scratch his head.

Jenny had recognized Ra the moment she saw him curled up on a rug in the dayroom at Carolyn's feet. Ra was an old friend from a past life in Egypt. She picked him up and she knew he recognized her too as he started to purr and rub his head against her cheek. She began to take him to her room, but Carolyn, who called him Ernie, told her to put him down.

Jenny refused, saying Ra had appeared at the halfway house so they could be together again.

"He did not!" cried Carolyn as she tried to take him away. Jenny pulled away from her and Carolyn lunged for the cat. But Ra settled the disagreement by scratching them both, running away and staying away for two days and nights. During that time, Jenny was instructed by voices to give up attachment to possessions. She was told Ra had been put in the house to show her that nothing could be owned, the universe was to be shared by all, ownership was a concept that caused division. She accepted the voices' explanation and gave Ra up. The next morning, the cat pranced into the day room and leaped into her lap as if nothing had happened. When Carolyn walked into the room, he jumped down from Jenny's lap and rubbed against her. "Lesson time," Carolyn grinned. "Its always nice to meet another new-age nun."

"What do you mean?" Jenny asked her.

"I just figured we both understand the reason for Ernie's disappearance - to give up the concept of possession."

Jenny smiled. "Yes."

"Therefore," Carolyn continued, "I assume we're treading a similar path."

Jenny feared asking, but knew she must. "Do you hear voices?"

"Shh," Carolyn whispered and glanced around. "If anyone hears you say that they'll do a report and bottom line you're tagged as "crazy". That happens and you lose the possibility of getting out that front door. Anything that can give them the excuse to keep you here will be used for that purpose. Never forget you're in a research hospital, and though it's plush and they charge you a lot, with the kind of diagnosis you've got, anything and everything will be used against you. Just mirror everything they want you to do. Don't give them flack, Don't stand up to them. Behind these walls, on this side of the door, without a key, you have no resource other than your self. It's a lesson in discipline. Don't talk about anything interesting because the staff will report it as delusional. Most of all, never mention the voices. They'll take them away from you electronically or with medication. I know. They tried to do that to me. But the voices helped me to shut the others out so now, for the most part they are my sole means of emotional strength and support.

They both exhaled at exactly the same time and broke out simultaneously in giggles, which made them laugh even more.

"Do we have the same voices? " Jenny asked .

"I don't know. I haven't been trained in reading minds yet. I've got to get all the groundwork done first, like selflessness and love. You know, the basic elements." She waved and walked away. Ernie/Ra started to follow, then changed his mind and jumped up on the windowsill for his morning's sunbath.

Jenny thought about the first time she heard the voices. It had been shortly after she was raped. Afterward she thought she had been pushed so far that she had made them up, or it was a hysterical reaction. But when they continued to come unsummoned and sounded so rationally clear about emotional things, she began to listen to them with great objectivity. She found encouragement in their words and a feeling of being blessed by their caring, knowledge and understanding. The voices were never to be taken lightly. She called them her "Guides."

Feeling uplifted Jenny walked toward her newly decorated room, when suddenly a shadow of anxiety made her stop. She didn't want to leave here. She valued the friends she had made in the hospital, that handful of people who understood her and with whom she could share these perceptions. And because she had the voices to advise her she felt safe and protected.

She paused in the doorway of her room. How different it was from her home in Los Angeles. It was sparsely furnished, Spartan almost, filled only with the bare essentials. Yet it was softer somehow and a bit more personal and feminine. The iron bed was covered with a pink silk Japanese quilt a friend had given her when he left the hospital. There was a picture of stars and comets painted by Billie a patient who spoke only through her art, and little rows of seedlings that she had started after the voices told her that plants were important for survival. Little things, yet so precious.

She drifted to the window, and gazed across the lawn toward the setting sun. A soft white mist covered the grass and had begun to climb the trunks of the massive oaks bordering the edge of the gardens. She pressed her forehead on the cool glass of the window, as the fine white mist rose up in front of her. How different this clean white mist was from the gray smog that covered Los Angeles. Al Rudnik, her boss at the newspaper had an office that was dirtier than the inside of a chimney. Al smoked enough cigarettes during the fourteen to sixteen hours he spent in his office each day to permanently coat every square inch of wall, furniture, and floor with enough residue tar that the smell would not be gone till years after the building was razed.

His smoke echoed the smog outside as he ignored the no smoking ban initiated almost everywhere in Los Angeles,

Jenny was having trouble breathing. Perhaps her shortness of breath was from anger instead of smoke.

Rudnik had wanted to kill one of the best and most controversial stories she had ever investigated. Perhaps he had been right. Her life would have been very different had she listened to him. But would it have been for the better or for the worse? Would she give up what she had learned if she was given a second chance?

She leaned heavily on the windowsill. Suddenly Rudnick's office was directly in front of her. He was sitting behind his scarred and battered desk, the lit cigarette dangling from his lips, waving a sheaf of papers with the proposal she had just written. "What is this?" he shouted not waiting for an answer, "Baby Factories? It's bullshit! Yellow journalism! You're writing for the Los Angeles News, not the Inquirer." A flush of red was spreading from his neck to his chin, racing across his nose to his forehead. Jenny knew his danger signals and didn't say a word.

"**Electro Magnetic Energy Chips**?" The editor was almost choking on his words, "**Implanted transponders to monitor minds**! What the hell are you writing here - the sequel to BRAVE NEW WORLD?" He thrust the pages back into her hands with a glare. "You're supposed to be writing a series on bio-genetic engineering, not crap about mind control."

"Al, if you'd just read it all the way through..." she began. But Rudnik wasn't in the mood to be crossed, not now.

"If I could read it all the way through," he interrupted, "I'd be the only person in LA to get beyond the first paragraph. This isn't a feature; it's secondhand science fiction. And if you were a rookie, I'd fire you."

Jenny took a deep breath, trying to suppress the anger rising in her throat. "Al, I have a friend who is working in genetics at Anson Industries. She has been giving me a lot of information about what's going on there."

"Like what?"

"She can bring us documents proving there is technology available that measures the output of electronic activity in a person's brain and can break it down into graphs that interprets it into words. It's mind reading."

"What do they do with it?"

"You must be kidding!" She was incredulous. "Everything!"

"Why?" He was looking at her amused.

My friend is afraid she'll be in danger if someone finds out she talked to me.

"Industry theft is a fact of life." His tone unsympathetic."

"Al, it's not as if she's working for the KGB! Anson Industries is a public company."

"Corporate secrecy is cut throat."

"But - danger? She didn't mean losing her job. She meant physical danger. Her life."

"You're naive."

She took a deep breath and decided to compromise her friend's confidence. "She's working on something that has to do with artificial blood and sperm."

Rudnik shrugged. "I'm surprised it hasn't been done already."

Jenny wasn't sure if he was joking. She continued. "Do you realize how advanced they are and nobody knows it. In addition to Mannie's work combined with the technology to read brain waves, Anson can make a component small enough to implant in a mind to send and receive signals."

He leaned in a bit closer, leaning across his desk with interest. "Right, keep going."

"If they can read minds they can reverse the process and replace the thoughts they've read with different ones sent by electronic impulses. Do you realize how mind boggling this is?"

He didn't react to her attempt at humor. A professional skeptic who disbelieved most things until every option was exhausted; Jenny could see that he was beginning to turn off. She decided to try again. "Al, this gives them total power over the world! When thoughts can be read and then manipulated, populations will be monitored and controlled. This technology makes it possible."

He shook his head. "It's too bizarre."

She looked at him steadily. "When one can control another's mind, one controls everything."

Rudnik shook his head no, his chin in his hands, his mouth in a frown.

"Look." She moved in closer as she pointed out the text. Rudnick's tension was contagious. She forced herself to stay calm.

"That's Schizophrenia." He drew away from her.

"No it isn't." She lowered her voice. "It's reality. Our world has become what we used to call science fiction. Think about the atom smasher, television, astronauts building stations in space. How about flying around the Earth in a few days in a single engine airplane, or circling in a space ship in just a few hours? What about satellite transmission? That was a science fiction concept not so long ago. How about heart transplants or e-mail? Anson has been developing artificial conception and gestation."

Rudnik pushed away from his desk and lit another cigarette. "Who is this friend?"

"Someone who got very angry with me when I wrote the article on animal sacrifices in the temples of science. Remember that?"

Rudnik let out a sharp laugh. "How can I forget? My grandchildren still lecture me when I use certain products or eat meat. You certainly had an impact!"

"I'm glad."

"That wasn't meant as a compliment.," he growled.

"I'm glad it had an impact." They were starting to get off track. "This article could be very important."

"Visions of Pulitzer dancing in your head?"

"No. You know I don't think like that."

"O.K. Mother Theresa, go on." He sighed and leaned back in his chair, his eyes closed.

"With this kind of technological advance we can all be thrust into an adolescent state. The danger in that is that if we all think alike, act alike, and thus feel alike, then one catastrophe affects us all. That is quite a weapon!"

Rudnik sat up. The concept of a single source of control on a world wide level sobered him. It was possible.

She knew she had gotten to him. "Who are these people trying to play God? How do they think? What do they want to do? The News should find out." She handed the paper back to him. "This is important Al, it can't be dumped. We're talking about domination here - complete world control."

He pushed his chair back. "And you sound like an episode out of "X-FILES.""

She shook her head. "Al, science fiction has become reality."

He started to interrupt but she wouldn't let him. "What this means is some day you or your heirs could be sitting here totally manipulated, your minds being used like a keyboard for some strange player's thoughts and beliefs."

"That's impossible!" He was growing redder, his lips pursed in a tight pout. This meant major anger. He took off his glasses and pinched the bridge of his nose so tightly it left two red marks. "Who's your source?" he asked wearily. "I need a name."

She hesitated.

His face puffed up like an adder. Another bad sign.

"Give me the name of your man or forget it. The story is killed."

Quickly before he exploded she answered, "**Her** name is, Dr. Manuela Cristal de Sebastiane. We call her Mannie. She's a scientist working with biogenetic engineering at Anson laboratories. She was my roommate at Radcliffe, and her credentials are platinum."

Rudnik started to interrupt, but Jenny went on. "She's a dedicated scientist and she's concerned about what is happening at Anson without any kind of monitoring."

"Great, another whistle blowing conspiracy monger," he growled.

Jenny continued quietly. "Mannie is concerned her program will contribute to incalculable danger." Jenny looked at Rudnik sharply. "She thinks someone should stop it before it happens."

Rudnik turned away. "Nothing's happened."

"Yet. Look, Mannie and I have been good friends for a long time. I know she can be trusted. She's more like family to me than the one I had."

"Well that's a great reason to give you the go ahead for a story that will bring lawsuits against this paper," he said sarcastically. "You're talking innuendo, not facts."

Jenny ignored that and went on. "In the mid 1970's a woman in Nebraska claimed she was going blind because of microwave beams being sent across her farm from one Army base to another. She sued the Army. They're still trying to keep the story under wraps."

"I don't blame them. What does that have to do with this story?" He rubbed his eyes and they began to water.

"Microwave beams cause behavior modification." She paused, unsure whether to go ahead, then decided to go for it. "You're getting headaches aren't you?" I noticed you were pressing the bridge of your nose like you had one."

He started to protest.

She kept on. "Do you remember what the Russians did to our embassy in Moscow? Since the late Sixties they beamed microwave transmissions at the Ambassador's office and so far three Ambassadors died of Leukemia. The fourth is in a naval hospital in Bethseda, getting chemotherapy treatment. And it's not from gallstones."

Rudnik looked at her, his hand over his mouth.

She continued. "At first our government thought the Russians were transmitting microwaves to jam transmissions, but it was later proven the microwaves caused changes in behavior. That is public information."

"I remember reading about it," he conceded.

"Now a microscopic chip has been developed capable of receiving and sending information like a transponder. Used in the various zones of the brain the simple stimulation or lack of stimulation could alter and control behavior. They no longer have to use microwave. This is easier. They've been doing it with monkeys in the labs. Remember my animal abuse story?"

"Yeah" he rubbed his chin, thoughtful.

"Think of what Stalin or Hitler or any of the other tyrants could have done with this technology. The person or group that develops this first will have control of the world in days."

Rudnik shook his head, allowing a smile to pierce his red-veined cheeks. "Conspiracy theories. Who are THEY? I hired a novelist instead of a reporter. You better check with our medical editor. You'll find your theories are classic schizophrenia. This won't be printed and I can't give you the time or budget for it. It's impossible." He looked away.

"This information has to be published! It can't be kept secret!" She pulled her chair closer to his desk. "Our minds will become open books."

"Will you be a hard cover or paper back?" he teased.

"Hard," she answered back. Suddenly her eyes widened. Clear silver streaks cut through the room, humming a charged electrical sound. She squinted and the beams grew clearer. All sounds from the newsroom stopped. The humming became louder as the grid of silver streaks grew dense and encapsulated the room. They were both wrapped inside it. "This room is filled with electricity!"

"What? Of course it is!" He flicked the desk light on and off a few times. "It's what powers modern civilization." He pulled the cigarette out of his mouth, incredulous. It was burned down to the filter. His hand trembling, he stubbed it out in an overfilled ashtray of dirty filters and burned a finger. "God damn it."

The stench of stale cigarette smoke filled Jenny's nostrils. The room was getting close and hot. She tried to dismiss the unpleasant sensations, but her skin was getting prickly. "Mannie has further information for me."

Rudnik pushed his chair around and looked out the window at the smog-covered city below. "I don't want this discussed with anyone. We need lots of clearances if this can be published. Understand? Half of me thinks you may have gone totally out of your mind." He looked past her at the wall. A shiver went through him. Passing a hand over his face he became aware Jenny was watching him.

A jolt went through her body. She jumped up and started toward the door.

"Jenny!"

She paused, her hand on the knob.

"Do you want me to put Siegel on this with you?" he asked. "He's available."

"Is he ever! No thanks. If I run into trouble I'll let you know. Meanwhile, it's best if I work with Mannie alone."

"All right." He picked up a paper on top of a stack along with a pencil and started to read. Jenny watched him. He had totally cut off. She left.

Stopping for a moment, she squinted, looking for the lines of energy she had just seen in Rudnick's office, but couldn't see them. She walked past rows of cluttered desks to her own, pausing to look back at Rudnik through the glass wall. His head was bent in deep concentration, the light on his desk turned off. Had she really seen those streaks a few moments before? She kept squinting as she walked to her desk.

The phone was ringing at her desk and she hurried to it. "Jenny Webster" she answered.

"Am I interrupting?" It was Tim. She felt lighter, better, Her cheeks burned with excitement and she smiled brightly,

"You could never interrupt me." She ignored the reporter at the next desk trying to get her attention. She turned her back, her blush growing deeper.

"Listen," his voice sounded gruff and throaty. "I've got to be in Washington first thing in the morning, so I'm taking the 4:00 p.m. flight this afternoon. Want to have lunch before I leave?"

"I'd love to."

"I haven't much time."

"That's all right." She looked at the bank of clocks lining the wall, the time of day for each major city in the world. "Do you want me to take you to the airport?"

"No. Roxanne hired a car so we can go over some last minute details."

She felt herself stiffen. "Is she going with you?"

"Yes". His answer was matter of fact. If only she could feel that way about Tim's beautiful and supposedly "brilliant" assistant. Unwilling waves of jealousy swept over her. She tried to get them to stop, but she couldn't do anything about it. Roxanne was efficient, ambitious and was doing everything she could to get Tim away from her.

"How long will you be gone?" Her voice was tight.

"Let's talk at the restaurant. There isn't much time."

She looked at the clocks in front of her. Time! It was already tomorrow in Tokyo. It was too late for lunch there, too early in Hawaii. Why did one always measure time? It was so relative.

"Right now?" He sounded annoyed.

Her heart clutched. "Of course. I have one call to make. Tim, I must tell you. I just had a really tough talk with Rudnik. I want to..."

"Please Jenny," he interrupted. "Wait till we see each other."

"All right." Rejection sank in. He was always cutting her off lately. No longer did he want to hear about her work or share ideas with her. She kept catching herself doing monologues to unheeding ears. And as far as their sex life, they could be brother and sister. There was no longer the touching, the little stolen moments in public where he put his hands in places she hoped no one could see. She inhaled deeply, "La Scala? It's still early."

"Roxanne called and got Simone to reserve a table." Jenny's jaw clenched tighter.   Reservations were never taken at the boutique restaurant. It was first come, first serve. Even famous Hollywood faces had to stand around and wait in the tiny entranceway. Jenny didn't know how Roxanne managed to reserve a table. Pushy and tenacious she believed she could do anything.

Tim hung up the phone before either said good-by. She held the phone close, swallowing the swelling bitterness. She felt so lonely, so distanced from him. Now, when they were together, she felt lonelier than ever. Something had happened and she didn't know what.

The second hand of the clock labeled London swept away another minute of precious time. She picked up the phone to call Mannie. She had almost forgotten. That was happening a lot lately - she got so carried away with the way Tim was behaving, or usually not behaving, that she would forget to do things Emotion was demanding her focus and time.

The phone rang nine times before the Anson operator finally answered. Jenny noticed that her own voice sounded angry when she asked for Mannie. She was tempted to tell the snippy operator she could easily be replaced by a computer, but was disturbed more by the thought then the operator's rude behavior.

"Yes."   Mannie's soft weary voice sounded pre-occupied and thousands of miles away.

"Mannie, it's Jenny. Are you all right?"

"Jenny! I want to talk to you."

"I've got to talk to you too. Tim's going out of town, how about dinner tonight?"

"When?'"

"Seven."

"Fine. Do you mind if we go to my favorite greaser's palace? I'm on a junk food binge. I'll tell you why when I see you."

"Whatever you want. But I get to make the next choice after this one."

"Done."

The long-haired reporter at the next desk started to come over. Jenny quickly buried her head and searched through her purse, pulled out a mirror and freshened her lipstick. She didn't want him to start talking. He could talk for hours unless he was on deadline. Then he'd scream at anyone who coughed or closed a drawer too loudly.

"Got to go." She jumped up as he approached her. He backed away bowing. Behind her she could see one of the clocks - it was growing later in every part of the world. Guiltily she put back the mirror and snapped the lock of her purse, heading for the stairs next to the elevator before Rudnik or anyone else could call her back.

CHAPTER FOUR

People spilled out the door of La Scala Ristorante jostling each other as they waited for one of the coveted tables inside. Jenny managed to weave her way through the throng, slipping past two less than thrilled designer-clad matrons as she walked directly to the welcoming arms of Simone the hostess who guarded the tables beyond.

"He's waiting for you. I gave you the quiet booth in the corner," she smiled, always the romantic.

"See," whispered one matron to the other. "He *is* somebody - sitting there alone! No one gets a table till their whole party has arrived." Their eyes followed Jenny to Tim's table.

Tim's face was set in a frown, his head turning nervously from side to side. Moving quickly to him, Jenny kissed his cheek and slipped in beside him. He was still the picture of perfection, she thought, his aquiline nose, angular cheek bones, even the few strands of gray in his dark blond hair and the tiny lines that creased the corners of his eyes gave him an air of wholesome distinction. She took his hand and squeezed it. "How are you darling?"

He shrugged, his face a mixture of emotions that had a strange quality teeming beneath its poster-like perfection. A chill fluttered through her. In the past few weeks she had tried to discuss the barrier she felt raising between them, but communication was growing more difficult with the love of her life. Tim would shrug and say she was imagining it and was insecure for no good reason, Perhaps she needed a lift he would say, offering to pay for a day at a spa or a new dress,

"It isn't *things* I want, "It's you." She cried. He ignored that and with a sympathetic smile offered his credit card. She had turned and walked away without another glance. The anger didn't last long.

Tim had been Jenny's dream come true. He was her Prince Charming, her Knight in Shining Armor. Even now, with the problems they were having, her heart always leaped with excitement when she saw him. Could it be her imagination that his heart had closed and his eyes were cold? Was it her own insecurity that something negative was happening between them? Was she creating problems where there were none?

She had tried to expel her heavy feelings, telling herself that Tim was getting ready to run for his first election and was under a lot of pressure. He had been groomed since a child to run for public office, and his first big political goal was near. He had a group of professional handlers hired by his father to lay out a plan of action since the time he graduated Harvard Law School. They placed him in the old-line law firm of Laramie, Rogers and Fowler, a powerful company with political and financial connections all over the world.

In his first year Tim was made a junior partner and plans were made for Tim and Jenny to be married after Tim's nomination to run for Congress. It would be an ideal time to garner publicity and build Tim an image of stability and romance patterned upon the image of the Kennedy/Camelot era.

But at this moment all Jenny wanted to ask her promising young politician was how he would feel if she got up and left the restaurant and walked out on him? Would he follow? Would he become more responsive?

"No" she answered herself, he probably wouldn't. So she stayed, frozen in the booth, trapped by her own assumptions, passive beneath their uncomfortable blanket of silence.

Tim took a piece of paper from his jacket pocket and studied it carefully.

"What's that?" Jenny asked.

"My itinerary for Washington," he said.

"May I?" She held out her hand and reluctantly he gave it to her. She took a match and struck it then held the flame to the paper till it was fully engulfed. People at the next table turned to look. "There," she giggled," now you don't have to leave me and go to Washington. Your schedule is up in smoke!"

Tim didn't laugh. "You shouldn't have done that." With annoyance he signaled the waitress.

Beverly Hills' perfect flesh and blood version of a Barbie Doll slithered to the table. "Hi Tim," she purred seductively, "Are you trying to cook your own lunch?" She ignored Jenny, holding her pad and posing with an assurance that every man in the restaurant was watching her.

"Just sending smoke signals to get you over here," Jenny interjected.

The waitress tossed a silky head of hair that had been cut and colored to give her plain face the illusion of glamour. She inhaled deeply to recite the lunch- time specials, the silicone mounds she called her breasts stationery despite her well- choreographed deep breaths to make her nipples rub against her flimsy jersey blouse. Sucking in her cheeks she widened her eyes, her green contact lenses glistening under the lights. But Tim's head was bent in deep concentration over the simple menu they both knew by heart.

Jenny and Tim dined at La Scala two or three times a week, usually more since neither of them had the time or inclination to shop for groceries or cook them.

The waitress caught Jenny's eye and together they waited for Tim to say something. Sensing their attention he put the menu down. "Bring

37

me Jean Leon red."

"Bottle or glass?"

"Jenny, would you like some?" he asked.

She nodded.

"A bottle."

The waitress shifted her weight against the table, her crotch practically resting against Tim's arm. "Do you want to order now? I know you have a plane to catch."

"Has it made the afternoon news already?" Jenny asked, wide eyed with innocence.

"Roxanne called to reserve a table."

"Of course." Bitterness rose in her throat as she thought of Tim's Executive Assistant. Dressed for success and spouting canned philosophies, the woman appeared to entrance Tim with her pulp level intelligence. Roxanne had a sponge-like mind and laser sharp ambition. Combined with a lack of scruples she was a prototype for a new kind of woman. Why couldn't Tim see that? Or was Jenny being suspicious and maybe jealous?

"You know we never hold a table for anyone," the Barbie Doll was saying, "but Roxanne has a way of getting what she wants."

"Veal Piccata", Tim interrupted.

Betrayal hit Jenny. Ever since she had investigated the beef slaughterhouses and wrote a series of exposes on the atrocities in them she couldn't think of eating meat – especially veal. Tim had respected her wishes and never ordered itl. Now he had. Why?

"I'd like the chopped salad, with basil and no salami" Jenny ordered and noticed she was leaning away from the love of her life.

The waitress left the table, with a hole between them. Jenny turned back to Tim and tried to fill it. "Are you all right?" She touched his arm but it felt stiff and unyielding.

"I have a thousand things on my mind," he said, adjusting his body so they could not touch.

Jenny's words flew out of her mouth. "Obviously I'm not one of them. Why did you want to meet me for lunch?"

"Because I'm hungry, and wanted to see you before I left."

See me? You haven't looked at me since I sat down."

His face grew tense. "Are you anxious to start a fight?" he asked. "I was hoping there wouldn't be problems before I left, but if a fight will make you feel better, I'll be happy to oblige."

"It doesn't matter if you leave," she said, taking his bait. "You're not with me anymore. You're like an empty form."

"I don't know what you're talking about."

"Of course you don't." Bitterness threatened, *change the subject* raced through her head. "Al read my proposal and there is a chance he will let me go ahead with the Anson story."

"He won't, he can't."

"I think he will."

Tim's voice was low and impatient, "I don't want you to waste your time or destroy your reputation. Your friend Mannie has had too many experimental drugs. She's paranoid and is leading you down a blind alley. You're going to hit a wall."

"That isn't true. How can you say that?"

"Can you prove her story that Anson is using her program to control minds? She probably deleted it from her computer herself

39

and forgot about it. No one has to use devious technological means to control people. Madison Avenue is the Mount Olympus of Mind Control. What do you think marketing research is all about? No one's going to bother with complicated technology. Mind control has been built with pictures and words. The technology is called marketing and advertising."

Jenny leaned closer to him. "Advertising does not control minds." She kept her voice low "it persuades. This technology replaces normal thoughts with implanted, manufactured ones. There is no chance for personal choice or individual thinking or feeling. This is a weapon and it's an extremely dangerous one."

"I wish I had one right now."

That's not funny."

"It wasn't meant to be. But you must admit the delivery was cute." He grinned at her in his most adorable way. It usually worked but his disposable charm wasn't working. Like a good warrior, he saw his failure and gently took her hand. This time he looked deep into her eyes. "Your thoughts my dear, are not rational. I think you should talk to a doctor."

Jenny felt like poison had been poured throughout her body. She searched for the waitress. She needed a drink.

"Why don't you re-focus?" Tim continued. "Work on something positive. Richard Laurence is going to create a big political upset in the coming election. I know him. He's good - a winner. You could become one of his speechwriters or even his press secretary. But you've got to start working for him now. It can be arranged. Just give me the word."

"Tim, Washington and power is your game, not mine. Why are you so concerned about my doing the story on Anson's genetic engineering if I'm wrong?"

"Because I love you and I don't want to see you ruin your career or our life. My God Jenny, it's not as if I'm trying to keep you from your work. I'm suggesting you focus on real issues, join with the sources of genuine power, be a success."

"You want me to turn my back on what I know is the right thing to do. On most levels I hope this information is wrong and I've wasted some time. But if I'm not and this technology exists, then it could change the world, as we know it. A Presidential campaign would mean nothing. I know you don't believe it, but it's possible. Can't you appreciate what I'm saying?"

"It's insane." he shook his head sadly.

The tone with which he said that sent a chill through her . She felt her jaw clenching, her stomach tight, she was seething. Taking a deep breath Jenny closed her eyes and tried to make her anger go away.

"You're walking in a field of land mines," Tim was saying, but she wasn't listening. Her head was spinning.

Tim bumped her arm as he reached for the bottle of wine. She had been unaware the waitress had brought it. He was starting on his second glass, she hadn't touched her first. She picked up her wine glass. He lifted his and drained it before she could say anything. A sharp pain hit the side of her head. Recently, every time she wanted a sip of wine a headache would hit her. She put the glass down and sipped water. Her eyes blinked shut. A red light appeared. She blinked again, it turned white.

"Are you all right?" Tim asked.

"Yes," she answered coldly."

"You look like you have a headache."

"One is starting. I can't drink anymore."

"Nonsense. You should have your eyes checked. You're getting too many headaches. Maybe that's why you're acting so strange. Why don't you call Dr. Friedman?"

"That's the second doctor you suggested since I've joined you for lunch." Her eyes had started giving her trouble. Sometimes, when she was doing an interview, the person she was talking to would start to look fuzzy and she thought she could see different colors emanating from their bodies. Then she would forget what they were talking about and focus on their colors. Afterward when she played the recordings back she seemed to be fully engaged in the interviews.

Tim watched her. She smiled slightly, but he didn't smile back. "Where are you going this afternoon?" He asked abruptly. "Back to the paper?"

"No, I'm going to the UCLA bio med library to read up on genetic engineering."

"I wish you'd find another story."

"Are you starting?"

In response Tim looked over her shoulder and rose to greet a small square shaped man who had suddenly appeared at their table. He wore a three-piece suit with padded shoulders and a nipped in waist, the top of his sunglasses were tinted dark so his eyes were hidden. His smile appeared frozen as his voice came from his throat. Tim introduced him as Melvin Phillips and invited him to join them.

"Only for a quick drink," he said sitting down.

Strange shivers ran through Jenny as Phillips sat a little too close to her. Tim motioned the waitress over and the man introduced as Melvin Phillips ordered a Bloody Mary with a voice so deep and smooth it appeared to be calibrated like an announcer, to cover what he was thinking or feeling.

"Synchronicity," Tim came up with loudly. "We were just talking about Anson, Melvin." He turned to Jenny, a friendly smile on his face, a smile she knew he wasn't feeling. "Melvin is Senior Vice President of

Human Resources at Anson."

Jenny nodded. "Yes, I recognized your face from pictures and of course your name." She smiled. "I've done a bit of research on Anson."

"So we've noticed. We have read all your articles, " He pulled his thin lips into the guise of a smile.

"Jenny," she said. "Please call me Jenny."

"How do you feel about fraternizing with the enemy, " he asked, punctuating the question with a sharp staccato laugh. Tim chuckled in harmony. She looked from one to the other, mirroring each other, playing a duet with her mind.

The waitress brought the Bloody Mary. Phillips grabbed the glass so tight, she feared it would break in his hand. He raised it in a toast.

She felt off guard, a bit frightened, hoping she could hold her own. "We're not enemies, Mr. Phillips," she said. "The article I had written about company influences over employees by no means targeted Anson in a negative way. Anson was used as an example because of the vast extent of your social services for employees. As far as the questions that were raised, public companies have to be held up to public scrutiny, don't you agree?"

His tight smile spread wider. "Anson is an honest company."

She smiled back. "Then you must be pleased."

He matched her smile. "We prefer positive publicity."

Jenny's smile faded. "Mr. Phillips..."

"Melvin," his lips stayed upturned like an ancient Toltec mask

She nodded acceptance, "Melvin," "that depends on the inference

43

you take."

The man adopted a pose of sincerity. "Our commitment to excellence stands up to your kind of scrutiny."

She ignored that. "I'd like to do an in-depth story on what Anson is about -- the day care centers, nurseries, low rent communities, pre and post natal care as well as your health services, and of course, your advances in genetic engineering." This last was slipped in quickly. She noticed a tiny twinge cross his face.

Composed he answered calmly, "Anson's employee benefits are quite wonderful."

"I'd like to visit the labs," she added.

He didn't react, "I want to impress upon you the fact that Anson's housing and benefit packages are strong incentives for our workers."

"I'm sure they are." Jenny smiled brightly at Tim who glowered over Phillips' shoulder. He clearly wanted this conversation to end.

"Your gated compounds where thousands of people depend on Anson is like a modern feudal system," Jenny stated. This time Phillips didn't return her smile. She went on. "Your employees depend on you for almost every necessity."

Phillip's head stretched up to ease the tension in his neck. "They don't have to take advantage of our services," he said.

Jenny studied him carefully "Families who have a good part of their income deducted for their special mortgage packages, whose children go to your company schools and day care centers, who depend on your health care plans and insurance, are investured to you. If they leave they lose their pension plan, their tenure, and maybe even the deed to their homes. I researched this thoroughly and that is fact." Tim poured himself another glass of wine and glowered at Jenny. She smiled at him and turned her attention fully on Phillips. "I think it's interesting that every six months your employees receive training videos in the Anson philosophy," she tilted her head and waited for his answer.

A wall started to build and secure itself around Phillips, chill surrounding his words. "Those are incentive builders for workers to move them forward. We don't like the status quo. We want every worker to move up to the next level. We want the lowest paid worker to believe that with hard work he or she can eventually become CEO of the company."

"Is that realistic? Has it ever happened at Anson, or any other large company?" she asked. "Has a janitor or someone from an assembly line or even a secretary made a Vice President or even a top level executive?"

Phillips was unflappable. "That takes time."

"How many generations? I'm questioning the reality of your company promises."

"The drive to succeed is what this country as well as Anson is founded on."

"Education and lucky genes have much to do with executive appointments," countered Jenny. "What I question is the exploitation of dreams without the hope of tangibles."

Tim closed his eyes and leaned his head back on the banquette. Jenny continued. "Your workers have to sign pledges to conform to Anson guide lines. They can't even smoke in the privacy of their own homes. They can be fired if their child or someone who doesn't like them snitches. Isn't that Fascist, a bit like Nazi Germany?"

"That policy has been instituted for health insurance reasons."

Jenny shook her head. Tim started to say something, but Phillips waved him off. "It's fine Tim, Jenny is trying to justify her unjustifiable distrust of our company. Perhaps we can make a believer of her."

Jenny noticed Tim's growing impatience. "Let's cut through the sound bites, " she said to Phillips. "I'm asking if there is a danger you're creating a despotic situation cloaked in the guise of corporate America?"

"Your articles have that tone, but you're mistaken. We're talking about corporate standards - every company has them. No one is forced to work for us. We get hundreds of applications daily. Our salary scale is higher then most. Our workers follow company policies because it gives them security and pride, as well as perks. For the most part the Anson group is one large, happy family."

"As long as they don't behave like black sheep, then they join the ranks of the homeless." Jenny purposefully avoided Tim's piercing glare. She decided to change the subject. "Why won't Robert Jordan give interviews? He used to be terribly good at them."

"Perhaps you'd like to ask him that question yourself?"

"I certainly would."

"I'll arrange it."

"That would be wonderful." She stayed cool though inwardly she was brimming with astonishment. Robert Jordan, President and CEO of Anson Industries had stopped giving interviews three and a half years before. The last time he had appeared on a program he had been assaulted with questions about Anson's ties to government. He never allowed another personal interview.

An attractive man in his early fifties Jordan was a Patrician - with graying hair, strong, sharp features and a trim athlete's build. He was a Yale man who had once sailed in the America's Cup, but beyond that he concentrated only on Anson Industries.

Jenny had known men like Jordan all her life. She had grown up in a community where many of the men were top executives in the Fortune Five Hundred companies. When she was a young girl and attended some of the grownups' parties she would hear policies being discussed that would benefit the companies or individuals who were guests there. The grownups assumed she and her friends were too young to understand what was going on. They were wrong. The power astounded her, it didn't seem right. Jenny questioned why people who took the public trust compromised the very people who put them there? For money? Power? All that betrayal just to feed a high overhead?

Once she became an investigative reporter Jenny interviewed many executives from large corporations, but she rarely got a straight answer about simple responsibility. Perhaps at times her questions stepped over the line of tact, but she felt strongly that these multimillionaires who lived in sublime security and comfort should be in touch with the people who did the real work for their companies and who supplied the consumer base for their products and profits.

A few times she had asked Tim to help her with political connections but he refused. But now, the man she most wanted to interview was being made available. She had little time to wonder why. "How soon would you like to meet Robert Jordan?" Phillips was asking her.

"Yesterday!" she smiled, not trying to conceal her excitement.

"I'll see what I can arrange." Phillips slid out of his chair and went to a private place to make the cellular call.

Jenny wiggled over to Tim and gave him a quick kiss, "Thank you, thank you," she hugged his arm happily.

"Don't thank me," he took his arm away. "You shouldn't be going on the offensive with these people. You should be using these contacts positively. This can backfire. You're throwing away opportunities."

"Life brings opportunity, not Anson industries."

"Will you stop? You should be their partners, not their opponent. It could be beneficial to both of us."

"I'll keep it under advisement, counselor."

"Do that." He patted her hand. "When I get back from Washington, we'll go to the mountains, to Winrock. We need a vacation."

Parker returned to the table. "Tomorrow, 11:00. Is that good for you?"

"Perfect," she said, "thank you."

Phillips turned to Tim and gave him a little nod. "Thanks for the drink Tim, good luck in Washington." He turned back to Jenny, a cold smile on his lips. "Come a few minutes early to get your credentials. I'll be there."

"I will, thank you."

Tim signaled for the check. Jenny put her hand on his arm. He gently removed it. "Sorry darling, I have to go, I have another appointment. Finish your lunch." He seemed upset.

Jenny looked at his half eaten lunch, resenting the slaughter of the unappreciated baby calf that suffered and died only to be left on the plate as table scraps. She started to get up to kiss him good-by, but paused when she noticed him stiffen. "Have a good trip darling. Call me when you get there. All right?"

"Jenny," he stopped and took her hand, "take care of yourself." He kissed her cheek. "I love you."

"I love you too." A warm flush filled her. She wanted him to sit back down with her, forget the appointment, Washington, everything but their love. She reached up to kiss him, but he had drawn back, any emotion he had been feeling was already shut down. The good-by was over.

She picked up her wine glass and held it in front of her face, blocking the tears that fell down her cheeks.

CHAPTER FIVE

Cameras were mounted everywhere. Jenny assumed the photo on the i.d. tag she was given at the security desk had been taken the moment she walked through the door. She was reluctant to pin the plastic sealed likeness of her face onto her expensive Jil Sandor suit, however, a gust of immediacy impelled her to push the pin through the buttery soft wool when she saw Melvin Phillips walking quickly toward her across the polished lobby floor. She locked the pin in place and rose to greet him.

Phillips was stiff and businesslike, quite unlike the smiling personable man she had met the day before. After the briefest of pleasantries, he escorted her to the penthouse where a pair of uniformed security guards accompanied them from the private elevator to a reception area on the penthouse level. The guards were burly, a Caucasian and an Asian, and Jenny guessed that physiologically they were probably lethal weapons. Melvin Phillips had confirmed her suspicions that the bronze pillars at the elevator door contained x-ray equipment. "For weapons," he explained.

The penthouse was vast, and monastic in its severity. Two-story marble pillars reached up toward vaulted ceilings that looked like they had grown out of the polished marble floors. The only sounds were from elevator bells and the soft hum of skyscraper technology. The Anson Industries headquarters was a contemporary cathedral of commerce, she thought. Perhaps she would title her article "The Temple of Trade". She hoped she'd remember that because she had no time to write it down. The guards were walking too fast for her to stop as they led her through a labyrinth of stark white hallways with recessed lighting that made the ceilings glow. Turning and twisting like a maze it appeared the design intention was to cause disorientation. It did. Without an escort, Jenny would never have been able to find her way.

Jenny noticed that everyone, including Phillips, the elevator operator, the receptionist, and the guards, wore I.D. tags with photographs that had been taken that day.

Robert Jordan didn't need a tag or even a picture to identify him. There could be no mistaking who he was. He had intensity, a power that could weaken others.

Jenny took a deep breath. She was used to powerful men, but Jordan's presence was overwhelming --a soul crusher. He was also very handsome - much better in person then on film.

Jenny had been struggling to control her emotions from the moment she first walked into the towering glass atrium outside Jordan's private office. Inspired by a rainforest the two-story atrium had a waterfall, tropical plants, and a sprinkling of exotic birds that occasionally flew through the foliage. The effect was breathtaking. She thought of the genuine rain forests Anson Industries must have destroyed in order to afford this simulation on the top of their high-rise.

It was all impressively disturbing., like Robert Jordan's appearance - beautiful -- but only on the surface. Perhaps such a mundane thing as love had never touched him. His face seemed to contain no sensitivity, no compassion. She detected only cynicism etched in his eyes and across his sulky lips.

Jenny had wanted to record the interview, but it wasn't allowed. She had to leave her briefcase at the secretary's desk and was told not to take notes. *"It would break the flow of the interview,"* she was told.

Jordan's private office looked out over Century City the way one would see it from a bird's point of view - all laid out perfectly beneath him, scaled with precision, thought and planning. Even the tiny dark specks she could identify as people from that height appeared to be strategically placed as a reminder to Jordan that ordinary humans did, after all, inhabit his empire.

Jordan rose from his chair but did not come out from behind his desk to greet her. Instead, he motioned her to sit on the large cushioned sofa on the other side of the room. She noted the distance gave her a feeling of vulnerability.

Before she could speak, an impeccably dressed butler in a three-piece suit brought in a silver tray with a tea service that could have been on display in a museum.

"Lemon?" the butler asked, his tones dripping with elegance.

"Cream," she answered, trying to match his tone.

Formal and methodical, the butler served the tea and offered biscuits, which both Jenny and Jordan refused. Neither spoke a word till the butler left the room.

When Jordan took a sip from his cup then looked up, Jenny took the initiative. "Mr. Jordan, is there any connection with the quarterly retreats you host at your Adirondacks estate for executives? People from multi national corporations and your advertising campaigns? They seem to have marked similarities."

"Really?" His eyes narrowed. "Why would you think that?" He sipped his tea.

She tried to ignore her quivering nerves. "Your advertising campaigns focuses on the ways ANSON treats workers, rather than on the products it produces. It's almost advertising for a way of life – not for a consumer product."

"I have no idea what you're talking about. Our advertising has always been focused on product."

"Mr. Jordan, we only have to look at your television and print campaigns to see that *The Anson Family*, as you call it, is being featured rather than the company's specific products. That's a departure from your previous advertising strategy."

"Ms. Webster, it wouldn't be in our best interest to ignore our own products. It would do no good to sell only the corporate name as you suggest."

"But in your recent commercials, you go into employees' homes and schools and personalize the products with them."

That's right. What better advertising than our workers using the products they make." he interrupted. "This is a silly line of questioning."

Jenny took a deep breath. She had studied Anson's new advertising approach as well as several others, and all seemed to be pushing the same message - we can take care of your lives better than the government.

"We're giving customers background on who makes the products they buy," Jordan said. "I like it, it's a new approach, peer oriented. Different. Surely you can't find fault with that. We don't sell our name like General Electric or IBM."

"Oh, but you do." she insisted. "That's why I'm asking you about this change of direction."

"This is ridiculous," he snapped. "You're wasting my time."

He was shutting down. Jenny had to keep the meeting going, change the tone. She shifted her weight and took a sip of tea. "Mr. Jordan, You appear to be focusing on achieving a certain kind of public confidence and support."

"Ms. Webster, you're naïve.," he nearly snarled.

"Is it a political confidence you're seeking?" She suggested quietly.

His eyes turned cold, almost lethal. "If I wanted political power, I would run for President, wouldn't I?"

She pushed ahead, ignoring the lines of anger forming between his eyes. "In your last series of television commercials, you compared the superior quality of your planned communities to government projects.

"That's right. They are."

"The impression was that your workers have better working and living conditions than the government can give them."

"We do. Especially with the present administration. Successful business people are geared to run things more efficiently and profitably than government. A community is no different than any other product. But I think you're reading more into this than necessary."

"I don't think so."

"I do." He sat back, his eyes gleaming with a cobra-like stare.

Jenny tried to hide her shiver, but he had seen it.

"You have an interesting mind, Ms. Webster," Jordan said softly. "Very imaginative. If you'd like a position with this company, I'll personally arrange it."

She tried to look flattered. "Thank you, I'm happy with my present work. But if anything changes, I'll take you up on it," she paused a quick beat. "What are Anson's future plans?" she casually asked.

"To continue creating products and systems that benefit mankind," came his automatic reply. He started to rise, indicating that the interview was at an end. A bland smile had begun to mask his face, shutting her off like a faucet.

Jenny hesitated. It was now or never. She must ask the most important question of all, before he called his secretary to show her out. His hand was already reaching for the buzzer on his desk.

"Tell me about Anson's work on genetics." Her voice sounded calm, but her heart was pounding

His hand stiffened and he straightened and gazed at her. His stare was ice cold.

"We're very diversified, anything is possible. I'd like a copy of your article before it's printed."

She kept her face impassive, but her body tingled. Her question had struck him like a diamond bullet. Robert Jordan was shaken. The one word "genetics" had breached his defenses. By asking for a copy of her article before it was printed, he had revealed vulnerability. He was afraid of what she might write. Robert Jordan had been shaken.

Jenny managed a polite smile as she rose from the sofa. "Mr. Jordan," she cleared her throat, "I'm sorry. It isn't possible. It's against the paper's policy. But you know I'm always fair."

"Thank you for your interest in Anson, Ms. Webster," he said distantly. A secretary was coming into the room. "Please show Ms. Webster out."

As Jenny walked to the door, her mind was racing. She would have to be careful. She would have to keep this article as objective as possible. She could not indict this man in print. As she turned to say good-bye, Jordan had already started to read through some papers on his desk. "Thank you, Mr. Jordan," she said with a smile.

Robert Jordan did not look up or answer.

***

The click of Jenny's heels made a marching sound as she hurried across the marble lobby toward the candy stand to buy a chocolate bar. Without missing a beat, she headed for the large glass doors leading on to the park -like entrance of the building, settling on a small bench perched next to a pond with bubbling water spilling over marble and granite slabs.

Taking out her cellular phone she dialed Rudnick's private line and waited as it rang. She checked her watch. It was 11:45. He should be there. He never took a break. She hung up and re-called. It continued to ring.

She bit into the candy bar as she tried to recreate the essential parts of the meeting from her memory. She had not asked him about the surveillance in his employees' housing complexes, and she had wanted to question him more about the meetings at his mountain compound in the Adirondacks...

Rudnick's phone continued to ring. Uneasy she hung up and finished her candy bar. A humming in her ears was starting to fill her head. She swallowed hard trying to clear it, but the hum grew louder. She re-dialed the number. This time Rudnik answered, out of breath and in a bad mood. She braced herself. "Al, it's Jenny."

"Where are you?"

She took a deep breath. "I just left Robert Jordan's office."

"Was he there?" he snapped.

"Of course. Why would you ask me that?"

"He uses doubles. Been using them since he stopped giving interviews."

Churchill and Hitler had used doubles. But Jenny could not believe that the man she had just met was anyone but Robert Jordan. His presence was exceptionally powerful. "It was Jordan," she insisted.

"I just had a meeting with Eriksen." Eriksen was Vice President in charge of personnel, the Publisher's hatchet man.

"What did he want?" Jenny felt concern for the editor. She hoped he hadn't lost his job.

"Management says you're too opinionated. They want you to tone down. They don't want law suits."

"I've never caused one!" She was shocked..

"Not yet, but you're close," he sighed deeply. "Listen, there is pressure coming in about you from high levels."

"Probably advertising," she grumbled.

"I'm going along with them, Jenny."

That stopped her. She crumbled the empty candy wrapper, mad at herself for eating the candy, and threw it on the well-swept ground. Guilt rose up and made her reach down and get it. She shoved it in a crevice between the side of the cement bench and a cobblestone. Then she pulled it out again and put it into her pocket. She didn't know what to say.

Al filled the silence. "What about Jordan? Did he give you the blueprints for his plan to take over the world?" Rudnik was not even trying to coat his sarcasm.

Jenny steadied herself. "Not yet, but I think parts of the meeting were revealing." She was trying to stay calm, but it was an effort.

"Really? Which parts?"

"When I brought up genetics it seemed to throw him a bit. He asked to read my article before it was published. I told him that was impossible. The question unnerved him."

"Great quote. *Can I read the article?* Just what we want." His words dripped through the phone like acid. "You're going to be in the unemployment line if you keep on like this," he growled at her. You haven't given us anything we can print, and you're making enemies. You better ease up. I'm not going to be able to cover for you. If you're getting paid to write stories, and they're not published - you know what happens. I've been letting your last few articles slip by because I wanted to see what would happen. But we have to pull back. Understand?"

"No, wait a minute," she tried to keep her temper down. "I was hired as an investigative reporter. This is the kind of reporting the paper should want."

"Find another story," said Rudnik bluntly.

"Al," she answered quickly, "This is important. That's why we're running into flak. If it can be proven it has to be told."

"I have our science editor looking into it."

"You weren't going to tell anyone!"

"I gave him your research," he continued, "If he thinks there is any credibility, then you're going to work with him."

"Shit! You're pulling rank." She hated that. It seemed to be the core of everything. Some entitled to powers that others couldn't have. The condition maddened her. She had grown up never thinking much about rights or injustices, about the way people were treated, not till her mother became ill and was hospitalized. Then as a teen-ager Jenny had seen how her pampered, protected mother suddenly became vulnerable and lost her rights. How she was forced to let others take over her decisions and tell her what to do. Even though her mother was in a luxurious private room in the exclusive pavilion section of the hospital, the fear engendered by her mother's vulnerability had made a lasting impression.

That hospital experience was the first time she experienced her emotions being controlled by others. She had felt herself merging with the many patients and families in a common helplessness; like hostages ensnared in a medical maze of chemicals and foreign terminology, Scrubbed surfaces hid the chaos of the hospital's pain and disease. The environment seemed to threaten each one of them on so many varied levels.

The medical staff dressed in uniforms that set them apart had the power to use painkillers and tranquilizers to mask their patients' symptoms. When the inevitable happened and a patient died, they would pile pillows on the corpses to keep death discreet when they had to move it out of it's former resting place. No one seemed to tell the truth. No one seemed to deal in a direct way. The time Jenny had spent in the hospital with her dying mother had been an eye opener for her. The hospital had become a symbol for masking fear and reality with layers of boxed and pre-recorded responses.

Now her eyes were opening to another kind of fear, management's fear of losing their *three p's:* paychecks, pensions and power. Clearly, Al Rudnik feared more for his job then he cared for the truth. Up to this moment he had been a role model for Jenny: the selfless, dedicated newsman.

"Al," she heard herself saying, " We have to deal with this." She could sense his anger rising before his voice reached her.

"You're a journalist, for god's sakes. I need NEWS stories. If you want to write fiction, do a novel or get a crystal ball and set up shop elsewhere

"Oh, come on Al," she pleaded urgently, "You can't take me off this story - not now. Give me some time. Please, I'm begging you. I'll bring in information you just HAVE to print - it will wipe everything else off page one, it's Pulitzer time, I promise."

There was a long silence. When Rudnik finally spoke, his voice sounded hoarse. "I doubt it, but you have a week. Not a day more. If it doesn't knock my socks off you're going to become a statistic and join the unemployment line. I mean it."

"Al," she said almost giggling with relief, "did I ever tell you I love you?"

"One week," he repeated, "then you're going to start on something else. The primaries, that's your next assignment." The line went dead.

Jenny pushed the *end* button and leaned her head on her hands. She needed time to think. Everything seemed to be falling into a pattern.

First there was Tim wanting her to work the primaries, and now Al. Was there a connection? Could they be working together? No, that was ridiculous paranoia. She must stop thinking like that.

CHAPTER SIX

Jenny put the phone in her bag and started to walk away.

"Jenny, hello!" A well built man in his mid thirties with a close-cropped beard and mirrored glasses waved and walked over to her. She hesitated. He looked familiar but she wasn't sure. No name was coming to her. Dressed in an Armani sports jacket over a cashmere sweater and perfectly pressed jeans the man could have been one of hundreds she'd met.

He laughed. "You remember me but you're trying to figure out who I am. I'm Larry Martin, a friend of Tim's. We were introduced at a party some time back."

She smiled. "It must have been awhile ago."

"It was." His handsome face with its patina of expensive grooming glowed perfectly. He could have just stepped off the front cover of L'Homo Vogue.

Jenny was silent as she ran his familiar appearance through her mind.

"Well, I guess I'm forgettable." He waited for an answer, but Jenny didn't comply.

The man lifted his sunglasses for an instant, his piercing eyes unsettling her. He put them quickly back on. "Could it have been a fund raiser?"

"That's a safe guess."

He didn't blanch. "Maybe it was for Councilwoman Gail Major… the party in the Marina?"

I don't think so." Jenny's eyes narrowed. The man was fishing. He had never met her. If he had an inkling of who she was he would know that supporting a person like Gail Major for City Council was not even remotely possible. Once she had quoted Raymond Chandler in an article about money-powered politics describing campaigns like Major's as "taking a tour through a sewer in a glass bottom boat."

"It must have been somewhere else," The man who called himself Martin was getting tense.

"Whatever. Well, bye, I've got to run." She began to walk away.

"Would you like to have lunch?" he asked. "Maybe we can figure out how we know each other over food.

"Sorry, I don't have time."

"How about coffee?" He walked along with her. "Ten minutes?"

"It's ten minutes too long. I have to get to another appointment. Give Tim a call and we'll all get together."

"Tim is going to be away for awhile."

"Oh?" A chill passed through her.

He smiled confidently. "He said he would be in Washington as of last night and wasn't sure when he'd be back."

She studied him closer. She thought she knew most of Tim's friends. Every once in awhile someone would pretend to know one of them because of their high visibility. They'd use names of friends, references from their respective professions. But this man's nonchalant

61

intimacy with Tim's whereabouts grabbed her attention. She wasn't sure if it was mere curiosity or the focused energy one is capable of directing when there is danger. "How do you know that?" she asked, keeping her tone light.

Martin laughed. "He told me you had burned his appointment schedule in the restaurant."

She didn't like what she was feeling. This man talked too much, tried too hard to prove himself. Why? What did he want from her? Her reporter's training told her he had a definite agenda with her other then the one he purported. She was curious. She had to lead him on till she knew what he wanted. "Yes,"

"We're wasting precious time. One more chance at coffee? Seven and a half minutes top?"

She didn't smile at his humor and decided to walk away. "It isn't possible, but thank you anyway." Once again she started toward the escalator leading underground to the parking garage.

"Struck out!" He smiled boyishly as he took a long graceful stride and easily caught up next to her and walked beside her. She could feel heat radiating from his body. Or was it her nerves? .

"Are you parked in the garage?" He asked the obvious. She gave him a quizzical look then whispered, "yes". ...

"So am I. We can go together."

Jenny stepped onto the down escalator with the man called Martin a little too close behind. For some strange reason she caught a glimpse of the blue sky before they descended into the cement recesses beneath the former Twentieth Century Fox Studio lot.

"Still have your BMW?" He asked the back of her head.

Another chill ran up her spine. "Yes," she nearly choked the words out in her attempt to remain casual. "How did you know that?"

"We discussed cars when we met," he said. "Tim wanted you to buy a Land Rover."

Jenny stared straight ahead as she reached the bottom of the escalator then turned toward the next set to continue down even further into the catacombs of Century City parking. The man was still too close. Her heart beat faster, her breathing shallow, fear taking over. She remembered at one point some time ago Tim wanted her to trade in her car and get a Mercedes or a Range Rover. She would not acknowledge it to this man whose intimate knowledge of Tim was making her feel anxious. How could he know all this? What did he want?

She continued down the escalator deep into the depths of Century City, very aware of the man following her as she stepped off four levels below the ground in the direction of a silver arrow against an orange background that pointed toward a gray cavern marked Red.

"Nice to meet you," she said automatically as she started to walk away.

"My car's over there as well."

She paused. She didn't like the sound of his voice. A young couple emerged from around the corner holding each other around the waist. She wanted to call to them, but what could she say? How could she call for help? And why? They continued up the escalator.

The man put his hand on her arm. It startled her.

"I appreciate your company," she said, "but I think I can make it to my car alone, thank you." She started to walk away

His hand tightened. "I have to make sure nothing happens to you."

"It won't." She tried to pull away. He didn't let go. Dread began to swirl. "Please let me go."

"Relax. We'll walk to your car." His fingers closed tighter.

She pulled away, looking desperately for a guard. "Please," she said, her voice growing louder, "let go of me. You're embarrassing yourself."

"No I'm not," his hand tightened painfully, digging into her. "Keep quiet." His grip kept tightening till his fingers almost touched.

Faintness threatened from the fear and the pain. How could this be happening? Where were the people who belonged to these cars? No one was here. It was empty. Empty. "Please let go," she cried. "You're hurting me." She tried yanking away. He held her tighter. The garage stayed deserted.

"Don't fight, I've already won."

He started to drag her towards the white sedan in the far corner. How did he know it was her car? Terror had overtaken her. This man was not kidding, he had taken control.

Strangled with fear she began to shake uncontrollably. He grabbed her chin with one hand and the back of her head with the other. In a quick, whiplash kind of movement, he twisted her head and pain screamed up and down her back. She slumped and he scooped her up and carried her the rest of the way.

Everything grew hazy. This couldn't be happening. This happened to other people, in stories she had written, in statistics. Her invincibility had failed her. There was no one to see or hear her; no one to help her, she was totally alone.

The pain was excruciating, cold sweat damped her good silk blouse, her heart pounded so loud it seemed to reverberate outside herself. Squealing tires negotiating the ramps overhead mixed with a slightly familiar sound. Was she screaming, or was it the cars?

He shoved her into the passenger side of the car and strapped her in, twisting her head again to paralyze her. He got behind the wheel. She wanted to ask why he was doing this to her, but the pain was so intense the *why* was not so important. She wanted the pain to stop.

As he drove up the winding ramp, she tried to steady herself with her hand on the door, but he twisted it till it fell to her side. His white teeth glowed eerily as he turned and smiled. He was enjoying her pain.

"You're going to take pleasure from this," he smiled.

"No," she whimpered.

"You'll have your chance. Don't blow it, in a little while you'll be blowing me."

"Please,"

"That's right. You catch on fast. Always ask permission. Now don't say anything else because I could kill you."

She looked at the black leather gloves gripping the steering wheel and believed him.

He glanced at her, "you need a good fuck. Tim hasn't touched you in a very long time."

His words exploded inside her. How did he know? Bleak foreboding crashed down on her. She wasn't sure she could survive what she was about to go through.

The car stopped at the cashier booth blocking the exit. He handed the parking attendant a ticket and money, pulling away just as the barrier was raised. He closed the window, trapping the exhaust fumes inside with her.

Arriving in daylight, the man reached over and pushed an artery in her neck, sending the people in other cars into a fog of haziness as darkness closed in. She jumped on to the tip of a comet for safety. The comet tilted backward, and fell head first into space.

Nothingness grew blacker till it filled and dissolved into timelessness and she was caught in endless space.

CHAPTER SEVEN

Jenny's eyes began to focus as the car screeched to a halt. The man was saying something but she couldn't make out the words. Her heart was pounding. She felt sick. He was shaking her, telling her to wake up. Suddenly her eyes were riveted at the sight of her own apartment building.

The sidewalk was still damp from an afternoon shower so none of the old regulars were sitting out on the lawn. But it was definitely her building. The man must have driven her home. With her head spinning she reached for the handle of the car door, but the man pulled her back. Her fingers caught between the handle and the upholstery and a nail broke as he yanked her across the front seat, dragging her over the gearshift to the driver's side.

A gang of children were playing across the street - cosmic cowboys in yellow goggles firing toy laser guns. She tried to shout to them as the man pulled her out of the car, but he leaned in close and pressed his lips against her ear. "One sound and you're history," he whispered. Then he gripped her arm and propelled her across the sidewalk to the front door.

At the foot of the steps she tried to grab the handrail but he shoved her through the big swing doors. There was music coming from one of the apartments inside. She tried to call out but he clamped his hand over her mouth and frog-marched her down the long corridor all the way to her own front door. Her neighbor's cat scurried away as they arrived.

He held her against the wall and jabbed the doorbell with his thumb - two long rings. "Please," she begged, "If it's money you want..." but she got no further. The door was opened from the inside and the man hurled her headlong into the apartment.

The living room was dark. Someone had closed the oriental window screens. Jenny barely had time to register this before his next shove sent her crashing to the floor. She tried to get up but a stinging slap hit the side of her head. She reeled into the coffee table, knocking a silver framed picture of Tim onto the floor beside her.

"Not on her face," said a voice sharply, "No marks."

It was a woman's voice. A shadowy form was closing the front door. Jenny scrambled onto her knees but the man put his foot on her hip and pushed her back down.

"Anybody see you?" asked the voice.

"Er, no," the man grunted. He sounded strangely muted, almost deferential. There was a click of heels on the polished floor as a pair of pointed toe high-heeled stiletto shoes came to rest only inches from Jenny's face.

"Pick her up," ordered the voice.

The man grabbed Jenny's arms and yanked her to her feet. With her heart pounding and her breath coming in gasps, Jenny found herself looking into the pale face of a woman with dark wavy hair and a slash of bright red lipstick. She was about forty, well dressed, and there was an air of authority about her.

"Hold her still," said the red lips and the man locked an arm around Jenny's neck, lifting her onto her toes. She could feel his hot breath on her cheek. In the same instant, the woman reached out and tore Jenny's blouse open down the front. Her blouse! Her beautiful silk blouse, she thought to herself crazily, wondering at the same moment how she could possibly care about a blouse at a time like this. Angry with her thoughts she found a burst of new energy and struggled against the man's grip, her heart pounding so hard she thought it would burst. She tried to kick the woman away with her feet. But the man jerked her neck backwards till she almost blacked out. She could feel her skirt being unbuttoned. She twisted and turned but the man's grip was like a vise and she started to choke. She felt her panties rip as the woman pulled them down past her knees.

"Put her on the sofa," said the woman, "it'll be easier there." The man relaxed his grip for a moment and turned Jenny toward the couch. Sensing her chance, she pushed him away with all her strength and made for the door, but he tripped her as she moved and she landed face down on the parquet. Suddenly she yelled out in pain. Something was almost breaking her hand. The woman's pointed toe stiletto shoe wrapped in silver snake skin treaded on her right hand with terrible force. The pain was so sharp that Jenny's scream died in her throat.

"Get the rest off her," said the woman above her. "If she moves, I'll break her hand."

The man knelt down beside Jenny and started to pull off her bra. The woman's full weight on her hand was unbearable. She could hear her own voice sobbing uncontrollably "Oh God, no.... please no.!"

When the man had stripped off all her clothes, the woman slowly removed her foot. Jenny rolled into a fetal position, cradling her hand and sobbing and whimpering like a child. She was naked.

The woman's eyes roamed over Jenny's skin as if she was appraising an object in a display case. "Nice body," she said to the man. Then she walked calmly into the kitchen and reappeared with a cup of coffee in her hand. She stepped over to an armchair and sat down, crossing her legs elegantly. Then, like a scientist examining a moth in a jar, she gazed down at Jenny and slowly sipped the coffee.

Jenny was trying not to cry but it was a losing battle. Tears of pain were streaming down her face. After a few moments the woman carefully picked a piece of lint off her sleeve, then placed her cup on the low table beside the chair and lit a cigarette with a Dunhill lighter.

When she finally spoke, it was in an almost sympathetic tone, like a doctor talking to a patient.

"Calm down, Jenny." She said evenly. "Nothing's broken."

Jenny gazed up at the woman through her tears. She felt like a wounded bird in front of a cat. The pain in her hand had started to lessen, but a terrible fear now gripped her mind. The woman had called her Jenny. She knew her name. Who were these people? What did they want from her?

"Go and sit on the sofa," said the woman, "We need to talk." But Jenny didn't move. She just lay there, curled up on her side, still nursing her throbbing hand. With a silent sigh, the woman rose and stubbed out her cigarette. Her movements were slow, almost studied. Suddenly she jabbed Jenny's ribs with the snakeskin wrapped toe of her shoe. "On the sofa," she snapped. "Now." Jenny glanced quickly up at the man. He was standing over her like a sentinel, daring her to defy the order.

Hesitantly, Jenny began to move. Then she stopped and covered her breasts with her hands, suddenly aware of her nakedness. The woman snapped her fingers and the man took a pace forward. Without warning his hand flashed down and grabbed Jenny's hair. Hot pain seared her scalp as he dragged her backwards onto the sofa and shoved her down into the cushions. Instinctively, she covered her head with her arms to ward off a blow. None came.

There was silence in the room. She could hear the children still playing in the street outside - so near and yet so far. Had one of them seen her being pulled out of the car? Would they tell someone? Would somebody come soon and end this nightmare? The woman was speaking again. "Let's get something straight," she was saying, "I don't repeat things. Ever. Understand?" Jenny nodded quickly but she didn't understand at all. She didn't understand anything. Who were these people and why were they doing this to her?

The woman had moved away again. She was opening a large, black

Alligator Hermes handbag on the coffee table. Jenny had not noticed the purse before, nor had she noticed the black leather coat thrown casually over her desk. There was a half-filled glass on the mantelpiece, together with an open bottle of scotch. Jenny's crystal ice bucket was on the table. How long had this woman been in her apartment? Who had let her in? The woman was pulling a small, shiny object out of her purse. She tossed it to the man who caught it in the air and put it in his pocket. What was it? A pen, a knife? Jenny watched as the woman took a small can out of her purse and walked over to the window. She paused there and looked out. Jenny didn't move. Her nakedness had made her so vulnerable that she hardly dared to breathe.

After a moment, the woman turned to face her. "Now listen carefully," she said. "We can make this unpleasant, or we can make it rewarding. The choice is yours." Jenny drew her knees up, trying to cover herself. Her mind was racing. Someone had let this woman into the apartment, someone with a key. She had made herself at home here, poured herself a drink, even made coffee for god's sake. What was she doing here? What did she want?

"I believe you ride horses," the woman was saying, "so you'll know why they have to be trained." Jenny wasn't listening. She was eyeing the phone. If only she could reach the phone. "I use the word trained because it's much nicer than broken," the woman continued, "but the purpose is the same - helping the animal to reach it's potential. Well, that's what we do too," she added, "only we do it with people."

She stared at Jenny for a long moment, and then stepped slowly over to the couch. "You haven't understood a word, have you?" She sighed, "Forget trying to escape." She indicated the man with a wave of her hand, "He's very well trained." She stopped in front of the couch and shook the small can in her hand. Jenny could read the label now. It said Quick Foam. "Open your legs," ordered the woman.

Jenny tried to shrink away from her, along the couch, but the man moved like lightning. He suddenly gripped her knees, bruising her flesh

71

with his thumbs, and forced her legs apart. Almost simultaneously, the woman squirted the can between her thighs. The foam was cool, with a faint aroma of mint - shaving foam. "If you don't want him to cut you, keep still," cautioned the woman. The man was holding a slim razor in his hand.

Jenny's heart was pounding. What was the brute going to do? It was a silly question because she already knew the answer. She closed her eyes tightly, trying to blot out the nightmare, as she felt the blade touch her skin. "Mustn't move..." Whispered a voice in her head. "Don't give him any excuse..." Hot tears of shame and anger welled up behind her eyelids as the man began to shave her.

"Total nakedness leads to total openness," said the woman, "and thence to complete acceptance."

With swift and easy strokes, the razor did its job. From time to time the man rubbed the foam in with his fingers, touching her like a lover. There were other voices in her head now. One of them was saying, "You're going to survive..." And another said, "Stay calm..." She tried to imagine her mother standing over her, sprinkling talcum powder on her soft baby's legs, but it didn't help. The reality was too powerful. Openness? Acceptance? What did she mean?

"Finished?" Asked the woman. Jenny squinted through her lashes. She saw the man nod as the woman handed him her torn silk blouse. Then she watched while he carefully wiped the foam from her thighs. Some of it had run down onto the sofa and he wiped that up too. One of the voices in Jenny's head began to giggle. Despite herself, she understood why. This man had slapped and choked her as if nothing mattered to him, not even human life, yet here he was wiping flecks of shaving foam off the sofa. Jenny started to close her legs together.

"Wait till you're told," snapped the woman. Then she leaned in and felt the newly shaved skin with her fingers. "Good," she nodded to the man. "The water's in the tub." Then she turned and picked up the phone.

The man grabbed one of Jenny's ankles and pulled her onto the floor. The woman finished dialing and started a conversation but Jenny didn't hear it. The man was dragging her across the floor by her foot. She clawed at a chair as she passed but the man was moving too fast. Her head hit the doorframe as they entered the bathroom, making her cry out in pain.

But her yell was stifled by shock as her body hit the water. The bath water was ice cold.

The moment he had thrown her in, the man plunged her head under the surface and held her down. She kicked her legs and tried to grab his arm with her hands above the surface. But it was no use - her fingers kept slipping. Her lungs were at bursting point and she started to panic. She felt sure she was going to die.

He let her up for a moment and she gulped in air. Then he pushed her back down again. She could see the undulating image of the woman behind him. The man let go once more and she came up violently, coughing and splashing water everywhere. The woman stepped back with a look of irritation on her face. A few stray drops had wet her jacket. Fastidiously she took a towel and carefully blotted them off. "She's had enough," said the woman, "Take her out."

Jenny was coughing desperately as the man pulled her out of the water. He slung her over his shoulder like a dripping sack and carried her into the living room. Then, with surprising gentleness, he laid her on the floor. She rolled over onto her side, still helplessly coughing and gasping for air, but the woman nudged her with her toe. "On your back," she insisted, "You were placed that way for a purpose."

Jenny tried to obey but her body wasn't listening. She felt the man's hands on her shoulders as he rolled her onto her back.

"This is your test of acceptance," said the woman, "so you'll offer no resistance. No resistance at all. Is that clear?" She stood there waiting for a reply. When none came, she suddenly shouted "Answer!" And Jenny managed a nod. She had no fight left in her now. She just lay there, shivering and coughing on the floor, while the woman tied her wrists with a cord from one of her bathrobes. She could see the man walking toward them with the crystal ice bucket.

"Acceptance is a very great virtue," the woman said quietly, "so just let this happen, okay?" Then without warning, the woman's fingers pushed an ice cube into Jenny's vagina.

Jenny screamed, and the man switched on the TV set. A game show filled the room with raucous laughter as Jenny writhed in pain. On the screen, a contestant was hopping up and down like a chicken while the studio audience roared their appreciation. Jenny gasped in shock as the woman pushed another cube into her. But she couldn't fight back. Her hands were tied and she had no strength any more. All she could do was lie there, weeping, as the woman filled her with ice.

The man had picked up Jenny's torn pantyhose and now the woman took it from him. She used it to bind Jenny's thighs together, just above the knees. "This takes ten minutes," she said to the man, "Go and pour yourself a drink."

When Jenny's legs were tightly bound, the woman stood up and casually smoothed her skirt. Then she walked away and left her.

For a long time Jenny lay there, crying softly, while the ice slowly melted inside her. The pain was greater than any she'd ever known, but she could hear the voices calling *"You're not alone ... we're with you ... we're here to help you through..."*

The woman was calmly flicking through a magazine as if this were her own home. After a few seconds, she picked up the remote control of the TV, zapped through the channels, and began to watch the news. The man had poured himself a scotch. "That's my glass," said the woman. "Get one from the kitchen. Top shelf on the left."

As the man wandered into the kitchen, he paused for a moment and gazed down at Jenny. She was lying on her side now with her knees drawn up, breathing deeply against the pain. He opened his mouth as if to speak to her, then he noticed the woman watching him, and he stuck two fingers in the sugar bowl, put a sugar cube in his mouth and quickly moved away.

By the time the man had returned and drunk some scotch, the ice had almost melted. The woman checked her watch, then switched off the TV, and knelt down beside Jenny. She swept some hair out of the girl's eyes and gently untied her legs. Jenny didn't move. She was breathing shallowly now and her body was limp with exhaustion. "You bore this bravely," the woman said approvingly, "I'll make sure it goes in your report." Then, with a silken touch, she began to caress Jenny's breasts.

"We must all learn acceptance, Jenny," she murmured softly, "then we can be accepted too. Imagine a world where everyone serves the same ideal - some in mind and others in body. Isn't that a beautiful thought?"

Jenny could feel the woman's fingers coaxing her legs apart, and she suddenly stiffened. But the voices whispered softly, "Don't tense up ... we'll help you ... we're here to guide you through..."

The woman's red nailed fingers were opening Jenny's shaved vagina like a flower, gently stimulating her as she laid there, eyes closed, in the quiet room. The man stepped over to watch as the woman leaned in to use her tongue. Jenny shuddered. "Don't fight it..." said the voices "let her have you ... give her what she wants..." The woman's tongue began to probe. And Jenny bit her lip.

For a moment, she fancied that she was on the ceiling looking down at herself, watching it all from above. But only for a moment. Then she was back in the real world, feeling the woman's tongue. She opened her eyes and saw the man gazing down at her, studying her face. But the moment their eyes met, he looked away and put another sugar cube in his mouth. How strange, she thought - he's embarrassed. "Yes..." said the voices. "That's your strength ... he's starting to feel your power.

The woman was sliding her lips up Jenny's ribs. She kissed her breasts and fluttered her tongue, encouraging her nipples to harden. Then she whispered in her ear "You're wetter now than in the bath. I think you're going to be easy."

Jenny froze. Could it be true? Was her body responding? How could it? She hated this woman, loathed her. She was brutal, disgusting. She had tortured her, hurt her, and forced her. How could her body respond? Or was it the siren voices that had betrayed her? Oh god, was she going crazy? Surely this was all a ghastly dream and she would wake up soon? Please let it be a dream. Please ...

"We can't..." the voices answered, "it's real and you have to survive." Jenny's mind was reeling now, and tears were beginning to come. Who were these voices and why were they telling her these things? Were they trying to drive her insane? "No ...!" they all babbled, "You're starting to win just give her what she wants ...

Jenny moved her hips a little, and the voices shouted, "Yes...!" Hot tears rolled down her cheeks as she forced her body to move, pulsing in rhythm with the fingers - slowly at first, then faster and faster. Her skin grew warm and started to tingle. She caught a glimpse of the man smiling down at her, and as she wrenched with anger her body arched upwards. "Now!" chorused the voices as Jenny's cries mingled with theirs.

Quite suddenly the woman was on her feet. "I said she'd be easy," she smiled to the man, "Put her on the door." Her voice was detached, professional again. She was wiping her fingers on Jenny's blouse.

Very slowly Jenny curled her body into a ball. She felt devastated. The woman had humiliated her, used her, mocked her, and she hadn't been able to resist. "God how I hate you," she whispered. She didn't care if the woman heard her. She didn't care what happened now. Her own body had betrayed her. What greater betrayal could there be?

The man's strong hands were lifting her to her feet, and Jenny's head swam as he carried her to the bathroom door. With surprising gentleness, he set her down and lifted her bound wrists above her head.

He threw the long end of the cord over the top of the door and pulled her arms up high. Then he tied the cord to the inside handle, and pulled the door firmly shut, jamming the cord tightly in the top of the door.

Like some medieval sacrifice, Jenny stood there on tiptoe. With her back to the door and her hands held high by the cord, she was utterly helpless. The woman came to stand in front of her.

"Sex is the greatest control mechanism in the world," she said in a clinical tone, "Things you hate, you can be taught to love. And things you enjoy, we can make you hate." Jenny could see the man undressing near the sofa. He had a magnificent body. Every muscle had been worked on and there was not an ounce of fat. "After this, you'll be a different person," the woman told her, "Our kind of person." The man was naked now. Slowly he came to stand next to the woman. He didn't look at her.

"Nice isn't he?" she chuckled. "He's my personal fucking machine." She had said it with the sort of throwaway pride that a rich person might use to describe an expensive car or a work of art. "Now, he understands acceptance perfectly," she added "which is why we use him so much." She lifted the man's penis and started to stroke it, taking care that Jenny could see every move. Jenny watched it rising in the woman's hand. It happened so smoothly, almost elegantly, that Jenny wondered if they were lovers. She searched the man's face for a clue but his eyes never flickered. He just stood there, letting her work him up, and avoiding Jenny's gaze.

"I've often wondered what it would be like to be him," the woman mused. "He's just an animal really," she smiled, "all libido and no brain. Still, he satisfies me when I need it. Let's see what he can do for you."

She's treating him like she treated me, Jenny thought. To her, he's just an object, something to be used. By now the man was as hard as a rock and the woman tested his readiness by flicking his penis with her long red nails. It made him wince and he took an involuntary step backwards. "Stand still," she ordered, and did it again. This time he didn't flinch. "That's better," she said, ""Well don't just stand there, go and fuck her. And make sure she breaks."

As the man came toward her the voices in Jenny's head gabbled "Use your body ... use your power ... use it now, and win..." But she didn't know what the voices meant, and panic gripped her heart. The man put his arms around her and guided each of her legs around one of his own. Then supporting her buttocks with his hands he entered her smoothly and started to thrust.

"He won't stop till I give him permission," the woman said, "so this could take a while." Then she turned away to the table and opened her big purse. When she returned, she had a miniature video camera in her hand. She aimed the lens at Jenny's face and tapped the man on the shoulder. "Now break her," she ordered, "and do it right. They need to see this on tape."

The man grunted and thrust into Jenny like a bull, pounding her into the door, as the woman started the camera. "Use your power..." Jabbered the voices, "use it now ... use it before it's too late..." Jenny's mind flew in all directions, trying to grasp their meaning. Use her power? What power? How? Then, in a flash, she understood.

Slowly, very slowly, she lifted her legs and wrapped them around the man's waist. "Yes...!" cheered the voices, "Take him from her..." Jenny fancied she saw a glimmer of puzzlement on the woman's face as she tightened her legs and clasped the man to her. But perhaps it was her imagination. Everything was moving so fast. The woman was stepping around them now, squinting through the lens and giving the man instructions. "Good, that's good. Now slap her. They'll need to see her cry."

But the man didn't slap her, and Jenny didn't cry. She was whispering softly in his ear "Just ignore her. Do it your way. Have me how you want."

The man moved his head and looked at her with puzzled eyes. And

Jenny knew the voices had saved her. He wasn't a robot, just a man. He wanted her for himself. She could feel his excitement mounting as she whispered, "Just enjoy me. Fuck me your way. Fuck me for yourself," and gradually she felt his whole body relax. His rhythm changed as he held her tight, then he pressed his cheek to hers.

"What are you doing?" the woman snapped, "Use her!" and Jenny laughed inside. She buried her head in the man's shoulder and murmured, "Really use me. Come in me. Come in me right now." And suddenly the man cried out. Like Jenny before him he couldn't hold back. She felt him explode inside her as he threw his head back and gasped. Then he buried his face in her breasts. The voices shrieked, "You've won...!" Sweat was pouring down his chest, trickling on to her stomach. Slowly Jenny unclasped her legs, and the man subsided completely.

The woman lowered the camera, her face contorting with rage. "You Cretan," she hissed, "get away from her." The man let go of Jenny and leaned heavily on the doorframe, breathing hard. Then the woman slapped his face. Jenny's heart leaped. She had used her body to conquer the man and now she would deal with the woman.

"You were right," Jenny smiled at the woman. "He's great. Shall we do it all again?"

The woman's eyes were like slits. "You don't amuse me any more Ms. Webster," she grated. Then she turned on her heel and strode away into the bedroom. Jenny could hear her opening the closet door. The man was still leaning on the doorframe, breathing hard and looking down at the floor. Despite herself, Jenny couldn't help a twinge of feeling. What had they done to him - whomever "they" were - to make him like this? Perhaps he wasn't a brute after all. Perhaps he'd been beaten and tortured like her. And perhaps he could help her escape.

But Jenny's thoughts went no further. The woman was standing in the bedroom door holding something in her hand. She glared for a moment at both of them, then strode over to the man and handed the object to him. It was Jenny's dressage whip. Jenny's mind went numb as she realized how this might end.

The woman stepped back with her chin held high, like a ringmaster about to announce the finale. When she spoke, her voice was shrill. "You use that on horses, don't you?" She said, pointing to the whip. It was a statement, not a question. "Well let's turn the tables, shall we? Let's see how it works on you." Then she snarled at the man "if you can't control your body, do it with that. Now break her."

The man swished the whip downwards, testing it in the air. Jenny could tell from the way he handled it that this was the first time he had ever held a whip in his hands. He seemed hesitant, undecided.

"What the hell's wrong with you?" The woman's voice was dry with anger and she was trying to moisten her lips. "Do it," she grated, "or I'll have you killed. Now thrash her."

Jenny tensed her body preparing for the pain. The man raised his arm, then WHACK! The whip slashed across her thighs. It was a glancing blow but it seared her skin like a hot wire. "Not her legs," the woman jeered, "her breasts. And I want to see blood."

WHACK! The whip stung Jenny's arms, narrowly missing her face. The man seemed agitated, uncoordinated. "Oh for god's sake, get out of here!" snarled the woman, and she snatched the whip out of his hands. Then as the man turned away she suddenly brought the whip up sharply between Jenny's legs. The girl let out a piercing cry and the woman did it again. Then she took a half pace backward and hit her across the midriff, leaving a thin pink welt almost a foot long.

"I'll break you if it's the last thing I do," she promised and raised the whip once more. This time, she found the target. Jenny felt an explosion of pain in her right breast, then an agonizing blow on her left. She screamed and the woman began to smile. Tiny traces of blood were trickling from two thin stripes across Jenny's breasts and the voices were calling again. "Use it, Jenny ... use the pain ... use the pain to fly...!"

SLASH! Her breasts were bleeding freely now. And the voices

shouted, "Fly...!"

"Oh god!" she sobbed, but she could feel herself rising. A force was raising her up. She heard the whip hit her again but she didn't feel the pain. She was leaving all that behind. With each new blow the force took her higher, and the voices chanted, "Fly...!" It was thrilling, it was ecstasy. Jenny felt lighter than air. She laughed out loud as the whip cracked down and she closed her eyes in bliss.

Then suddenly the voices faded. They just died away and stopped. Jenny opened her eyes. The woman was standing with the whip in her hand and confusion on her face. Far from breaking her victim, the whipping had made her laugh. The girl had actually laughed.

Jenny gazed at her tormentor and, in that moment, the battle was won. She whispered very softly. "Hurt me again, as much as you like. You're never going to break me." The woman stood her ground for a heartbeat, holding Jenny's gaze. Then she blinked. It was the smallest flicker, the tiniest movement, but it's meaning was louder than thunder. Jenny watched in silence as the woman turned away.

"YOU'VE WON!" screamed the voices, and Jenny laughed again. She laughed at the woman who couldn't control her. She laughed at the fear and the pain. And the voices chanted "yes-yes-yes." and Jenny was flying again.

Up and up she soared. Up through the ceiling and into the clouds, away to a secret place. She had left her body far behind. The man and the woman were mere flesh and blood, but Jenny was different from them. Jenny could leave her body - the voices had taught her to fly. She could see the world spread out below her, and even see her room, but she wasn't there at all any more. She was free, like a bird in song.

Jenny could fly like an angel!

CHAPTER EIGHT

Someone was tapping. Jenny turned her head and started with alarm at the sight of a man's face looking at her through a car window. A car? What was she doing in a car? She started to move, but she was strapped down. Then she realized she was held down only by a seat belt and her panic started to subside.

The man was wearing a hat - some kind of uniform. Who was he? How did she get in this car?

"You okay Miss?" shouted the man through the glass.

Jenny sat up straighter, her head pounding, groggy, she desperately needed some air. She started to open the window but stopped. What about the man - what if he grabbed her? He tapped the window again, "You all right?"

She wasn't. Her head was spinning and she felt very dizzy, plus her eyes felt grainy and she couldn't see very well. She wanted a drink of water. Why was she here and what was this all about?

The man's face showed concern. He had a badge pinned to his jacket. Could he be a policeman? He looked too old. Hammers were pounding behind her eyes, over her forehead, she couldn't think clearly. "Take a breath..." said a voice.

She did what she was told and the pounding slowly subsided. She then noticed the word SECURITY printed on the man's jacket, and

"ANSON" stamped on the badge. OH GOD! She was in Anson's parking garage. Why was she here? Had she passed out? She suddenly realized that she was in her own car.

The man frowned, "Do you need help?" he yelled and tapped again. Then he unsnapped a leather pouch attached to his belt and took out a cellular phone.

On the floor of the passenger side of her car Jenny saw the tip of a fingernail. Her hand on the door handle flashed through her mind and she remembered someone pulling at her, but she couldn't remember what happened then. She shook her head and yelled to the man, "No, I'm fine," then started to search for the keys to her car. She had to get out, she was going to smother. The keys weren't in her handbag, she pulled everything out. "I can't find my keys..." She called to the guard. He tapped the window and pointed. Her keys were in the ignition.

"Are you sure you're all right?" the guard shouted through the window. "Can you drive?" His words set her on edge, she had to get out.

"Yes, I'm fine."

Her smile was not from the heart as she turned the key in the ignition, a sigh of relief as the car started up. Giving the guard a small wave she quickly backed out of the parking space and made her way toward the exit signs. Her heart beating as the car pulled away, Jenny noticed in the rear view mirror that the guard wrote down the number of her license plate.

Jenny just missed hitting the barrier as she skidded to a stop in front of the exit booth. The garage attendant's eyebrows raised with annoyance as she watched Jenny sift through her things, searching for the parking ticket. Jenny opened the window, taking a quick gulp of the relatively fresh air, "Uh, excuse me," she asked the attendant, "but what does the ticket look like?"

"Like a parking ticket honey," said the attendant, "Try your glove compartment or the sun visor," she advised.

"Oh." Jenny felt stupid. Just the other day she had bought a large plastic clip to hold things like parking tickets. She remembered using it when she entered the garage. She paused, trying to grab a fleeting thought about the garage, but it flew past her. BLAM! The driver in the car behind blew his horn, he was losing his patience. She took the parking ticket stamped ANSON INDUSTRIES and handed it to the parking attendant who handed it back. "It's purple," announced the woman, "that's yesterday's."

"What?" Jenny could barely ask. "It can't be," she was incredulous.

"I just got it from your machine, uh - today," she stammered

"Nope, it's yesterday's," the attendant repeated. Today's tickets are white." She held one up for display.

"But, I - I got this today," Jenny protested, foreboding starting to creep in her mind. She couldn't have been here overnight, wouldn't a security guard have noticed her? "It has to be a mistake," she said, watching as the walls of the garage began to undulate and come close. "Never mind," she said as she saw the wall behind the woman move up, "I have to get out of here, how much do I owe?"

"That's sixty eight dollars, forty eight for yesterday, and twenty for today," the woman gloated, obviously relishing this aspect of her job.

Jenny fumbled till she found her wallet and pulled out three twenty-dollar bills. "Do you take credit cards?"

BLAM! The man in the car behind her used his horn again, BLAM! Then another one. Jenny's heart pounded as she stuck her fingers deep into the secret pocket of her wallet where she usually hid extra money for emergencies of this kind. BLAM, BLAM, BLAM - other cars were joining the dissonant band. She was shaken, embarrassed, and then relieved as her fingers found a hidden folded bill. She pulled it out and saw it was fifty dollars. Shaking with relief she handed the woman the fifty and a twenty. "Keep the change. Just let me out."

"Don't you want a receipt?" asked the woman, "it's a lot of money," she opened the cash drawer and extracted her tip then began to write a cash receipt for Jenny's seventy dollars.

"No, please," Jenny tried not to sound desperate "Just lift the barrier, I don't want the receipt"

"Oh don't let them bother you," the woman lifted her chin to indicate the other drivers, "it's good to make them wait. Makes you more desirable." She winked. "I read that in NEW WOMEN." She handed Jenny the receipt, which Jenny threw on top of the other articles strewn on the passenger seat.

She pressed the gas pedal to the floor once the barrier was raised. Squealing and peeling rubber she drove unsteadily up the dark twisting ramp, nearly bumping into the wall a few times as she searched for a radio station to give her the time and the day.

When she came into daylight, Pico Boulevard was filled with cars whizzing by at breakneck speed. Behind her impatient drivers blew their horns and inched forward to make her go faster into the oncoming traffic. She wouldn't take the chance. Her nerves were too shattered to drive aggressively and she couldn't see clearly – everything seemed blurry. There were other times when she would be macho with her car, but for now, she needed to go at her own pace.

A break in the traffic gave her a chance to turn, but as soon as she began she felt a terrible pain in her arms. The pain spread, her shoulders ached, as did her right hand. She noticed that whenever she took a deep breath a slight pull and burning crossed her midriff. In fact, her whole body ached as if she had been beaten. What was happening? Why were the cars going so fast? Was she unknowingly caught in the middle of some emergency exodus?

She held the wheel tightly, holding on for dear life, feeling like she was choking and needing to loosen her collar. Tentatively she took one hand off the wheel and reached for the top button of her blouse. Something was wrong - she adjusted the rear view mirror so she could see herself. The blouse she was wearing was not what she had on before. It had different buttons - the buttons on her Armani silk blouse had been pearl, these were plastic, in fact the blouse was pink instead of off-white and made of cotton instead of silk.

The car swerved. Somebody had changed her clothes! What was happening? She finds herself in her car in a garage with a parking ticket from the day before and wearing different clothes! Had she blacked out? Lost a day? What was happening? She had to pull over; her head was swimming so badly she could barely see. She had to stop this car.

She noticed her skin was hurting, burning under her blouse. The car was swerving, moving almost independently, the directional signal blinking wildly, she tried to pull over and finally managed to get to a yellow line. Turning off the ignition, her fingers shaking as if palsied, Jenny unbuttoned the bottom part of her blouse and lifted both the blouse and the silk camisole up to her breasts.

She saw the welts, heard once again the sting of the whip, the slashes across her flesh burning with anger. Once again she could see the ripping blouse, the bra, the man, her surrender and her empowerment, the terrible dread and utter helplessness. Oh God she sobbed as she traced the criss crosses of congealed blood across her midriff and breasts. They were warm and very sore. She sobbed as the memory of that nightmare continued to fill her mind. A nightmare she wished she was dreaming, but which the physical evidence made painfully real. She wanted to go home, She needed to take care of herself.

It took twenty minutes longer than usual till Jenny pulled in front of her apartment. The tires bumped into the curb, the hubcaps making a loud scraping noise. This time the gaggle of old people were sitting out on the lawn, turning as a single unit to watch as she badly parked her car. Where were those people yesterday when she had needed them? They were here to annoy, but disappear when they could help. Waves of despair and resentment started to grow in her and she fought to keep them away. She didn't want depression to control her, especially now. She needed positive strength.

She nodded a quick hello as she walked quickly to the front door, pretending not to hear the raspy voice of her neighbor Carol calling to her, seeing out of the corner of her eye as the hefty woman dragged a loaded shopping cart up the sidewalk with one hand and her squirming four year old son with the other.

Jenny's legs felt stiff as she climbed to the second floor. All she wanted to do was soak in a bath when suddenly a feeling of horror took over her. She remembered the bath. Slowing her pace she approached the front door. Hesitating and full of dread she put the key in the lock.

She hadn't considered, hadn't even thought about the possibility that those two people could still be there. She had been in such a rush for the security and the familiarity of her apartment, that she had forgotten what had happened there. She didn't want to go in alone and started to turn away just as the door opened. OH MY GOD! Was it one of them? She started to run. Would they shoot her? Was she about to feel the shock of hot lead going through her back?

"Meez Jeennie," a voice cried out. "Meez Jeennie." Jenny froze then relaxed. It was Clarita, her Guatemalan maid. The dark haired woman, once a beauty but marred now by hard work and pain stood in the hallway and called out to her, "you not come in?" she asked.

"Clarita," Jenny motioned to her frantically. "Come here. Venga! Are you alone?"

Clarita looking confused took a few steps towards her, Si," she said hugging herself, "No anyone, solo me."

"No other personas en la casa?" Jenny questioned. Clarita shook her head.

Jenny walked cautiously toward her and peered in the door. The apartment was sparkling and shining, yet different, like a stage set and very cold.

"Did somebody help you?" she asked the woman who stood nervously by her side. "It's muy bueno, very clean. You did a good job."

The woman shook her head, uncomfortable and embarrassed. "I no able to work today," she apologized. "My little boy sick. We go to hospital. He okay now, but I have no time."

"Oh." Jenny's heart dropped. But someone had cleaned. It was immaculate. Had they gotten to Clarita? Paid her to stay away? Was that why she was so nervous? "Que pasa?" she asked the woman what was wrong with her.

Clarita looked at the floor and wrung her hands. "Mi hijo," she began, and suddenly Jenny understood that the woman's problems had nothing to do with hers. "Do you need money?" Jenny asked.

"Si," she nodded, her eyes very sad. Jenny motioned her to come with her into the apartment. She would have paid anything to have someone with her at this time. The house felt alien, sinister. Were the deeds still alive in the walls? Since energy cannot be destroyed but only transmuted into another form, could the memories come out to haunt her if only she were there? Could it be the memories of what had been done? A shiver went through her. Her home wasn't hers any more.

Gingerly she touched her desk and pulled out her checkbook from the drawer. She quickly checked the numbers, everything was intact. It was not money or goods those people were after, it was her soul. She made out a check for a month's wages, and handed it to Clarita who hadn't expected that much. Jenny cased the room, trying to see into the bedroom as Clarita started toward the door.

"Clarita," Jenny stopped her. "Would you do me a favor? Would you come with me as I go through the house?"

"Ees problem?" Clarita asked, her eyes no stranger to atrocities and dangerous times.

"No, no problem," Jenny tried to soothe this refugee of revolutions and killer earthquakes, "I'm sola, no Tim," she shrugged with a shaky smile. The Guatemalan shook her head in understanding and together they toured the house. There was a strange new scent, a medicinal disinfectant that had been loosely covered with a cheap floral scent. It was the kind they used in hospitals and other public buildings. That was a mistake, Jenny thought, if they used professional cleaners then there was the possibility they could be traced. Suddenly a chill passed through her. They had to know that. It was obvious they just didn't care.

She noticed her bathrobe hanging on the back of the door, the cord through the belt loops, all clean and ironed and freshly done. The bottle of Scotch had been removed from the living room and when she looked in the liquor cabinet it had been replaced. The crystal ice bucket was back on the shelf. The ice - Could she ever touch ice or look at that bucket again?

Clarita was getting antsy. She wanted to leave. "Los muchachos, my boys," she explained, "they home from school now."

"Go ahead, Clarita." Jenny wished someone she loved would be home for her. She wished she could call somebody; tell him or her what happened. But who? She didn't feel comfortable calling Tim.

There were no messages recorded in the answering machine - or at least, none remained if there had been any. Was it possible Tim hadn't called? The announcement she had made was still on - at least they hadn't erased that. But what had they erased in her? What damage had been done? How soon would she know? She knew she was still in shock, and why had they taken her back to the garage?

She sat down on the sofa and ran her fingers through her hair. Leaning back she put her fingers inside her blouse and nudged her silk camisole up till she could feel the tender welts on her body still very warm. She surveyed the room, the bathroom door where less than 24 hours before she had hung like a primitive sacrifice. Could it have been a random act? Was she a victim of being in the wrong place at the wrong time? No, the man had known too much about her and the woman had been in her house. They had done a lot of research, it was very well planned. The woman kept referring to the "others." Who were those others, and who did the woman call? It was no use checking the telephone records because they must have already eradicated them. These people were professionals, they were not sloppy and would leave no clues behind that they didn't want left.

She needed to talk to someone, a friendly voice, definitely not the police or any other authorities. The last thing she wanted was to be treated without sensitivity, she needed a friend, not anyone who would probe.

Mannie! Why didn't she think of her immediately? She rushed to the phone. By providence she didn't have to wait long for the operator to answer and then Mannie picked up on the first ring. "Mannie," her voice caught in her throat, she couldn't contain the tears that covered her voice, "I need help."

"What's wrong? You sound awful. What's happened?"

"We can't talk on the phone, can we meet earlier?"

"Sure. My God. Are you all right? Do you want me to pick you up?"

"No, that's all right. I was able to drive home, I can drive now." She took a breath. "Your favorite place? In about an hour?" Everything was kept vague because of Mannie's tapped phone. It was probable now that Jenny's home was bugged as well.

"All right, but take care of yourself, all right?"

"I will," promised Jenny, "and Mannie, you too, drive carefully."

"I always do. You know I'm the best driver around."

Jenny laughed. She couldn't believe she was still able to do that. Mannie was one of the world's worst drivers though she believed she was the best. It always made Jenny laugh - even now.

God how she loved her friend. She could hardly wait to see her. She knew Mannie was good emotional medicine for her.

CHAPTER NINE

The car phone wasn't working. Every time Jenny picked it up, static made it impossible to hear anything. Although she had left early, construction on Wilshire Boulevard was causing a major traffic jam so it would probably take another fifteen minutes just to go a few blocks. Her hands tightened on the wheel. She didn't want to wait. She needed Mannie now.

She checked her watch with the one on the dash. They were both the same, It might be twenty minutes or more till she got to the restaurant. She tried Anson Labs again. The operator couldn't hear her, too much static.

There were so many cellular phones in Los Angeles the circuits were overloaded. Trapped in gridlock on the street and in the air, movement and communication stopped, she was terribly alone. What if someone tried getting into her car? Could she defend herself even with all these people around? She hadn't before. She gripped the steering wheel tighter

Should she have called Tim or did he already know? Anger crept into swirling despair as she made herself suffer with her own imagination. Why was she so ready to indict Tim, to cast him in the role of villain? Had he hurt her so badly and made her so angry she could only think about him negatively? Perhaps she was mistaken. The thought made her feel better.

Thank God she was meeting Mannie. She was the kind of friend with whom she could talk short hand. Mannie knew about rape.

Mannie's older brother had molested her when she was ten, then an uncle attacked her six years later. When Mannie left Brazil to go to school in the States, she changed her name from Manuela to Mannie and never wore dresses, high heels or make-up again. She cut her hair short and wore men's style clothing. But with her long legs, chiseled cheekbones and shiny black hair, she was a standout beauty despite her attempts to annihilate her looks.

Jenny had roomed with Mannie for four years at Radcliff and despite what the other coeds and even Tim used to say, she knew Mannie wasn't gay, just uninterested in dating. Her sexual energy went into her work, science was her passion, research her love. Her desires were only that she be allowed to use her brilliant brain in pursuit of scientific discoveries. After receiving her MD, Magna Cum Laude, from Harvard Medical School, Anson Industries offered Mannie a research position in their state of the art laboratories along with a fine support staff and a salary three times larger than offered by anyone else. Jenny had been relieved Mannie was in Los Angeles when she decided to move there with Tim.

A space was available in front of the restaurant as soon as she pulled up, the first good sign in what had been the worst twenty-four hours of her life. She checked herself in the rear view mirror and put on dark glasses. There was a slight chance she was holding up and could pass through civilization.

Grease filled the long narrow room of Mannie's favorite restaurant, Kaplan's Deli. She couldn't understand how her elegant cosmopolitan friend could possibly like a place where smoke permeated the ceilings and the plastic decorations. An edible smog. Next time she will choose the restaurant.

Jenny searched the room for Mannie but she wasn't there. A short heavy-set man wiped his greasy hands on a bloodstained apron and walked over to her. She backed away. "One?" he asked, a heavy scent of tobacco seeping through the gap in his teeth when he opened his mouth to speak.

"I'm expecting someone. I'll wait."

"You can have a table," he said, reaching out a hand to lead her.

She shrank away before his bloody fingers could touch her. "No thanks, I'd rather wait here,

"Whatever you want," he shrugged and went back behind the counter.

She examined the contents of the deli case. Orderly rows of red fish lay on their side, mouths opened in silent screams. She sensed someone behind her and turned, her throat closing before she could scream. A sinister looking old man stood too close behind her. He wore dark black glasses and a threadbare felt hat that shadowed his lined, mottled face. Strands of greasy gray hair stuck out from the bottom of it. Still and staring he stood too close to her. She backed against the deli counter, afraid, wanting him to move, but he stood his ground. The counterman came and took the man by the elbow and led him down the row of tables. It was then she noticed his red-tipped white cane.

She wished Mannie would hurry. She couldn't keep herself together much longer. She paced as she tried to think of the last time they had met.

It had been a three-day weekend and the two friends went to the mountains to get some fresh air and see clean snow. They had just come in to the lodge after a long hike and had been warming their feet in front of the large roaring fire as well as their bodies with steaming hot toddies. They had been discussing the ethics of sacrificed laboratory animals and Mannie had been trying to justify the practice. But Jenny wasn't accepting the word "sacrifice". She kept calling it torture and murder.

They were being careful with each other as they teetered between genuine anger and restraint for the sake of their friendship. Mannie knew that Jenny belonged to animal rights activist groups but she still insisted the use of animal sacrifice in laboratories was absolutely necessary for the good of science.

Then she told Jenny how she had been thinking about having a child but was unwilling to conceive with a man. She had added that she also disliked the idea of carrying a fetus in her body for nine months so she was working on a way to create artificial gestation and have it functional within the year.

Jenny had accused her of using an incredible amount of research money and animal life only to fulfill a personal need to circumvent her genetic inheritance – all because she didn't want to carry a child. "As long as there are children in his world needing homes and protection, it's incumbent upon anyone of passable intelligence to ignore their throbbing biology and adopt a needy orphan," Jenny had said

But Mannie insisted she was working in the interests of emerging generations. "A developing fetus surrounded by an artificial placenta in an artificial womb under optimum conditions fares a much better chance of having a fuller and healthier life once it's born," she explained to Jenny. "No drugs, no accidents, no tension, no pollution, and the female genetic contributor you call "Mother", is not faced with nine months of physical and emotional discomfort. Because the conception will be a conscious act it will cut down the burgeoning world population and also, why must a woman suffer? If I were pregnant I couldn't function as I do. It would affect my work. Being pregnant doesn't seem like a necessary enrichment to my life, and it doesn't mean I would be a better mother. Being a good parent is what is important, not how you become one."

Jenny didn't know how to answer that, but she thought the concept of artificial gestation sounded inhumanly frightening.

"An actual pregnancy costs a woman a minimum of six months," Mannie said. "What if she has no one to support her and she can't work because of complications? It happens."

"People shouldn't have children when they're in difficult financial circumstances, especially single women," Jenny reasoned. "Children should be brought into this world with every advantage possible."

"Great, but unrealistic. Anyway," said Mannie, "that's another argument. My financial circumstances are good and I have a lot to offer a child. So I'm bowing to my genetic nesting urges and using my scientific knowledge."

"I think you should adopt, but if not, what about a surrogate?" Jenny asked her.

"Well," the scientist answered, "I had planned to use one but all these law suits because of surrogate mothers changing their minds scared me. So I put my ovum in cryo storage until the artificial womb is ready, then I'll combine my ovum with the sperm of the best genetic type and use the artificial womb to gestate her."

"Her?" Jenny had said then quickly told her friend to forget what she asked. She hadn't wanted to know Mannie's answer. A shiver ran through Jenny and she looked around. She tried peering through the streaked windows of the deli but there was still no sign of her friend. Taking a deep breath she went back to the excitement Mannie had shown when she thought of a way to make money on the concept.

"I have a great idea," Mannie had told her. "Once the development of the artificial womb is successful, we can go into business and have baby factory franchises."

"Terrific," Jenny lied. "We can call them ***Manny's Stork-Inns***. But before that happens, how about letting me write a feature story about it?"

"I'm not sure. Let me think about that." Mannie seemed a bit upset. "Jenny, I want you to understand - I'm afraid of being intimate, having intercourse with a man. And as far as artificial insemination, I don't want to walk around for nine months in that hormonal and physical condition. Would you?"

"Well, yes, I do. Mannie, isn't this what the Nazis had in mind?" Jenny asked.

Mannie stiffened. "I'm not a Nazi... I'm trying to be practical and think objectively."

"Oh Mannie," Jenny interrupted. Don't get upset. Nothing's happened yet."

"No, you don't understand." Mannie looked anxious. "The creation of these artificial wombs isn't just for me, it will give great freedom of choice for so many women. The project has great financial potential for Anson and they have been very generous with research and development money." She smiled slightly, "they have also given me a small point participation on each unit. It could make me very rich."

"You already are."

Mannie had pulled a magazine over from a stack near the fireplace and started to draw on it. Excitedly she had sketched in the general outlines of a transparent artificial womb. "We're experimenting with lots of different chemicals till we have amniotic fluid. So far it kind of looks like chicken soup. But I know it's one of those things waiting to be discovered. I'm making the artificial womb look like an incubator but it will be soft and expandable as the baby grows. It's hooked up to a simulation of a human mother's body processes; breathing, heart beat, blood flow. Nutrients and other life supporting needs will be carried through the fetus' umbilical cord just like any ordinary womb for any ordinary fetus."

Jenny had felt strange surges going through her body "I would hardly call these circumstances ordinary. And I suppose more animals will have to die for their intestines or artery material."

Mannie ignored that. "The body processes and systems will be connected to a main computer terminal that monitors everything for the nine month gestation. When abnormalities occur that can't be immediately corrected, the gestation will be terminated. Back up eggs and sperm are going to be kept in case this happens and will immediately be combined in a Petri dish to start another life. Parents will not be notified till it is time for their child to be born."

"You mean disconnected," said Jenny.

"Yes, that's accurate. But it could also describe natural childbirth."

"Will the event be catered?" Jenny had quipped, remembering now how seriously Mannie had taken everything.

"As a matter of fact", Mannie had answered with enthusiasm, "the parents and invited guests will come to a viewing room. I want to furnish it tastefully with plush seating and low but pleasant lighting. Afterward there will be a bright and cheery party room so the new family can celebrate their baby's arrival."

Jenny felt blown away. The future would soon be here and she wasn't ready for it. Science had gone beyond her personal understanding.

Mannie had been so excited as she stood up to emphasize her future plans. "I hope to make the wombs portable so they will eventually be used in private homes hooked up through personal computers to a laboratory's main frame. However, for the immediate future I can see only clinics or, call them baby factories, where artificial wombs will be hooked up to computer terminals twenty four hours a day."

"What about love, nurturing?" Jenny asked. "Isn't it nice to have loving conditions when conceiving a child? Spiritual bonding could impact greatly on a child's psyche. But bonding in a Petri dish? What kind of spiritual enhancement is that?"

Mannie anticipated the question. "I intend to find composers and artists to create visual and audio stimuli to sensitize, teach and prepare the fetus for the outside."

"Artificially manipulated feelings." Jenny shook her head. "That is so dangerous. You could instill negative feelings with that kind of in-put as well."

"Not with proper guidelines," answered Mannie. "You know, I'd like you to write about this. A newspaper story might be good. It certainly would keep everyone honest. Some of the people at Anson have been breathing down my neck. Maybe they need to know that others are watching them."

"What do they want from you, besides immediate results?"

"Just that. They're trying to pressure me to use human subjects instead of animals. I think that's a way off, but they don't want to wait. When life can be created, strong guidelines and regulations should be kept." Her face darkened, as she grew serious. "Only if you write this, you can't use my name."

"I'll try not to."

"Try isn't good enough." She said.

"I'll do whatever I can." Jenny tried to assure her. "You gained some weight and you look tired." Jenny decided to change the subject

"I've been nauseous and feel awful."

"Maybe you're pregnant," Jenny joked.

Mannie laughed and Jenny joined her.

Jenny had then picked up her Hot Toddy and toasted Mannie. "To New Age immaculate conception. No more worries, no more infection. Find the color and type you want in a catalogue, shake the contributing father's hand for personal contact - tradition sake - and a signed check will make you a mommy. – No muss, no fuss." They clinked their glasses.

Wind and traffic noise signaled the deli door opening and Mannie came propelling through the door. Her wrinkled khaki raincoat flew behind her like a cape barely covering a stained lab coat and trousers. Her short dark hair was curled with perspiration yet she looked ravishing. Heads turned even though Jenny thought Mannie had not managed to conceal her extra pounds under the layers.

Mannie hugged her, apologizing, "Sorry about the time, but..."

"It's all right." Mannie hugged her again and Jenny almost started crying.

"It's so good to see you," they both said together, Mannie laughed, Jenny managed a small smile.

Mannie put her arm around her and Jenny forced herself not to shrink away as they walked together to the back and chose a large booth in the corner.

Settling in, Jenny noticed the blind man sitting opposite them. Something about him made her blood curdle. He spooned an inordinate amount of sugar into his cup, and then brought it carefully to his stationery lips. Jenny shuddered.

Mannie looked at Jenny soberly, no longer smiling. "I have to tell you something."

Jenny waited; she would let Mannie go first.

Mannie looked directly at her. "I am pregnant."

Jenny froze. "What?" The words could barely get through the swirling in her head. "How is that possible?"

Mannie shrugged. "I don't know. I've been trying to figure it out."

"Figure it out? You have no idea?"

"No."

"How about the artificial sperm you've been working on? Could that be operable?"

"No, we're years away from that." Mannie was almost impatient. "That's the creation of life. We joked about it last time, remember?"

"I was thinking about that before you came in and the feature article I want to do about your work. Jenny touched her friend's hand, "Mannie, I have to tell you what happened. Maybe this is connected, maybe not, but I'm very scared."

"You? Scared? That isn't possible. However I'm frantic. Here I am, the Virgin Mary working on ways to create babies without physical contact, and I get pregnant

Without a clue as to how it happened! I'm my own guinea pig, how's that for the greatest irony?" Her face was turning red, tears welled in her eyes.

"Maybe I've lost perspective," she continued, "but I don't think I got impregnated in the lab. It couldn't happen. We're not that far along yet. But the reality is, I'm pregnant and I don't know how."

Jenny felt angry and frustrated. She wanted to unburden herself to her friend, and her friend only wanted to talk about herself. Any other time she would have jumped in with everything she had to help Mannie. The situation was incredible - even though she had a theory about it. - Mannie was in denial. She probably had drinks or something with someone and was either slipped a "date rape drug" or she lost control of herself and blocked it out. But she didn't have the patience to try to get Mannie to listen. Jenny had needed Mannie; she hadn't counted on it being the other way around.

"Do you remember Peter Ballard from M.I.T?" Mannie was saying, "the one who used to follow me around and ask me out?"

Jenny nodded, feeling a flicker of resentment at her friend's continuing insensitivity.

"Well, Ballard is working for some large Japanese pharmaceutical and they give him so much money you wouldn't believe it.

He came over and we started playing with some genetic samples that Peter had brought back from Japan for his artificial blood research."

"Did you have anything to drink with him?" Jenny interrupted.

Mannie nodded. "At dinner. We went to the Beverly Wilshire. His company is very generous. He has a development fund that is richer than most third world treasuries. He also has an unlimited credit card for entertaining. Nice huh?" She smiled, but Jenny didn't smile back. Mannie didn't seem to notice.

"Maybe you had more to drink than you realized and went to bed with him. You did have dinner in a hotel. It's a trick some men use. They get you drunk then take you upstairs." She felt shivers running down her back. Sex. Would she ever have trusting and loving sex again?

Mannie shook her head. "Not possible. Peter Ballard is gay," she answered. "When he came out of the closet he decided to go into research so he wouldn't have to touch female patients." Mannie slunk down in the booth. "Look at me - I've been like a celibate nun most of my life, never let a man touch me, though at times I think I'd like to try. And now, I get fucked, and I didn't get to enjoy it or hate it."

Jenny couldn't laugh, she was feeling betrayed. Mannie didn't care, didn't remember what she had said, didn't hear anything she had said.

Mannie was like a baby, she could only think of herself. "So I'm pregnant," she was saying once again, "and I don't know how. Some scientist, huh?"

"Are you sure?" Jenny asked. "You've gotten a bit fat. Could it be a false pregnancy? Women sometimes carry every sign."

"I wish. I checked that out - had an ultra sound. There's a baby in here," she patted her stomach. "I could see it on the screen. Want to see its picture?" Jenny didn't answer but Mannie pulled out a Polaroid anyway. It was a video image that could be interpreted as a fetus, but it was very fuzzy. "I haven't got the wallet size yet," Mannie joked. "Can you tell it's a girl?"

"Mannie, you can't make out anything in this picture." Jenny was losing what little patience she had. A strange feeling hit Jenny, and it gave her the chills. She glanced at the blind man. He was bothering her - he was very quiet, unearthly still. Jenny didn't know how to cope with Mannie's information. Turmoil reigned in her head. Everything that happened in the past 48 hours was too much, too strange. Mannie must have blacked out that had to be the answer.

"I'm in my fourth month," Mannie was saying flatly, "and the weird thing about this is the moment it was confirmed this afternoon, I felt myself liking the concept."

"Concept. Terrific," said Jenny.

"Now, what are you going to do with this 'concept' that happens to be made of flesh and blood and your genetic parts? What about taking care of it? You don't know how it happened, who the father could be, or even if the father is human for god's sakes! Maybe it's one of your mutants from your laboratory. Look what happened when Albert Hofman discovered LSD. He was trying to synthesize Ergot for pregnancy, and somehow he either inhaled the substance or it went through his skin. A large part of the world was changed from that scientific accident. You have to be more responsible. Contact Peter Ballard. He may be working with other artificial things beside blood."

Mannie was chagrined. "I tried. He's in the Far East somewhere. I just ran up a huge phone bill trying to track him. He's dropped out of sight."

"What do you want to do?" asked Jenny, annoyed with her friend for not caring about her problems.

"How about a baby shower or shopping for a bassinet?" Mannie's lip started to quiver, "she's pretty isn't she?" she joked, holding up the Polaroid then bursting into tears. Jenny sat back and waited till her

103

friend stopped crying. Normally she would never react this way, but now her anger was growing.

Mannie pulled herself together. "Okay, I'm sorry, I've totally ignored you. What happened to you?"

Jenny didn't want to tell her, She thought the blind man might be listening. Anger toward his intrusion and Mannie's tirade had rattled her. Why should she feel this kind of anger toward a poor old blind man? A waitress circled and tried to stop. "Bring us a large bottle of Perrier," Jenny told her, "and two coffees. We're not ready to order yet."

"Mannie," Jenny took a deep breath. "The worst thing that could have ever happened to me did. You know how it feels and that's why I have to talk to you." She stopped, choked up. Mannie looked down, playing with the saltshaker, waiting for Jenny to speak.

"It was so horrible I don't know how it could be true."

"Maybe it wasn't," her friend suggested. "Maybe we're both caught in bad dreams. Maybe one or both of us is dreaming this, or maybe I've just made everything up. Maybe I created this to cover the fact I got fat from overeating or I'm pregnant to prove to the world that I'm straight."

"Are either of those true?" Jenny asked, a bit annoyed that Mannie had put the focus back on herself.

Mannie looked gray, like her energy had drained.

"No. I wish it were. Jenny, tell me what happened."

Jenny opened her mouth, and then stopped. If she told her she would have to relive it, every moment, each touch. She couldn't go through with it now, Mannie's problems had drained her, and the blind man was upsetting her. How she wished he would leave. What if he could hear everything they were saying, as he sat there pouring sugar into his coffee cup, like it would turn solid, Jenny looked at Mannie expectantly.

"What happened?" Mannie repeated.

The words dropped out of Jenny's mouth without thinking. "Tim and I are in trouble," she said skirting the issue. "He's turned into a real pain. He doesn't want me to do the story about your research; worried I'll step on the wrong toes. That's all he cares about lately, not stepping on the wrong toes. Since he has decided to go for the White House, he has forgotten about his reason for doing it, the important issues."

"You've lost respect for him." Mannie said.

"I love him," Jenny answered.

"There is no love without respect, Webster. You know that," said the beautiful, sad Brazilian.

Jenny didn't want to think about that. She motioned towards the blind man, "That guy over there is making my skin crawl."

Mannie leaned over to look at him. "That's because you can't see his eyes."

Jenny shook her head in denial. "And you, Miss Virgin Mary. Talking about not seeing, you must have been drunk or knocked out with that new sedative men are using on women to rape them. It's tasteless and they put it in their drinks in bars. It has to be. Think about it. Do some soul searching. Who have you been out with besides

Peter Ballard?"

"You."

"Can't you do a genetics' test or something?"

"Not without knowing who the father is."

"Right." Knots were growing in Jenny's stomach. She felt as if she were going to scream. She noticed a strange sweetness sweeping over Mannie, she looked peaceful and happy, then suddenly fright crossed her face."

"I'm so scared," Mannie said.

"Of having a baby?"

Her eyes swam with tears. "Will you be the Godmother? If anything happens to me, will you take care of her?"

"Of course I will," but somehow none of what Mannie said seemed real to Jenny. She wondered if Tim was right - that Mannie lived in a fantasy and much of what she said could not be taken seriously.

Mannie snatched a napkin out of the holder and crumpled it against her mouth. "I know you're angry because I'm acting badly. But something strange is happening - I'm being pressured to use human fetuses, " she paused and looked at Jenny, tears streaming down her face. "I haven't been totally honest. I've known that I'm pregnant for a few weeks. So do some of the others in the lab. But I honestly don't know how it happened. They're trying to convince me to let them remove the fetus so they can grow her in the artificial womb. I don't want to do that. No one can be sure it's safe yet and I don't want my baby to be the guinea pig. I can feel her. She's alive, connected, and dependent on me. We have a kind of communication already, I know that sounds crazy but it's true. My Supervisor is threatening to transfer me and have someone else take over my work. Of course they won't say it's because they can't use my fetus, they'll say something that will destroy my reputation and then I'll never find first class work. These people are ruthless."

The lights flickered and Jenny jumped, but Mannie didn't seem to notice, she kept talking. "I need you to write the article, to keep an eye on them, expose. You're the only one I can trust not to reveal my name."

Jenny's breath stopped. Guilt rose up. "I'm having problems. My editor doesn't want to do the story unless he knows more facts. I had to give him your name, I'm sorry."

Mannie's looked shocked. "It could be my death warrant," she mumbled. "But I do think that the article should be done, even if it's dangerous for us." She took a shaky breath. "I'm so conflicted. Maybe we should wait till the work is finished and I have permission to give interviews. I have a child to think about."

"Mannie, I won't use your name again, I promise. And I think I can trust my editor." She felt a thump of dread hit her chest. "I hope I can. But then." tears blocked her throat and she turned away. "Look, I'm sorry," she managed to mumble.

"Don't cry, it's all right," croaked Mannie. "Boy, are we messes, sitting here crying." She started to giggle. At first Jenny stiffened, then she started to shake and her tears turned to laughter. Both of them laughed, prompting the other, escalating into whoops and shrieks of uncontrollable laughter. Tears poured down their cheeks, other patrons turned, the waitress stopped her approach towards them, and the blind man continued to stare.

They got themselves under control. ""Don't worry," said Mannie, patting Jenny's hand. "I overreacted. I'm more scared about childbirth. Will you be my partner at Lamaze classes?" Jenny started to giggle and nodded her head, Mannie picked up the laughter and the two howled again.

Mannie shook her head, still laughing, "I can't believe this - when I saw that baby on the screen - a real person," her voice caught and she suddenly grew quiet. "Don't let them take the baby from me," her face was a portrait of fear, "you're right, they probably drugged me. It had to be. But why?"

The waitress came over and started to interrupt. "Please wait," said Jenny, her mind racing. She leaned across the table and looked into Mannie's blue eyes. "Don't be scared. They can take our bodies, but they can't have our minds. Don't lose yourself emotionally. They'll never touch you then. Believe me." She felt a strength raising inside of her, the kind of strength she first felt when she left her body. "Don't give yourself away, listen to yourself and you'll survive."

"If I get pregnant unknowingly," said Mannie, very serious now, "then any fertile woman can be impregnated without her knowledge, or consent."

But the big question for now is - why you? We've got to find out who did it and why. I think there is a connection to what happened to me."

"What did happen to you? It's more than problems with Tim, I know that. I'm sorry, I've just been so self-indulgent. Forgive me. What happened Jenny?"

Jenny started to shake. "Not now. Let's finish with your problem. One problem at a time. We have to be very careful what we're saying."

Mannie put the menu down. "I'll get you names, information,

everything you need. This break through should be made public. But please, try not to use my name, I don't want to lose my job or be black listed. It can happen very easily."

"Don't worry. I'll do everything to help you." Jenny put her menu down on the seat beside her. The last thing she wanted to do was eat right now. "I'm not thinking very clearly. But I do know that if you give me names and information the more credibility I'll have and the more we can accomplish. Your genius may have unleashed a monster that needs to be controlled."

Jenny leaned back, pondering. "I wonder if there are researchers doing more than we know?"

"I hope not."

Jenny shook her head. "This isn't about ego. We need to think deeply about the new technology. There is great power in it. Look at us. We're professionals, yet when we question it, we become fearful."

Mannie took her hand. "Don't get more upset."

Jenny took her hand away. "So many people take their lives for granted and put their working brains to sleep in front of their television sets. When they're not doing that they herd through shopping malls in half wakened states, amassing huge charges on their credit cards then they go to drive in chapels and pray by rote for money to pay for those charges. They never give a thought about the deeper lessons of life. There is no seeking for truth, no desire for meaning. Profitable survival is the goal of their existence."

"Jenny, you're on a soap box.

She shrugged, "I have a messianic complex, but I mean it. You do too or you never would have given me this information."

Mannie shook her head. "I'm a scientist, not a savior. I just don't want this getting out of hand, that's all." She drew herself up and seemed to grow stronger. "I'll get names for you. I'll have to do some bribing to get into that area of the computer programs."

"Great." Jenny reached over and squeezed her hand.

"Now," Mannie asked. "What are we going to do about food? She looked around for the now non-existent waitress. "I'm not very hungry. Especially here. Why do we come here?"

"Habit. Let's change it right now and leave." Jenny started to push herself out of the booth.

Another waitress with platinum blonde hair piled high and thick mink eyelashes approached them. The plastic nametag under a flowery handkerchief read 'Dotty'. "Wanna order?" She asked, her gravely voice deepened with years of cigarettes and booze, her eyes testimony to a hard life.

"We've changed our minds," said Jenny. "Sorry."

The waitress wasn't backing off. "There's a minimum charge in these booths. Your Perrier doesn't cover it, and you've been here awhile."

"Is this a time share?" Jenny resented her attitude. "We'll be happy to pay for the water plus the minimum."

"That's all right," said Mannie. "I'll order something."

"Don't be bullied into eating if you don't want to. We're talking principle here," argued Jenny. "And you shouldn't be drinking coffee. Caffeine is bad for my goddaughter."

She stood up. "I can't stay here anymore. It's claustrophobic. I've got to get air." She threw down a ten-dollar bill. Mannie picked it up and stuffed it back in Jenny's purse.

"Jenny, do you want to come back to my house? Stay with me so we can talk?"

Thoughts of Mannie's small-overcrowded apartment made her feel more depressed. Unspent rage was threatening to release. "No thank you, I can't, I really need to be alone. I want to get out of here."

Jenny looked over at the blind man staring soundlessly like a George Segal sculpture. She didn't know why but there was something about him that she hated. Her hands were in fists. Why that blind old man? What did he represent to her?

Mannie looked stricken. "I'm worried about you," she said

Jenny shook her head. "I'm sorry. It should be the other way around. It's just personal stuff - I'm feeling sorry for myself. I'll be all right. I feel suffocated. Got to get out. I'll call you when I get home, all right?" She threw her a kiss and left.

Mannie put her own ten-dollar bill on the table and followed her out. The blind man started to slide out of his seat as soon as Jenny went out the door.

Mannie left the delicatessen and hesitated on the sidewalk. There was no sign of Jenny, she had disappeared. Then she saw Jenny's BMW turn the corner. Troubled by her friend's behavior, she paused at a newspaper stand and pulled out a late edition of The News. She scanned the headlines, then looked through the front and Metro Section for Jenny's by-line. Not finding it, she threw the paper into a wastebasket just as the blind man tapped his way over to her.

"Could you help me?" he asked, his head tilted to the side and up, as if trying to see around his dark glasses. "I don't hear any traffic noises and I'm not sure whether the light is red or green."

"Which way do you want to go?" she asked.

"South, across Wilshire."

Mannie took his upraised elbow and began to lead him toward the corner. The man brought his other hand up and steadied himself against her arm. The thin needle hidden between the first two fingers of his hand easily penetrated the raincoat and jacket she wore. She didn't feel the sting when the blind man stumbled and expertly pushed the needle into her forearm, the motion of the fall and his grasping hand diverting her from the pinprick going into her flesh. He stiffened slightly when they reached the other side; and a police car pulled up and stopped. One of the officers got out and went into the delicatessen while the other waited. The blind man quickly tapping his cane against the sidewalk, left. Mannie ran back across the street. She stopped when she got to her car and grabbed the handle. She felt woozy. Trying to shake it off, she opened the door, and got in and started. Pulling out of her parking space she barely missed the car that was already using that lane. The policeman on the opposite side saw what happened and put his red light on. He made a u-turn and went after her, his lights blazing.

Mannie didn't see them. She continued down Wilshire Boulevard toward the ocean, her car swerving as though she were drunk. Ringing filled her ears, her driving glasses fogged, the windshield steamy. Straining her head to peer through the window, she became captured by the red ball of the setting sun sinking into the ocean. There was a red light in her rear view mirror as well. Flames danced in her head, a high-pitched sound massaging her, as she blinked her eyes and started to relax. The licks of flame reached through the window, forcing her eyes to stay open and focused upon them.

She didn't blink again as her car went through the crossed arms of the statue of Saint Monica, perched at the dead end of Wilshire Boulevard. Her hands clutched the wheel firmly as the car continued through the shattered remains. Unblinking, never shifting her focus off the sun, Mannie didn't see the two elderly people sitting on the park bench enjoying their last sunset. The runaway car crashed through them, separating them in their last moment of life. It glanced off the panicked mother and her baby carriage, squashing the white Scottish terrier trapped by its leash. The battered car paused for a moment at the stone retaining wall that lined the grass parkway overlooking the ocean, then flipped over and floated free in mid-air till the forces of gravity brought it crashing down onto the last vestiges of rush hour traffic on Pacific Coast Highway two hundred feet below.

CHAPTER TEN

The tangle of colorful metal and glass mixed with pieces of limbs and blood, appeared less horrific when reproduced electronically on a television screen. Jenny glanced at it as she turned the television on, then went to her desk.

As she waited for her answering machine to deliver the message recorded there, the words of the perky blonde newscaster came blasting at her. "A friend and co-worker of Dr. Manuela Cristal de SEBASTIANE could not believe she was personally responsible for this tragedy."

Jenny turned the answering machine off and edged closer to the TV. A picture of Mannie came up on the screen. Jenny's head exploded, she sank to the floor, she couldn't breathe, she could barely see; another part of her world had just been destroyed.

The newscaster, blue eyes sparkling with eye drops and well-placed pin lights reported "Dr. Cristal de Sebastiane's friends and co-workers said she had been nervous recently after learning of a pregnancy." She paused, the blue eyes sparkling with a hint of tears. The camera pulled back revealing the roundness of the newscaster's own pregnancy.

The screen now had eyewitnesses to the accident telling their versions to the network minicam. This was their "moment of fame" pop artist Andy Warhol had predicted - the 15 minutes all shall one day achieve. An excited Latino man wearing a bright blue Adidas jogging suit told the camera he saw the car swerving erratically before it crashed into the statue of Santa Monica. He paused to cross himself, milking his "moment" then declared, "the driver was drunk, boracha." Someone waved at the camera from behind.

The perky blonde newscaster, turned back to the camera announcing her next interview, a spokesman from Anson Industries, Melvin Phillips.

Jenny couldn't believe he was on that screen. This had to be some cruel idiot's idea of a joke - a DVD had been put there to freak her. She changed the channel, but Phillips was being interviewed on another network as well.

"It had been suggested," he was stating, "not mandated, that Dr. Cristal de SEBASTIANE, take a leave of absence. She had refused, citing she didn't want to leave her work." Phillips faded off the screen and the camera came in again on another blonde newscaster who wiped off her smile and replaced it with a serious and sad look. She wrapped up the segment with Mannie's birthplace and survivors. No mention was made of her genius and her contribution to society. It would take years for any of that to come out, if at all. For now, her work, her contributions, would be overlaid with the stigma of this accident and the lives it took whether she was innocent or not. Her life and accomplishments would forever be stained by these events.

The newscaster was signing off with a huge smiling, "We'll have more later." Then the logo came up for the ten o'clock news. Jenny rolled back on her heels and tried to breathe, but her emotions were crashing, blurring her thinking. The accident must have happened right after she left the restaurant.

Mannie, her dearest friend, she'll never have that trust with any one ever again. The flood of tears for Mannie and for herself added to the overwhelming emptiness filling inside.

The phone rang. She let it ring. It wouldn't stop. She had turned the answering machine off. Her mind reeling she reached for it, Tim's voice was there. She couldn't speak, tears flooding all attempts.

"Are you all right?" Tim asked firmly for the third time. She shook her head and attempted the word "yes".

"Darling," he cooed gently. "I heard about Mannie. It was on the news." His voice grew harder, anger seeping through. "I warned you to stay away from her but you wouldn't listen."

She couldn't answer him. How could he be saying that?

"I'm coming home."

"No!" she shouted, surprising them both.

"They'll stop at nothing.," he said softly.

Was he warning her? "I know."

"Where were you tonight?"

"With Mannie."

"After."

"I went to the beach house, then decided to come back here."

"Well, thank God you weren't in that car. Did anyone see you with her tonight?"

"In the restaurant."

"Let's hope they don't put you two together. You don't want to get involved."

"I am."

His voice grew low, sympathetic. "I'll get you out of this, but you have to help me."

"Out of what?"

He didn't answer that. "Don't leave the apartment. I'll call a friend, Elaine Jefferson. She's a registered nurse, trained in crisis intervention and, if necessary, has her black belt in karate."

"Why would I need someone like her?"

"To protect you. I want her to stay with you. Do you understand? I want someone with you. You're not to be alone."

She couldn't talk, her throat had closed.

"Don't be scared. You'll be taken care of." he hung up.

She wiped her tears, turned on the phone machine and walked out the door.

***

The Santa Monica Police Station was packed with the aroma of twenty-four hour use, harsh fluorescent lighting grossly illuminating the kind of seedy, dark aspect of police life most people see only on TV.

Jenny didn't want to be in this place of dense chaos. It had been these kinds of dingy environments that made her switch from being a news reporter to investigative reporting.

As a rookie reporter covering the city beat, she would often go home suffering from what she reported; the ragged, nerve-splitting events that refused to leave her once she was inside the relative safety of her own home.

So she had switched to cleaner crimes - the white-collar kind -- committed in the conference rooms and private clubs of the corporate and political worlds. She focused on abuse of position rather than street crime, though at times she had trouble drawing the differences.

But now she was back where she had started, investigating a multiple homicide. But this one was different. The person accused had been her very best friend and it was important to investigate this without emotion. She had to -- if she wanted answers.

Assuming a steel coated assurance she didn't really feel, she headed for the detectives lounge and walked in without knocking, assaulted immediately by the musty odors of stale smoke, body odor and old beer.

A chunky middle-aged man jumped up as she entered, his hand automatically reaching for his gun.

"Relax." she flashed her press pass, mustering the toughest attitude she could. "I'm Jenny Webster, THE NEWS. I'm covering that fatal traffic accident in Santa Monica on Pacific Coast Highway.

"Yeah," wheezed a thin detective, his skin bleached by years of fluorescent lighting "Kamikaze Mama! That was a mean one."

Jenny forced herself to stay quiet. She couldn't give herself away. Managed to stay controlled.

"Lady," the older detective said, his hand still on his gun, "we've already talked to the NEWS. We had a press conference. Didn't you see Terry O'Malley? He covers this beat. And as far as you coming in here like you just did, this is for police only. We come here to rest and think about things we want to think about. You gotta get permission from one of us to come in. Understand?"

She nodded, "Yes, I'm sorry but..."

He interrupted. "Talk to the Sergeant." He gestured away from himself as he mumbled, "outta here."

She felt so stressed she was mute, so she turned and started to leave.

Wait." A tall thin man, his face scattered with freckles framed by curly red hair came over to her. His dimpled smile, bright blue eyes, and high-sculpted cheekbones made him comfortably appealing.

I'm Detective Parker. I'm working that case

His smile was refreshing, his diffident manner disarming. Light, and compassion seemed to flow from his eyes. Jenny felt stirrings of comfort coming from him.

"Let's have some coffee and talk," he said, ushering her out of the Detective's lounge.

They chose a bench near the end of the hallway where it was quiet.

"I am a reporter for THE NEWS," she told him, "but I'm also a good friend of Mannie Sebastiane. I was with her tonight." This was not what she had planned to say. She was here to get information, not implicate herself.

He sat quietly, listening without reaction.

"Mannie wasn't despondent," she told him. "She had verification of her pregnancy this morning. I saw a Polaroid of the fetus from the ultra sound. She was very proud of it, joked about making copies." A sob threatened to come out and Jenny dug her nails into her palms. "Mannie had the Polaroid. Did you find it?"

"No." He made a note. "I don't think it's possible anything could have survived that crash, but I'll see what we have."

Tears welled up, she tried to hold them back, but they spilled over her lids and down her face.

"I'm sorry. I shouldn't have said that," he awkwardly looked through his pocket for a handkerchief as she wiped her tears with the backs of her hands. I'll check the list of items we have." He moved a few inches down the bench from her. "Go on."

"I left the restaurant, Kaplan's Deli, before she did. I was going through one of my personal pity parties. I had been..." She stopped. She couldn't tell him. If she did, a whole other can of worms would be opened and she couldn't deal with it now. "If only I had stayed with her," she continued, "this wouldn't have happened."

"It was her time," he said.

"What?" She looked at him closely. Jenny was not accustomed to hearing a policeman talk like that. Their eyes locked with unspoken understanding and despite everything that had happened, she had a sense that she was growing stronger.

"Mannie could not have killed herself," she told him, "she was filled with new life, excited about her work - besides, pregnant women almost never commit suicide not with the life force within them."

She suppressed the next threatening sob. "You know," she looked up at him, tears streaming from her eyes, "even though she complained about feeling tired and stressed and gaining a lot of weight, there was a difference in her. I think she was seeing herself in a whole new way, as a woman for the first time. No," she shook her head emphatically once more, "there was no way she could have killed herself. It isn't possible." She looked up at him. He seemed so caring, so sympathetic. He urged her to go on.

"Contrary to what her co-workers said, it wasn't the baby Mannie was upset about, it was how she got pregnant and by whom that concerned her." He made a note. She continued. "I think when she saw the shapes and outline of that baby inside her, she was feeling true love for the first time in her life. I didn't see that at the restaurant. I wasn't really relating to her. I was too concerned about how she wasn't relating to me, listening to my needs, and I felt resentment. Oh God!" a huge sob overtook her and she buried her face in her hands, sobbing. The detective found some napkins near the vending machine and gave them to her. She wiped the tears away. "I was dealing in my own feelings, accusing her of doing exactly what I was doing. How could I be so insensitive?"

He patted her hand. "Don't be so hard on yourself. Besides, be grateful you have such a beautiful memory of your friend. That is the woman to remember." He paused delicately, "why was she so concerned about the pregnancy?"

She told him about Mannie's fear of men and her desire to have a child and the work she was doing: the artificial placenta and wombs, the computer programs,

Everything. He didn't say much but took a lot of notes. "Didn't Anson tell you any of this?" she asked.

"We just did a preliminary investigation. We're going b a c k there tomorrow."

121

"Give them enough time to destroy evidence."

"The lab is sealed."

"That doesn't mean anything." She took a deep breath, barely able to get the next question out. "Where is ... where are her remains?"

"The morgue. I don't suggest you go there. It's gruesome. Remember her the way she was. It isn't necessary for you to see what is left."

"No, I guess not. Is there evidence of a fetus?"

"Ms. Webster, I don't have that much experience, but from what I saw of that wreck, I doubt they can find anything except from tissue reports and that takes time."

"But..."

"Impossible," he interrupted.

Jenny didn't know why, but he was calming her. He was in a position to interrogate and bring up things that would upset her, but instead, in the midst of an area usually associated with fear and violence, she was feeling better.

"I promise I'll do everything possible to find out what happened. By the way," he blushed a bit and swallowed, "I know your work."

When I was deciding whether to move to LA I read THE NEWS every day, I used to read your stories. I think you're a fine writer."

"Thank you," she said.

"Mannie's accident didn't feel right to me. I don't know much except what physically happened. But I don't think this was a willful act. She doesn't seem to have that kind of psychological profile. Especially after what you've told me. We'll do everything possible to learn what really happened."

"I know you will." She thanked him and left, glad he hadn't offered her a ride home and wondering why he hadn't.

CHAPTER ELEVEN

Bed never looked so inviting. The sheets felt soft as silk, the mattress seemed to reach up and embrace her, cuddling her against the world. Jenny floated in a world of soft darkness and enveloping comfort.

The bed started to shake. She sat up. Was it an earthquake? Her heart pounded. Nothing seemed to be moving. She took a deep breath and laid back.

The bed started to shake again, her body vibrating with an intensity that seemed to shut off the separation between her and the bed. She merged with it, became a part of it. She was the bed. Then suddenly her body stopped shaking. Nothing else moved in the room. She was scared. It must have been a nightmare she told herself. It was the stress.

"JENNY!"

A blast of painful fear shot through her chest. She bolted upright. Someone was in the room. The woman who had beaten her had come back for her. She had been hiding somewhere in the house.

Jenny clutched the blanket to her chest, fighting the impulse to pull it over her head. Scanning the room, listening for a telltale sound she tried to calm herself, depress her beating heart. But she knew she had distinctly heard the voice. It sounded as if it had been next to her ear. It had not been a dream. Oh my God, someone had to be in the room. It had to be that woman…

She turned on the light, grabbed a letter opener next to her bed stand and got out of bed. Minutes dragged into eons as she forced herself to walk from room to room and look in every potential hiding place – sometimes twice. But the apartment was empty. She crawled back into bed and propped the pillows up against the wall and leaned against them. Closing her eyes, trying to still her beating heart, she tried to convince herself it was only a dream. She couldn't fall victim to paranoia, she lectured herself. Yet it had seemed so real; in her own bed, this bedroom, her apartment. Everything that was familiar. How could it be illusion?

She wished she could talk to someone. Not Tim. He wasn't sensitive to her any more. That was part of their problem. Reaching for the phone she dialed the Santa Monica police department. "Detective James Parker please,"

"He's not here."

"Could you reach him at home?"

"Who is this?"

"Jenny Webster, THE LOS ANGELES NEWS. I talked to him a few hours ago."

"Isn't it late for an interview?"

"I have information for him."

She could hear paper rustling in the background. The noise made her nervous. "Look, never mind. Please leave word I called. I'll speak to him in the morning."

The sergeant's voice changed. "Jenny Webster, right? LOS ANGELES NEWS?"

"Yes."

"All right, he'll get the message."

"Thank you." Jenny put down the phone.

The phone rang. Her head snapped up. It was light outside. She had fallen asleep and her neck was stiff. The phone was shrill. "Hello?" She was breathless.

"Ms. Webster. Jim Parker here. I hope I'm not calling too early. I received your message and wanted to get to you. The desk sergeant should have called me right away."

"I told him not to, it's okay." Her voice was deep and low. "Something terrible happened to me just before Mannie died and there might be a link. I want to talk to you about it.

"Can you tell me now?"

"I'm afraid to use the phone. It might be tapped or there might be hidden cameras – I don't know. I'm afraid and I think I can trust you." Her voice cracked. She tried to hide her uncontrollable emotion.

Parker scribbled a note to himself. "You can."

"Thank you," she said.

The doorbell rang. "There's someone at the door. I'll get back to you later."

"Do you want me to wait?" he asked

"No, it's all right." She hung up and pulled herself out of bed. "Who is it?"

"Elaine Jefferson. Tim told you I was coming."

Jenny went to the door and looked out through the peephole. A tall muscular woman, her head elongated by the lens, stood at attention, her hand grasping the strap of a large tan shoulder bag. With trepidation Jenny opened the door. Six feet tall and bristling with authority, Elaine Jefferson entered the room. Although no more than 125 pounds, she appeared hard and muscled and ready to fight.

Elaine put her large bag down next to the desk, filling the room with her presence. Jenny watched her silently, Slowly the woman unbuttoned the jacket of her corduroy pant suit, took it off and folded it fastidiously over the back of the desk chair. The woman's dark panther-like eyes held her spellbound. Jenny felt frail against the woman's raw power.

"Tim's worried about you. He thought you might want a sedative? I think that would be good."

"I just woke up. And Tim knows I won't take any kinds of medications, especially sleeping pills or tranquilizers." Jenny's anger took control. She didn't like this woman. Didn't want her here.

Elaine found the single hard chair in the living room and drew it up to face Jenny. "Are you feeling guilty?" She asked.

Jenny stiffened, her mouth twitched. "Why should I?"

"From the rape. That happens some times. I'll stay with you till you recover from the shock."

How did she know about it? Had she told Tim? Her head started to spin. She couldn't remember! Shivering Jenny pushed herself off the sofa. She was stiff and everything hurt.

Elaine watched her like a hawk as Jenny walked toward her bedroom. "Thank you for coming, but you can leave now. I don't need you. I have to get ready for an appointment."

"Go right ahead - if you can."

Jenny's head snapped up, exhaustion vanished. "What did you say?""

"I thought you might be too tired," soothed Elaine. She looked at Jenny questioningly.

Jenny's fingers stretched rigidly away from her body – like a cornered animal trying to defend herself.

Elaine walked over to the mantelpiece and examined the small Rodin bust of Tolstoy.

Jenny hesitated. She didn't want to leave Elaine in her living room. "Why are you here?" She asked again.

"I told you, Tim thinks you should have protection."

"Well I don't."

She shrugged. "Tim's orders."

"Tim does not give me orders. And I don't accept them through you."

Elaine turned from the sculpture and walked toward her. Jenny felt paralyzed as the woman slinked stealthily toward her. The skin on the back of her neck rippled unpleasantly. This woman reminded her of the blind man, the one in the restaurant. Panic was stirring - they were going to kill her. Was Tim involved?

"I want you to know you're safe," Elaine was saying.

Jenny fought for control.

Elaine watched her passively. "I'm trying to be sensitive Jenny, believe me, Don't get paranoid. No one wants to hurt you. These kinds of things are insidious. They can affect you more than you realize. You won't know who to trust. Like now, you don't trust me."

"That's right."

"There is no reason, correct?"

"Every reason" she answered, but what if the woman was right. There was no specific reason Jenny should not trust her. But something about her sent warning signs. Was it because Tim sent her? Was this her continuing paranoia about Tim, her distrust? When he returned she would tell him what she had been feeling. If he became angry and defensive, then maybe she was right. But if he shows understanding, maybe it would help to bring them closer again.

"Tim thinks you're in danger." Elaine's face was hard and set. "He sent me to protect you," she repeated. "I can and I will."

Jenny tightened with anger. "You say you come to help yet you're doing the opposite. Everything you say feels combative.

Jenny's eyelids grew heavy, the woman's black leopard eyes drifted into pools of infinity. "You're one of them, aren't you?" she thought she slurred, but she wasn't sure. Everything was drifting.

Elaine came over and picked up her wrist to take her pulse. Jenny tried to pull it away, but couldn't.

"I want to help you, Jenny," crooned the woman. "You're not thinking clearly. You're refusing help and you're being self-destructive. You're punishing yourself for something you couldn't help."

She smoothed Jenny's hair. Chills went down her back.

"You're creating a situation that will make you entirely alone - distancing yourself with anger and self pity. I want to save you from that." Elaine's voice was chanting, hypnotic. "Give up your anger and distrust of me."

Jenny felt a surge of energy as she tried to deny what Elaine was saying. But the most she could do was shake her head weakly.

"Relax," said Elaine. "I'll make you tea."

Jenny dropped into the chair just inside her bedroom door.

"Is something wrong?" asked Elaine.

"Headache," Jenny slurred.

"Nauseous too, I bet." She took her pulse. "It's the shock. You better lie down."

"Can't. Pinwheels of fire are turning in my head. "

"Sit still, flow with it," suggested the nurse. "I'll help with the pain."

Jenny heard her rummaging through her bag, then felt the cold of an alcohol pre-moistened cotton square rubbed on her arm. She had no strength to protest as the sharp tip of a disposable needle pierced her sanitized skin.

"Flow with it," crooned Elaine, withdrawing the needle and patting Jenny's shoulders and neck. "Stay cool," she murmured in a singsong way, "You're stressed."

Jenny lowered her burning head to her hands. The rest of her body started to feel numb and began disappearing. "Help," she called out as the fiery pinwheels continued to spin crazily, drawing her deeper and deeper into them. Elaine rubbed her back and neck, working her way down her arms.

"Don't touch me," Jenny slurred.

"I'm here to take care of you." Elaine crooned.

The sounds of her words flew into space.

Jenny became very aware of her breathing. Momentum was building and she was flying to the right. Her eyes opened. A bright electric light pulsated, daring her to turn it off. She shuddered. The light seemed so real.

The bedroom door was open. Through it she saw a form on the couch. Elaine was on it, sleeping. She leaned back and stared at the light. It dimmed as if it was winking.

CHAPTER TWELVE

The light from the electric bulb faded into daylight as the many layers of urban civilization started to wake up. Children crying, laughing, silverware jingling, garbage cans clanging. A telephone rang, an alarm clock went off,

The cacophony of symphonic morning sounds woke Jenny up.

She didn't remember going to bed, but she could definitely hear the blaring sounds coming from apartments as traffic and weather reports accompanied the toasters and microwaves baking vitamin enriched compounds that were shaped like muffins and bread.

News reports coming through the window said the air people were breathing was "dangerous " It suggested that sensitive people stay indoors. Should sensitive people ever leave their homes? Jenny thought.

"It wasn't a dream," said a voice.

"What?" Jenny asked sleepily as she pushed herself out of bed.

"IT WASN'T A DREAM," said a louder, more grating voice. Elaine came into the room and stood looking down at her. "It wasn't a dream," she repeated. "Your friend was killed and you have to deal with it. I helped you into bed yesterday and you slept through the night. You were saying some very strange things. I thought it best to let you sleep. I hope you don't mind, I borrowed some blankets and stayed overnight."

"I noticed."

"Come on," Elaine took her arm. "Time to deal with life."

"Please, let me get up at my own time," Jenny lay back against the pillows, woozy.

"Sorry." Elaine stood stiffly at the foot of the bed. " Guess I can be a bit controlling."

"Not with me." Jenny tossed the bedclothes aside and tried to get up. A pain struck her in the lower part of her neck, traveling till it enveloped her head. Elaine watched her a moment then walked out.

Dizziness and pain made getting up difficult. She was weak and needed a shower. The bathroom door was closed and the shower was already running. Elaine was in there. The pain in her head intensified. She went into the living room and sat down. Elaine put her on edge. She appeared to be neutral, but Jenny knew in her heart that she wasn't. Tim had sent her - that suspicion again. She couldn't help it, it kept popping up. Chills ran through her. She wasn't sure if she was cold from the breeze coming through the open windows or because of fear. Maybe both. Elaine affected her the same way the blind man at the deli had. The blind man! Mannie. She went to the telephone.

***

Detective Parker was on the phone taking notes as Boyle returned from the vending machine, unwrapping a Hostess Twinkie. Parker hung up the phone, his brow furrowed in concentration as he looked at his notes, then became aware of Boyle standing over him, the end of a Twinkie in his mouth.

"Eating Twinkies can be dangerous, Sergeant. Remember what happened to Mayor Masconi in San Francisco?"

"Huh? " Boyle asked.

"The Twinkie defense - the guy who shot Mayor Masconi said that eating Twinkies made him do it." Explained Parker.

Boyle took another bite out of the cake and licked the crumbs off his fingers. He held what was left out to Parker. "Want to live dangerously?"

"No thanks," Parker tried to hide his revulsion. "I don't want to lose control." His brow furrowed again. "I just received a call from Jenny Webster, that writer from the News who came to the station last night. Told me she was with Sebastiane just before the accident. Said it couldn't have been a suicide, Sebastiane was upbeat and excited about the baby, only confused as to how it happened. She remembers a blind man at the restaurant who seemed to be eaves dropping. She said he made her feel uneasy, as if he was watching them and not blind at all.

Boyle shook his head, "I don't know. Sounds screwy." He opened a can of orange crush and took a sip.

"It's worth checking out.," said Parker. "She also said that she thought the guy could be a regular at the restaurant. What do you think?"

"Be my guest, said Boyle, stuffing the rest of the Twinkie in his mouth. "See if you can buy me a few packages of these over there. Maybe they'll give them to you wholesale." He chuckled. "I feel like living on the edge."

***

The pain in Jenny's head was so terrible it was making her sick. She dug her fingers into the sides of her temples. It didn't help. She had taken an aspirin, something she rarely did unless she was very uncomfortable, but this headache was going to be one of those resistant ones that didn't respond to the feverfew herb.

Parker had asked her to come to police headquarters and provide details to a police artist for a composite drawing of the blind man in the restaurant. She felt a comforting glow after she hung up with him, and then became aware of Elaine standing in the doorway, watching her. She wondered how long she had been there.

"Finished?" she asked the large woman who seemed to have no problem with staring at someone without blinking. "I want to take a shower."

"Not a bath?"

A chill ran through her. "No." She didn't like that. Was that supposed to have double meaning? She wanted Elaine out of here.

"Do you mind if I put some coffee on?" Elaine was saying.

She did mind, but she didn't know how to tell her. What if she was wrong? "Go ahead. Uh," she paused, then forced the words out of her mouth. "How long do you plan to stay here?"

"As long as you need me."

"Well then, you can leave. I don't need you."

Elaine looked at her steadily. "I'll talk to Tim."

"So will I."

Jenny went into the bathroom and closed the door. She was shaking. Elaine was intimidating her. But maybe she was feeling paranoid because of all that happened.

When Jenny emerged from the bathroom Elaine was sitting on the sofa, sipping coffee, looking very much at home.

"You don't have to wait for me," Jenny told her. "I'm going out now. I'm fine"

Elaine smiled as Jenny left and closed the door behind her. Holding her coffee cup she went back to the kitchen for a refill.

***

"Stringy shoulder length gray hair, kind of dirty looking but not really a vagrant." Jenny perched on a high stool next to the police artist, her shoulders hunched stiffly as she watched a close approximation of the blind man come up on the computer's color monitor. "His glasses were extremely dark and he had on a black hat and overcoat. The kind of look you can't ignore or forget too easily. Like a cartoon character."

A funny kind of dread went creeping through her it was crazy. The blind man and the rapist were probably 25 years apart in age and had little in common except an unsettling quality. But they seemed the same. She wanted to tell Parker about the rape but the brutal reality of the police station and the insensitivity of detective Boyle kept her quiet. She felt too fragile.

Parker touched Jenny's elbow lightly. His touch sent warm shivers through her arm to her heart.

"Would you like coffee?"

"I don't think so. I think I better go home." She was starting to feel uncomfortable with him.

He looked surprised. "Didn't you want to tell me something about a link…"

She had wanted to tell him about the rape but she shook her head no.

…

Jenny could tell Rudnik was lighting another cigarette as he continued talking to her. "You can't do a first person piece. This is a criminal police case."

"But Al, the stories you're printing about Mannie are not true I know that woman better than anyone else." She walked around the room trying to find a more comfortable spot.

Rudnik was annoyed. "Jenny, we are getting our material from police reports and eyewitnesses. We don't care about her education and how nice she was. She killed a lot of innocent people in one of the most gruesome accidents I've seen since I've been at this desk."

"That isn't fair. You're condemning her before you know if it was intentional or an accident. Maybe she was dead before she got in the car. Have you ever considered that? You and everyone else are so anxious to point your finger and accuse. She may not have committed suicide. She could have been murdered too. Maybe Mannie was used as a weapon." She lowered her voice as if it were going to make a difference over a telephone that was probably bugged. 'Maybe it was because of my investigation."

"Well then, why not you Brenda Starr? Or did your man with the patch and the black orchids come to your rescue?"

"In a way he did," she thought of Tim sending the nurse to protect her. In the light of day she could appreciate how he had been concerned and was trying to help.

"Forget it. You're not going to write her apology. You're not going to plead her case in print." He hung up.

Jenny felt exhausted. Seeing the picture of that blind man come to life the way it had on the computer screen was more upsetting than she had anticipated. His face was haunting her -- the way it had when she first saw him that night. What was it about him that was so familiar - almost touchable? She was starting to feel panic. She wasn't thinking clearly. Everything was blurry. Could she be in shock as Elaine had told her?

Elaine had been at her apartment when she got back and Jenny had a strange feeling she had been going through her things though nothing looked out of place. She wasn't feeling well and when Elaine handed her a glass of orange juice she took it and drank it thirstily.

"I'm going out for awhile," Elaine told her. "I'll   check in with you later.

"That won't be necessary."

"I will anyway. I left a pot of coffee for you."

"Thanks, but I don't drink coffee. " The veins in her neck began to tighten. Her head felt heavy.

***

Parker wrinkled his nose as the smell of grease blasted through the open doorway of Kaplan's Deli. People were coming in and leaving, taking seats at tables and the counter, moving with the cadence of familiarity, the motion of routine. When the woman behind the counter finally looked at Parker she told him to take a seat wherever he liked.

"Actually, I'd like to talk to you," Parker said politely.

"Can't you see I'm busy?" flirted the platinum blonde woman whose thick makeup didn't quite fill in the lines and creases mapping her face.

"This will only take a minute," Parker said, flashing his detective's shield.

The woman's face fell with disappointment. "What do you want?" she asked tersely.

"Does this man come here often?" he asked, holding up the police computerized rendering of the blind man.

"I've never seen him in my life."

"Take a closer look."

"I did. I've never seen him."

"Do you have the receipts from this week?" he asked, his voice tightening, his resolve growing.

"No. The accountant has everything. It's all on computer. We don't do anything here except push buttons."

She would have continued but Parker interrupted. "Who else was working two nights ago?" he asked

"I wasn't."

"Okay, then who was?"

She pointed with her chin to an old counterman behind the deli counter. Then, without turning her head she tilted it to the right toward the large open room. "And Stella, she knows everything."

"Which one is she?" Parker asked, looking at the two waitresses sauntering through the tables.

The woman swiveled her head. "She's not here. Must have her day off."

Parker stared at her a moment, started to say something then changed his mind and went over to the counterman.

"Yeah, I'm here every night," answered the scarred, tattooed man, his tobacco-stained teeth grinning in an unfriendly smile at the detective. "No one's replaced me in over thirty years - birthdays, Christmas, anniversaries, it doesn't matter. I'm always here. And I don't recognize that man's picture. Not at all."

Parker checked with the two waitresses, but neither remembered seeing a blind man. Dotty did however remember Jenny and Mannie. She told him that Jenny "seemed a little too nervous for her own good."

Parker left the restaurant and traced the route Mannie's car had taken. The debris from the statue of Saint Monica had been cleared, though remnants of yellow police tape fluttered in the wind. It was hard to imagine the devastation that had occurred here just a few days before. He started to walk toward the edge of the cliff then stopped and turned away. "Such beauty, such horror," he murmured softly to himself as he walked to his car.

***

A key turned in the lock. Could it be Tim? Jenny's heart was pounding as she waited for the door to open. Her overweight, frenzied red headed neighbor Carol wobbled in, dragging her four year old son Davis who clung to the rotund calf of her leg like a pilot fish clings to a whale.

"Hi! Hope I didn't scare you. I used my key because I didn't want to disturb you." She talked loudly, as if Jenny were three miles away, the large chunk of gray gum in her mouth teetering toward the front of her teeth. "Could you do me a favor?" she shouted as if her ears were stuffed.

"It depends," Jenny answered softly, hoping to lower the volume of Carol's voice with her own.

"Would you mind watching Davis just a few minutes? He has a slight fever and I want to go to the drug store and get him Animal Farm aspirins. They're the only ones he'll take. He likes their commercial, can sing all the words. Sing them for Jenny, Davis."

The little blond boy stared defiantly at his mother, snot running from his nose and over his pursed and pouting red lips.

Carol hiccupped a giggle. "I forgot. He's sick. He won't entertain when he's sick. It's in his contract." She giggled again. The little boy watched his mother silently.

Jenny felt drawn to the person inside the little boy. He seemed so bewildered. She could feel his mind working. He was very mature for a four year old. She wondered how Davis would be affected as time went on. What kind of women would he be attracted to? How would they treat him? If she had a mother like Carol and she was a little boy, she probably would end up hating women.

"I'll put the television set on." Carol shouted, and turned it on loudly, so loud Jenny understood why her natural volume was a shout.

Jenny went over to correct the sound. "Carol, I have to leave in an hour. Please hurry." Carol propelled Davis close to the set and pushed him in front of it. There was a scene from a war, a real one, going on.

"Don't you think he'd rather watch cartoons then CNN?" Jenny asked her.

Carol ignored her then paused at the door. "Can I get you anything?"

"A newspaper please."

"Why buy one?" she shouted. "Don't you get them free?"

"I'm not going to the office today."

"Okay", she looked at Jenny like she was crazy. She paused at the door and looked back. "It's easier to watch the news on television." She slammed the door shut.

Happy music came on. Davis had switched the channel. "Cream, Cream, Candy Cream. The Sweetest Thing You'll Ever Need!" Pink pellets danced on the screen. Davis mouthed the jingle silently; his nose tilted 2 inches from the television set. Jenny tried to pull him back, but he wiggled out of her grasp and moved as close in as possible. She started to object but decided against it. Davis was prone to tantrums and she didn't want him to start one. He looked like a gnome hunched up on the floor, a brown terrycloth towel tied over his shoulders like a cape, brown corduroy pants pushed up and pinned under his knees like knickers, and his long straight blonde hair brushing the shoulders of a brown and red striped shirt. Jenny shook her head sadly as she looked at the child so close to the set. She had written an article on the effects of television rays on humans. Close proximity to a television screen could result in eye damage. Carol should know that, she had given her the article to read before it was published.

Davis looked over his shoulder at Jenny and smiled. She smiled back, his infectious personality making her feel better. He didn't have to be as demanding and as spoiled as he was. He came over to the desk and leaned against it. She smiled again and patted his hand. He came close and she hugged him, then pulled away and took some paper out of her desk drawer to put in the printer. The little boy moved in closer, leaning over the arm of her chair.

"What are you doing?" asked the wide-eyed child.

"Going through the motions of trying to write."

"Huh?" he asked, bewildered.

"Nothing. When you're older I'll explain."

She looked at the computer keyboard, but her fingers refused to reach for the *on* switch. Tears filled her eyes. She was overcome with grief. She couldn't write.

Davis rested his head on her shoulder. She gathered him up and put him on her lap. He grunted happily, reached around and hugged her. She hugged him back. His little arms gripped her tighter. He was so loving, so sweet as he nestled his lips next to her shoulder. Floods of warmth and well being moved through her. She hugged him tighter. He pushed himself up, his knees resting on her lap, and put his arms around her neck, kissing her wetly on her face. She laughed, dodging the avalanche of wet kisses from the child's juicy full lips. He grew more insistent, and it turned into a game. Jenny would dodge his kisses and he would try to find her face as she turned her head quickly from side to side, a heavy wet kiss his ultimate gain. As fast as she moved her head the child managed to kiss her face. He held on more tightly and leaned up against her.

She tried to pull away, to pry his hands off her neck, but they were locked tightly like iron handcuffs. She pulled and pulled but they wouldn't come apart. Davis' face grew bigger and fuller, his shock of blond hair surrounding pink wet lips and a fat pink tongue. His nose ran and the saliva dripped and bubbled from his large open mouth, wet bubbles slipping over an open smile, over his small perfect white teeth. The mocking smile met the scream in her ears as it left her throat. "Get away. Get away from me" she yelled as her head thrashed back and forth. Caught in his grip her neck could not move as the wet pink tongue came closer and closer. He was no longer Davis, no longer Carol's little boy. He had become a monster, a huge crushing force, holding her down, wanting to devour her. He eased up for a moment and pulled back, showing her his face. The face of the child had become the face of the rapist. She screamed and pushed him away. The creature fell onto the floor. The child's cries joined her own and competed with pounding coming from the door.

Jenny stopped screaming, the child did not. A key in the lock opened the door before Jenny got to it. Carol came crashing through the room like a crazed buffalo. Hesitating a moment till she got her bearings, then rushed to the screaming child lying on the floor and kicking in a tantrum. Lines of dark smudges covered the surface of Jenny's sleek desk, where he pounded against it with his mud-caked sneakers. Carol picked him up and hugged him.

"Baby, sweetheart, what's the matter? Why are you crying?" She rocked him. "What is wrong with him?" she glared up at Jenny, ready to blame her.

Jenny leaned against the doorframe, her face ashen, hands clasped as in prayer. "He wouldn't let go so I..."

"She pushed me," Davis screamed. "She hurt me." His small angry red face looked at her accusingly. Carol cooed to him, her eyes glared at Jenny.

How could you? He's only a child. Are you crazy?"

Jenny withheld reply. Her hands covered her mouth. She watched the mother and child, removed from her reality as if they were two-dimensional figures on a life size screen. The living room set appeared to be painted behind them, the bright light flooding the scene came from the bulb of an artificial sun. The scene looked right except she couldn't hear the player's words. The frizzy haired woman called Carol was moving her lips and grimacing her face as she smoothed the head of the two dimensional little boy whose mouth was still open catching bits of the tears streaming down his face. Yet she heard nothing.

She did feel the cold air however when the two figures – the mother with the child in her arms rushed past her and slammed the door shut. The blinds quivered and she watched as in slow motion a lithograph of Jean de Ark fell to the floor.

A glint of metal coming from the ceiling behind a heating vent caught her attention. A television lens, she thought. Someone was taping her in her own home, she was being watched. The sound of heavy breathing filled her head. She inched toward the coffee table and picked up a heavy Jade Peruvian head, and threw it at the vent. It splintered into pieces of green and white plaster. She didn't react to the fact it was a fake. Pulling the desk chair over to the wall she climbed up and tried to reach the vent with a hanger. It wasn't long enough. She got down and ran to the utility drawer. A game show audience screamed as three contestants dressed as babies careened in a fast moving circle and started to fall down. Jenny threw a hammer at the screen just as they fell. The screen exploded into thousands of pieces of glass and the laughing stopped. She retrieved the hammer from the pile of glass and smashed the stereo and the speakers Tim had just put in there. She noticed the telephone. That was probably bugged too. She pulled the plug out of the socket and sent the phone smashing through the remains of the broken television set. An interior pop marked its final demise. Poising in front of the overhead vent, she took an arsenal of household weapons and threw screwdrivers and awls against the wall, trying to hit the malevolent eye staring down at her travail. Paint cracked and pictures fell as she missed time after time. She finally hit the vent with a wrench but the metal covering didn't move.

Exhausted and shaken, energy drained, she went to the kitchen. The pitcher of juice was on the counter next to the sink. She poured a glass and gulped it down. Her shaking hands poured another and she swallowed it, then another, and still another. She didn't stop till the pitcher was finished. She barely made it to her bed before she collapsed.

CHAPTER THIRTEEN

Layer upon layer of heavy steel mesh parted as Jenny floated up from the island of her bed. Furniture and walls disappeared as she went through them, their solid reality dissipating into swirls of rotating molecules. She felt no fear as she moved free of gravity, free of any of the laws of nature she had known before. She perceived a curtain of white light was shielding her from evil. She had no fear.

Glancing down she saw an elongated body stretched like a grasshopper beside a pool of water, knowing the long green lizard's body had once been hers.

A clear bubble appeared behind her left shoulder. She had never seen anything like it, yet it filled her with such overwhelming peace and happiness she knew this was one of the voices that spoke to her.

"Why do you need that body?" It asked silently.

Jenny looked down at the lizard, green as a palm leaf, and knew she could not give up the physical, the time wasn't right, not enough had been mastered. A warm affectionate connection for the green reptile welled in her. She could never consciously give up her body. The pull of physical experience was too powerful.

She started to spin, speeding till she lost awareness.

A split of bright energy tunneled into her brain. Her eyes opened. A row of bright lights glared directly above her, straps pinned her arms to her sides, pressure from a foreign object against her esophagus. She pushed her head against hands that held it and saw six pairs of eyes staring back at hers, faces hidden by green cloth masks. Directly opposite, between the rows of heads, a plaster statue of Jesus Christ with tortured eyes and splashes of simulated blood on his forehead, hung suspended on a plastic cross-nailed to the wall. Beneath the statue, a round digital clock read 11, but was it 11 in the morning or 11 at night? Jenny didn't know. The six heads leaning over her obscured any time reference - day or night in this stark white room there was no difference.

One pair of dark eyes caught her attention. They were panther eyes, with an energy flow distinctly their own. It was Elaine. Jenny acknowledged her. The green head and black eyes nodded. A green shirted figure reached over and put his fingers down her throat. She gagged as the unrelenting rubber coated fingers pulled at the object inside her.

"How you doing Jenny?" the figure asked, preventing any answer. She blinked her eyes, tears gathered. She could see the tube being pulled from her throat, leaving a burning, throbbing sensation behind.

The hard surface she lay on started to shake. The six heads pulled back as the line-up of lights converged behind them. Two aluminum racks holding bottles with plastic tubes running to her arms, jiggled and swayed as they were wheeled down the corridor. The back of her head bounced from the vibration of rubberized wheels against hard tile floors.

Roomless doors whizzed past. The green mask she had identified as Elaine walked next to her - Elaine's hand resting heavily on her shoulder as if to keep her in place. Loud booming voices accompanied the journey calling for "Dr. Stone in ER" Red and green lights flashed over streaks of colors painted on the sides of the walls. Jenny couldn't move, tight sheets held her down. She could feel pulsating aches in the tops of her hands where needles were inserted and taped to her flesh.

"What happened?" she managed to ask the mask called Elaine, as steel walls encased them in a space moving upward.

"You took an overdose."

"No, I didn't." The light hurt her eyes. She hadn't taken an overdose. She could not conceive of wanting to kill herself. She firmly believed that if she couldn't face up to the problems she was enduring and took her own life, then she would have to come back and do it all over again. She believed in re-incarnation, and for that reason she would not commit suicide.

Elaine took off her mask exposing her face etched into a mask of disapproval. She turned her gaze away and looked straight ahead as one of the walls opened before them.

They wheeled the table into a tiny green room. Jenny sensed the mustiness of disease and death. Hands reached under her and moved her to a bed - her arms outstretched, connected to the bottles a virgin sacrifice for a medical ritual. She couldn't resist, couldn't even try. She was too tired. Her heavy lids closed. Hands reached over and pulled her blanket back. She was startled.

"Take it easy. I just want to take the needles out." Drugged sleepiness swelled her thick eyelids. She could barely make out the features of the man, only the fine blonde hair covering his arm. She tried to push him away, get the man away from her.

"Hey!" he called out, "take it easy. I'm sorry I'm hurting you but you'll feel better with these needles out of your arm."

"Get away. Don't touch me. Get away.," she screamed, fighting him with all the strength she had. A needle dangled, half pulled from her arm.

Footsteps rushed into the room, a blur of white uniforms came closer into focus. A pinching burn jabbed her arm. Immediately, once again, gray mesh walls closed in around her.

She found herself in the airport. She was confused. How did she get there? Then she saw Tim stepping off the red eye flight from Washington DC. He looked exhausted and cranky. She noticed that nearly everyone on the plane wore campaign buttons of some sort. They were coming here for a rally. Tim was disheveled and was coming out of the plane behind quite a few others. This meant he most likely had not been able to sit in first class – he wouldn't like that. A heavy set man clamped a beefy hand on Tim's shoulder. "Nice talking to you. Kept me from getting too bored all night."

Tim mumbled something without directly looking at the man

Jenny called to him and tried to touch his shoulder, but it was as if she was invisible, he didn't respond at all. Vexed Jenny followed Tim into the men's rest room where he went to the washbasin and turned on the hot water.

As he studied his face in the mirror, Jenny did the same without registering that her own face was not mirrored back at all.

Tim had been flying around the country with his father to campaign stops and political rallies since he was a little boy His father had never been elected to public office but with his financial and corporate acumen he was a prized adjunct to many politician's entourages. Jenkins Senior was proud that it had been he who had started young Tim on the campaign trail at such an early age. From the day he was born, Tim's father had been determined that his son would be President of the United States and it was under the umbrella of this obsession that Tim's whole life had been directed.

149

Jenny remembered Tim telling her on their first date that before he was five he had been able to put together a puzzle map of America, and recite all the state capitals. Before he entered first grade, he could write the names of all the Presidents of the United States in the correct order and without a single spelling mistake.

Tim's father had shown Jenny pictures of Tim's tenth birthday celebration in which he attended his first dinner at the White House. And though she loved Tim madly, she was always saddened by the fact that his father's ambition had taken over his life. But she also accepted the fact that by the time Tim was twenty he believed in his destiny and if she wanted to be his wife, she would have to accept that and be a part of it.

In the last semester of her senior year in High School, Jenny had visited Tim at Harvard when he returned from the London School of Economics for his PHD dissertation. It was a politically chaotic time in which the old world order had begun to crumble; the Berlin wall had been torn down precipitating a crumbling of Communism over a vast area of the world. The Soviet Union broke up into separate and sometimes acrimonious divisions while the threat of religious wars, dictatorships, and economic collapse loomed through Asia and the Balkans.

Before it could spread to the West Tim's father acted with characteristic flair and summoned together a group of friends to discuss the disturbing changes, which threatened the peace and prosperity of the United States.

The men who attended the private meeting held at the California home of a former president, represented the full might of America - a chief executive of one of the world's largest multinational corporations, a media giant, a serving member of the Joint Chiefs of Staff, two Nobel Prize winners, four bankers, and no fewer than six ambassadors. Their deliberations lasted three days; at the end of which their conclusions were so startling that even Tim had been shocked by them. For it was he who, one day would be expected to carry them out. But first they would make him President.

Tim barely noticed the young soldier who had come out of a stall in the bathroom to wash his hands. The harsh fluorescent lighting painted a ghoulish portrait with dark circles on his cadaverously pale face. Tim was staring into the mirror, thinking about what his father had told him. When Jenny realized she could hear his thoughts, she tried not to listen, but she couldn't help it. There was no place to go, she was stuck to him like some invisible Siamese twin.

Tim smiled at his reflection, thinking that although he had no sleep and felt exhausted, he still looked pretty good. Jenny watched her fiancée's conceit as he studied his profile. She could hear him thinking that he was starting to look more sincere and trustworthy every day.

"You have the kind of charisma that cameras love to catch," he told his image in the mirror. "A media dream -- you're Robert Redford in "The Candidate", but for real." He gave himself a dazzling smiling in the mirror and checked his profile.

Jenny remembered the first day they met at the St. Charles Hunt Club. Tim had come back for Thanksgiving, and members of the hunt had been out cubing. Cubing was a way to train young hounds for the hunt by dragging a dead animal from the back of a four wheel drive vehicle so that the dogs could learn to follow a scent. Tim had noticed Jenny immediately, far away from the others, trying to school her unruly horse. When the horse refused a jump and started to rear, Jenny didn't react the way most riders would. Instead of kicking the horse and hitting it with a crop, she leaned forward on the horse's neck and whispered and the horse seemed to relax under Jenny's skilled hands.

"I don't know what you said to him, but that was one of the most interesting pieces of riding I've ever seen," Tim had told her as he rode over to her. She blushed, and smiled her thanks. As they rode back toward the others, Tim could not take his eyes off her. He was captivated by her radiance and, in that instant, he knew that he had found his perfect mate.

The door to the men's room opened and a man dressed in madras trousers and a shirt printed with red lips came in, the smell sweet of after-shave lotion unsuccessfully covering his body odor, Jenny felt sick but then heard Tim tell himself that he would go straight to the hospital instead of going home. He wanted to see Jenny. Feelings of anger and disappointment were beginning to creep in on him. He was angry with Jenny for not listening, and angry with his political team. They had wanted him to stop Jenny writing articles about Anson Industries, but Jenny wouldn't listen. Tim had been exasperated by her stubbornness, but the group's reaction had shocked him. Even now, he could hardly believe the harshness of their judgment. This was the girl he was going to marry, not some ordinary journalist. They should never have said those things. Not in his presence.

As the cab pulled out of the airport, it passed the private area where Tim had boarded his father's plane to take him to Maryland for a special training course. It seemed so long ago, but it had been at this retreat and training center that he had learned the elements of a new governing order based on intellectual capacity. From a group of eminent scientists, politicians, and thinkers, he had learned of a grand design to wipe out poverty, war, and starvation in the world with a breathtakingly radical solution. The plan hinged on a rigid concept of personal worth, and that was to be programmed at the moment of conception - not in a living womb, but on a scientist's bench. In a Petri dish. Tim was to be groomed and trained to be one of the leaders entrusted with preserving this vision and keeping it in place. Jenny grew cold. The people who were plotting his career had warned him that Jenny was a danger. They assured him that frightening her off was essential, and he had to trust them to do it right. But he had been shocked when she had told him about the rape when he called her in the hospital. Even these people wouldn't stoop to that.

"Don't cry, I'm here," he whispered, holding her by the shoulders.

"Are you all right?"

She shook her head. "No."

"I'll get you out of here."

"Please," she whispered hoarsely.

"I'll talk to the doctor now." He paused and looked at her. "I knew this story you were chasing would lead to disaster."

"Why?" she stared up at him, tears still streaming.

He drew in his breath sharply and held it a moment. "I don't know."

When he left the room, Jenny got out of bed, forcing her rubbery legs to carry her into the bathroom. Bright sunlight poured through the windows. The ritual of washing her face made her feel better. She could concentrate now. Tim seemed strange, calm yet disturbed. Was she being paranoid? Nothing was right anymore. What once was solid and "real" now appeared duplicitous and surreal. Only her dreams and visions had the solidity of reality. Fantasy had become reality, and reality was mere fantasy.

She gave her cheeks a pinch to bring back their color. She was alive. She felt better. Because Tim was here? Revitalized, Jenny went back into the room and saw a contingent of doctors clustered grimly near her bed. Tim stood off to a side, talking to the eldest and most distinguished of the group. The others, identical in green shirts and pants, stood mutely by, their arms crossed and heads lowered as they listened to the two principal's conversation. They snapped to attention as she entered the room. All conversation stopped. She walked to the opposite end and sat down, weak but smiling. "Do I get to hear the verdict?

If you want to leave, you may. You can be discharged," the elder doctor said, "medically. However I would suggest follow up. You did a very dangerous thing."

Jenny was hurt by his words. "I didn't try to commit suicide. I didn't take anything! I don't know how it happened! If I wanted to die I would have been successful."

The doctor stared back with no expression. He didn't believe her.

The head doctor handed Jenny the release and showed her where to sign. As she started to put her signature on the document he faced his group but continued talking to her. "If you want to leave the hospital we are no longer responsible for anything that might happen."

"Thank you doctor, but you never were." She tried to hide her hands so he wouldn't see them shaking. She handed the clipboard back to the doctor and Tim walked them to the door, assuring him he would take full responsibility for her.

She started to say something then bit her lips against the words. Now was not the time to defend her individuality. Nor was it the time to ask Tim how the attacker had known such intimate things about her, things only Tim would have known.

He came back in, smiling.

"Tim, it's possible the fetus survived."

"The fetus?" He froze for a moment, shocked. "Darling! I didn't know!"

No, not me." She felt terrible. He had been genuinely excited and now she would disappoint him. "I'm sorry. I meant Mannie's baby."

"Mannie's baby? She couldn't have been pregnant!" he shouted.

"She was near the end of her fourth month when she had the accident," she paused. The pictures of the accident came back to her. She wished she could dissolve them, never see them again. It was beginning to sink in that her friend Mannie was gone; the one person who always cared about her, the one she knew she could really trust. If Tim was betraying her, she now had no one. No true friend, no confidant, no checks no balances. "They may have saved her baby."

"Darling, Mannie was a full blown Lesbian. She wasn't pregnant."

"Yes she was. I don't know who the father is, and she claimed not to know either. I have to find out. I owe this to my friend and possibly her baby. If the fetus was saved I want to know what happened to it."

"Darling, let's get out of here. You're upset and I don't blame you. I'm very tired. I had a miserable flight."

"I know."

He looked at her strangely but she had turned her head so he wouldn't see the tears in her eyes. She had been kidnapped, beaten and raped, her best friend was killed, and Tim was complaining about a five-hour plane flight.

He hugged her. "I have a surprise." He ushered her out the door. She followed obediently. "Look." Tim pulled an airline ticket out of his coat as they stood in the elevator. She looked at it, questioning. The doors opened and they walked out. "This afternoon we're flying to Puerto Vallarta, Mexico. When we arrive we grab a taxi to the Bay of Tortugo, rent a boat, a "ponga" to be exact, and race the dolphins down the coast to a private cove where my friend has been kind enough to give us his fully equipped hacienda for as long as we like. I know the place well. I used to spend a lot of time there on school holidays and it's heaven."

She threw her arms around his neck and kissed him. For the first time in many months, he didn't stiffen. "Perfect! More than perfect. You always know how to make me feel better."

"I love you."

"I hope so."

He was about to question that statement when his attention was drawn to her focus, the limousine waiting for them.

"Good touch," she said as she settled gratefully into the plush beige seats of the stretch. I needed this. Much better than that hospital bed! You're bringing me back to a nicer reality. I like this. I love you."

He smiled, "I'm glad."

CHAPTER FOURTEEN

The sparkling salty water massaged her body and refreshed her mind. She rolled on her back, stretching out lazily. A huge wave came up and knocked her over. Jenny laughed and swallowed water. Pebbles washed into her bathing suit. Mexico was salvation.

The estate on the private cove was primitive in the sense it had no phone, electricity, or transportation. The only way to reach it was by boat and any extended journeys into the jungle were on foot or riding one of the small burros kept in a large enclosure at the far end of the estate's perimeters.

The entire area was saturated with such a palpable peace of such deep dimensions that it was able to embrace and comfort her so she could pull back from the jolting events that were too fresh to be mere memories and helped to soften their excruciating pain.

Using powerful strokes to catapult herself out a few yards more, she pushed her body under the next wave, reversed herself and floated back to shore. Coming out of the water she felt the hot sun begin to dry her immediately. She saw Tim straight ahead, wrapped in the cocoon-like netting of a tightly woven *matrimonial* hammock that swung between two large date Palms. He appeared to be sleeping soundly, arms crossed over his chest, a sweet smile spread restfully across his face.

Her heart lifted. Tim looked so peaceful. He had needed this rest nearly as much as she had. Was it possible she had been wrong? Had he not been the one to change, was she the one?

Frowning with the thought Jenny went into the bathroom, peeling off her wet bathing suit and decided not to light the coconut shells doused with kerosene in order to heat the water. She stepped under the cold shower. The decision was wise. The cold water on her warm skin felt good.

Stepping out of the shower she put a towel around herself, hung her bathing suit out to dry and looked around, deciding what to do next. It was still morning and she certainly didn't feel like taking a rest. Sunbathing was out of the question, her skin was too fair. Reading might break the spell she was under.

Feeling compelled to pick up a piece of paper and pencil she watched as the pencil began to move in her hand, putting down words that became thoughts and looking very much like she was writing them. But she wasn't.

"YOU CAN FIND THINGS TO TRIGGER THESE FEELINGS IN YOURSELF – NO MATTER WHERE YOU ARE. USE THEM AS SYMBOLS. GO OUT AND GET A ROCK. SOME TIME IN THE FUTURE THE MEMORY OF WHERE YOU GOT IT WILL BRING YOU BACK HERE."

The writing stopped. Jenny folded the paper and put it in her diary along with similar notes and decided to go out and find a rock or some such momento to take home with her. Pulling a long-sleeve gauze shirt over her bare torso she slipped into soft linen drawstring trousers but her sandals were nowhere to be found. She'd go barefoot.

Stepping through a wall of heat on to the verandah Jenny paused to look at Tim, but her eyes were drawn immediately to a thin black snake slipping silently through the grass, it's tongue flicking in and out -- searching for scent samples in the air. Stopping at the foot of the hammock in which Tim slept, the snake appeared to find the source of its scent and coiled its forequarters in preparation for a strike.

Afraid to call to Tim, fearful any sound might cause the snake to strike, Jenny searched desperately for someone to help them. But once again at a crucial time in her life there was no one around. Inching her way toward Tim and the snake she hunted for something to throw and scare it away. But the movement startled the snake and it reared even higher, spreading its neck into a threatening hood like a Cobra. But were there Cobras in Mexico? Jenny had no time to think about that. She had to help Tim and called out to him without a second's hesitation.

Lurching up at the sound of Jenny's stricken voice Tim immediately saw the object of her alarm.

"Don't move," Jenny called to him as she aimed a large rock she could barely hold and heaved it underhanded like a bowling ball toward the snake. The rock barely missed the hypnotically dangerous snake that hesitated a brief yet timeless moment till its instincts made it slither away into the surrounding foliage.

Heedless of the sharp hot stones cutting her bare feet, Jenny raced toward Tim who sat with eyes glaring resentfully.

"Great —" Tim croaked, holding on to the sides of the swaying hammock like a rowboat ready to capsize. "Now we don't know where it's gone."

Jenny was too shocked to say anything. She thought she had saved his life and now he was angry, unmindful of what she had done.

Swinging his legs over the side of the hammock and gingerly putting his feet on the ground Tim didn't say another word as he rose and walked swiftly away toward the estate compound.

Holding back tears Jenny plunged through the jungle not stopping till she was far into the interior and only then to cool her burning feet in a cool mountain stream running alongside the path. Calming down she surveyed the vegetation and noticed three thatched roof huts nearly hidden in the thick foliage.

"Hola," she called out in Spanish, but no one answered. Curious, she walked to the nearest hut and peaked in. On the dirt floor a large cooking pot rested on a pile of smoking logs. In the shadows were hammocks strung close to the walls. All was tidy, efficient and primitive.

Sensing something behind her she turned and saw two Mexican Indian women sitting in the doorway of another hut. A third was on the rocks nearby. Their cloudy gray eyes hooded from inspection they watched her carefully,

She smiled and started to walk toward the single woman, but as soon as she did a piece of spiked cactus went into her toe. Gasping as she fell to the ground, grabbing her foot in pain, she was shocked to hear a giggle coming from one of the women. Startled she forgot her agony and stared as one of the three smiled sweetly and offered her a cup of what appeared to be a steaming liquid, a tea.

Jenny shook her head but the woman gestured again and pointed to her foot then to her mouth to drink.

Reluctantly Jenny pulled herself into a sitting position and took a sip of the brew. It was bitter. She started to put it down but the Indian woman gestured emphatically for her to finish. Jenny sipped a bit more as the bitterness disappeared and was replaced with a flowery sweet taste that coated the bitterness on her tongue.

.   Waves of loving calmness seemed to pour from the old woman and everything started to dissolve into sweetness as the edges of the craggy faced woman softly blended into beauty. Jenny sat dreamily in front of the woman obediently sipping. For a moment the face of the old woman become that of her mother. Then a ray of light made its way through the thatched hut and burnished the Indian woman's wrinkled skin into a mask of copper.

The walls of the reed hut began to shimmer, becoming luminescent pillars, impelling Jenny to rise and walk through them into what had become a temple of shimmering gold. In the far distance she heard what sounded like a giggle. Tempted to look back she ignored the urge and continued forward, impelled by a force she could not question or name.

Reaching a vaulted room that contained only a large crystal in the center of it, Jenny noted that the crystal was faceted with triangles and flat surfaces which drew her close to examine the interior.

"It's a *story keeper,*" said that voice that had been coming into her thoughts so clearly since the terror of the last few days. It had been the energy of the voice and not so much the things it said that had caught Jenny's attention and made her listen. It was a separate knowledge that she knew without question was apart from her own.

"If you look carefully you will see the past and the future." The voice was saying as Jenny walked through a luminescent passageway she felt she had known before. Overwhelming feelings of purity and love made her vow to herself that she'd never leave this place or question those voices because she knew that the forces that were leading her were those of the good.

"Look ahead," came a soft command in her head. "If you look back or down you might get scared. Keep this experience. Don't tighten or turn back."

She obeyed joyfully, taking the advice with a full heart. Never had she known such peace and happiness.

Little semi-transparent shapes like butterflies appeared and flitted around her – lilac and gold, scarlet and blue, green and magenta -- a cacophony of pure visual harmony, a ballet of mind lifting proportions.

She knew Earth was beneath her - far behind, and that she had entered the inner resources of space that were hidden and stored in her mind. Clear light surrounded her, the force of "true life". This was where she really lived, really belonged. This was reality -- more real than the vague existence she experienced with life on Earth.

Her natural power had returned, a power she had given up while living in the gravitational confines of the three dimensional planet. How could she have forgotten this remarkable world inside her?

"You don't really have to eat anymore," said the voice within her.

"Why?"

"To quickly reach this place you have to train yourself to take the power from plants and the sun and turn it into your own energy. That's what Buddha did. So do many of the great masters."

"But how do I do it?" she asked,

"Be observant about what you eat. See anything you put into your body as a pure unit of energy. Your instincts will lead you there."

"But what if I forget?" she asked.

"What's to forget?" the voice inside her questioned.

"How do I make sure I'll never lose this knowledge again? How do I hold on to it when I return to Earth?"

"Trust and honor your feelings. This truth will never leave you."

"But how do I do that? I want to know. "

"Don't worry. You will be reminded, you will be shown," consoled the voice. "Trust your instincts, those are your guides. You can call them love," said the voice, starting to fade.

She could feel herself slipping, back through the atmosphere to a denser space.

"Love will bring you back here even if you're not aware like you are now."

Warmth covered her heart and she stopped sliding backward. The dense air dissipated and everything once again was clear.

"Remember what you know," the voice was saying, "by using symbols if you need them. But don't get caught in them. They are only vehicles. Remain a clear thinker -- keep access to the purity that is your freedom.

You've been here before and always have been. Anything else that happens is just a pit stop toward your complete enlightenment. To stay here takes training. It takes time to get it. That's what this voice is for, to guide and teach you."

"But wait a minute – " she called out in the void. "Can I always trust it?"

"Yes, but trust your doubts too. Everything is perfect no matter which way you see it. Good or evil are manifestations to reflect each other. Without evil we wouldn't understand good."

"That's hard to accept," Jenny said, tightening and pulling back from the pure joy she had been feeling.

"Following the good is easier and faster," the voice went on. "Evil will secede to good. When you equate light with goodness and evil with dark, light has power over darkness and can dispel it. With light, illumination, there are no shadows, there is no dark."

Jenny felt confused.

"Sometimes you must be pushed to the limits, taken to the darkest areas of consciousness and tested so these truths of the universe can make an affect on you."

"Please...! No more testing!" But Jenny could feel herself tilting and plummeting back to Earth.

***

Bells and wind chimes tinkled in the breeze filling the air with brightness and sweet sounds as Jenny rushed along the hot jungle path, unaware of the heat or sharp stones beneath her bare feet. She was worried, felt Tim waiting for her, felt a little scared.

He had left angry with her and would be doubly annoyed because she was probably late. Actually she had no idea how much time had passed --it could have been five minutes, three hours, six days. Time was meaningless in light of the momentous experience she just had.

It had been a rebirth of sorts, a clearing of her cerebral veils. It was most definitely an epiphany in which truths were revealed. Whatever she would call it when she would tell Tim about it, she would explain to him that it was the birth place of all her future thoughts and belief systems. Her perception of reality would never be the same.

The path curved and the rooftops of the main house came up through the jungle, a man - made oasis in the ancient, lush foliage. Troubled she paused. Had the brew the Indian woman given her put her into an altered state so she only fantasized what she thought existed? Or was she being tested with doubts to refute what she had seen and experienced?

She would have to deny her own feelings, her happiness and bonding with positive energy. Her body cringed at those thoughts in her head.

No, she told herself. She had begun to perceive reality in a new and different way and Tim was a test, a trigger point because her emotions were so caught up with him. She was in love with TIm and had opened physically and spiritually to every aspect of him. But the thought of talking to him gave her strong misgivings.

Should she tell him what happened, describe the journey? What if he laughed and didn't believe her? Trying to describe it could cause an argument. Perhaps she should keep the experience secret. Unease was pervading every choice she could think of.

Stopping and turning away from the main house Jenny began pacing in circles, her breathing short and labored. Suddenly a gust of wind swirled up and enveloped her with soft warm energy, reminding her she had been given a new world to digest and live in.

Tension drained out of her body and positive vitality entered within her. Mother Nature had taken over and was going to protect her. What she had experienced was real and these doubts were the beginning of a whole string of tests. She understood if she stayed plugged into positive feelings, everything would have an answer, every moment the opportunity for a profound life lesson.

She quickened her pace. She could deal with Tim. Then she heard the sound of voices. The few words she could make out were in English. She stopped. One of the voices was Tim's but there were other people with him.

Reaching the clearing Jenny saw two people sitting on the verandah with Tim, a man and women. Jenny smoothed her hair and approached them. In deep conversation Tim didn't acknowledge her till the two visitors shifted their focus to her.

The man was small and thin, almost frail. He had a clean-shaven, bullet-shaped head and wore small round glasses with tinted lenses clipped on to the frame. But it was the woman who claimed Jenny's attention as she stepped onto the verandah. As the woman turned her face slightly, Jenny gave a sharp little gasp and stopped dead in her tracks. The woman, her hand poised on the verandah rail, met her eyes with Jenny's.

Even though her dark hair was pulled severely back and tied at the nape of her neck, there was no mistaking the pale oval face, nearly luminescent in the fading evening light. Nor was it possible to mistake the reed thin body and those cruel red lips. The long manicured nails were another give away as was her arrogant stance; the way she leaned slightly back from the hips, the disdain as she twirled the wine glass in her hand.

It was the woman who had tortured her in her apartment!

For an endless second, Jenny's eyes locked with those of her tormentor. Then the woman smiled brightly as if she had never seen Jenny before in her life.

"Its a test..." The words chimed in Jenny's ears, swirled around her head. Tim's body swiveled lazily to greet her, a welcoming smile painting in slow motion across his handsome face. His eyes were not smiling. Jenny's breath caught in her chest. She could hear the jungle insects buzzing loudly – they sounded like drills, the buzzing filled her head.

A large white motorboat bobbed in the cove off the beach, flying the Mexican flag. She would have liked to run away and almost tripped when Tim took her hand and pulled her gently toward him.

"Darling, we were concerned about you."

He wasn't. She had heard this insincere *sincere* tone hundreds of times before.

"Jenny," he continued with a smooth silicone coated voice. "I'd like you to meet Doctors Jan and Felix White."

Blood rushed to her head and stayed there pounding. She could scarcely breathe. Tim's phony voice continued. "The Whites are old family friends."

All she could hear was *family* and *friends*.

"They have a lovely vacation home just a few miles from here beyond that point." He waved his hand in the direction of the North where the shoreline jutted out,

The woman called Dr. Jan White watched her steadily, breathing through her mouth. She flicked her tongue to wet her dry lips, her head stationary, scarcely breathing, her back rigid.

"Excuse me," Jenny's voice found itself, "Tim, may we talk?" She turned and walked back toward the jungle. Tim excused himself and suggested the two guests have another drink.

Jenny tried to breathe, praying the lightness in her head would not make her faint. She stopped at a large palm tree; it's trunk bent and leaning low to the ground so she was able to sit down on it. Tim approached her.

"What's wrong?" he asked, squatting next to her and taking her hand.

She held the tree firmly as the ground seemed to sway. "Are those really your friends?" She asked, trying not to lose control.

"Yes," His face was a portrait of innocence. "Why?"

Tears refused to stay contained and poured down her face. Everything was burning as she struggled to speak. "Do you know who that woman is?" she asked.

"Of course I do," he looked impatient, "Jan White. I told you, they're old family friends."

"Family doctors?" she asked.

Tim chuckled, his look of innocence intact. "Not really darling, Jan and Felix White are psychiatrists." He squeezed her hand.

Jenny pulled her hand away from his, the stark implication teeming through her head.

"Every once in awhile my father would send an employee to the Whites' clinic if they needed psychological help. But our relationship has always been personal and social."

"*Clinic.*" Jenny repeated. The woman's cool, assertive approach suddenly made sense.

"I knew they were going to be in Mexico the same time we were," Tim continued, "so, considering what you have just been through I thought it would be good for you to meet them so I invited them to dinner." He stood up and put out his hand to help her stand.

Jenny stayed rooted to the trunk. "Tim," she said. "That woman," she paused, afraid to say it.

"Yes?" Tim's eyes had a cold glare, anticipating her words would hold a negative attitude.

Jenny forced herself to continue. "She was the one in my apartment."

"That's ridiculous," Tim said coldly.

'It's the truth." Her voice sounded very high.

"Impossible." He searched her face. He was genuinely surprised and concerned.

"No, it isn't. It's her. I could never forget her. I wish it were a mistake. I know her..." she took a quick breath, "intimately." Jenny turned away, hot tears flowing down her cheeks.

Tim reached down and took her hand and kissed it. "Darling you've made a mistake," he gently pulled her to her feet and brushed away her tears. "You're in a highly charged emotional state. In fact I was happy to learn that the Whites would be able to come meet you. I want you to talk to them. They could be very helpful."

Jenny stared at Tim in disbelief. How could he be saying this? Was he involved or completely naïve?

"Look, " Tim when on, "I realize that Jan has a classic look and can be mistaken for someone else. In fact, I've seen it happen to her time and time again. It's an easy mistake darling, especially now." He hugged her and patted her on the back like a child. "Don't worry, I'll say something to them to smooth this over. But hurry, we mustn't keep them waiting any longer."

"No!" she pulled away.

Tim's mouth drew into a thin hard line. "Darling you can't stay in the jungle all night. It's too dangerous. Really darling, pull yourself together and stop this now."

"Tim?" she asked, and then stopped, afraid to go on.

"Yes?" He was brushing leaves and dust off his trousers and palms as he waited for her to speak. He checked in the direction of the compound and seemed to be satisfied his guests were all right. "Please Jenny, pull yourself together. You're embarrassing me as well as yourself."

"Tim, I wonder..."

"Yes, come on darling, out with it, our guests are waiting."

His indifference was crushing. Who was this man she thought she loved? What was he made of? She looked into the sky for a moment and thought she saw a blue butterfly. Instantly all the beings came back to her and she felt a new power. "Tim," she heard her voice saying, "I don't know if you're involved, but that woman is, I know it."

"Now I'm involved! Was I in the apartment as well?" His face was angry, his voice harsh. "Did I rape you too?"

"Tim!" His words hit her like a physical blow. She had never seen him so cruel. Crushed she realized in an instant that she was on her own. Tim would not help her. She turned her face away. "Go ahead, I'll be there in a moment."

Tim walked away.

Jenny leaned against the Palm tree. There was no way she could get off this island alone. And even if she had access to a phone, who would she call? How could she direct them to where she was? She had no idea, hadn't paid much attention. She would have to get through this by remaining observant and emotionally still. If she showed weakness they could tear her apart.

Slowly she walked back toward the compound. She had beaten this woman once before and she would do it again.

"Jenny," said the woman with the same polite and professional voice, the same cool sophistication and demeanor as Jenny stepped on to the verandah. "We understand you've mistaken me for someone else. I'm terribly sorry," she smiled sympathetically. "We know about your recent misfortune. Tim did tell you we're doctors in the psychiatric sciences, didn't he? I don't know if this will allay your fears at all, but we're not villains, quite the opposite, we'd like to help." She smiled sweetly. Her eyes glittered.

Chills ran up Jenny's back.

Tim's head was turned away. She did her best to stay calm, but her heart was pounding. There was no escape. "If I had known you were coming, I would have been better prepared," came forth from her mouth.

"Darling," Tim dripped tones of charm on to his words, "Would you like a drink?"

Her mouth was very dry. "Please. Juice or mineral water."

"Why don't you have something stronger, more hospitable to make amends for this embarrassing mistake."?

"It wasn't a mistake," Jenny said turning to a maid holding a tray with Margaritas. "Una sin tequila, "she told the woman who went back toward the kitchen.

"Ah," said Jan White. "You're cheating. No tequila."

Jenny nodded, her mouth quite unable to smile.

"Tim has told us quite a bit about you," Jan continued, conversationally.

"Has he?" Jenny asked, disciplining herself not to say anything about the way the woman already knew her.

The woman maintained her polite smile and adjusted the dark glasses on the bridge of her nose. "We have been hearing about your latest series of articles."

"The ones Tim disapproves of?" Jenny asked pointedly.

Jan ignored the sarcasm. "He's quite proud of you," she turned to Tim who smiled back at Jan over his glass.

"I'm glad," Jenny said as she watched Tim with the woman. He never discussed her work, especially work that was in progress. He was smiling without substance. The dinner bell broke the tension and everyone rose very quickly.

Jenny didn't want to eat anything. Her feelings of betrayal and absolute horror were worse than anything she had ever experienced. There was something else going on as well, a fearful sense that nothing she was seeing or feeling was actually real. It made her feel empty, all alone in the world. There were no voices to advise her, nothing to help her, only herself. Was this graduation, was she supposed to survive this completely on her own?

She followed obediently into the large open space that was the dining room. Its thatched roof sent down criss-cross rays of light creating a mosaic pattern over the table and walls. Even the servants standing stiffly behind their assigned chairs looked part of the pattern. When everyone was seated, trays bearing platters of tacos, enchiladas, chile rellenos and iced pitchers of Sangria, red wine with fresh fruit, were presented.

"Blood," muttered Jenny.

"I beg your pardon?" Jan politely questioned.

"Blood. In the pitchers. Sangria. That's what you're drinking."

"Oh. Well, here's to us Vampires!" Jan announced gaily, picking up the glass of wine Tim had poured for her.

"That's right," said Jenny. Conditioned feelings of hunger began to gnaw at her. She didn't feel hungry, so why was her stomach growling? She had just been shown profound secrets in the jungle, the process of photosynthesis, and had been told by the voice she had the ability to do that. However, the process required years of practice and discipline. She closed her eyes and sent a message to her stomach to remember what she had learned. The grumbling subsided. She looked up and the three were watching her. She decided to ignore them and looked at the food on her plate. The melted cheese and beans were overcooked and fairly dead looking. She looked for something else, something fresh to eat, but there was nothing - just some limp pieces of chopped lettuce and over-ripe tomatoes.

"Buen provecho," said Tim gaily, and they all dug hungrily into their food, with soft grunts of satisfaction.

Jenny sat quietly, her fork in her hand, watching.

Aren't you going to eat?" asked Tim. "It's delicious."

"Is there anything fresh to eat?"

"In the blood." He chuckled, and continued eating.

Without thinking she dug her fork into the fried chili relleno stuffed with cheese and bit into it. The pleasure of good flavor exploded and made her want to start eating. She ate greedily till she became aware of the speed, looking around to see if anyone had seen her. Dr. White was watching, but the other two seemed unaware. She started to eat again, making a point of doing it slowly, perceiving each piece of food as a component of energy. Dr. White had put his fork down and was boldly staring. She didn't know how to respond, it was embarrassing. Every time she picked her head up, she saw him looking. She put her fork down, folded her hands under her chin and stared back. He didn't flinch, like the blind man in the restaurant.

The thought brought tears again. She hadn't been at the newspaper, hadn't even thought about it or what had happened about Mannie's reputation since she left the hospital. She had been in a time capsule of her own making.

Dr. White continued to watch her. "What is happening in the world?" she asked him to draw his attention away from her.

"It's still revolving," he smiled.

She didn't smile back." "I mean politically, economically. I'm afraid I haven't been in touch."

"Still full of the mistakes and misjudgments of our current administration. Do-gooders trying to protect the masses who don't want to do anything."

"Those are harsh words coming from a man who took the Hippocratic oath to serve humanity."

"That's a totally different argument."

She had touched a nerve and he was growing angry.

Tim intervened. "Jenny, we're here to relax and enjoy ourselves. Must you start an argument?"

"I merely asked how the world was doing. It's called discussion, not provocation. I think you're the one provoking an argument." She pierced a taco with her fork and held it up. "Why don't we just enjoy this nice dead food and I'll be quiet." Her head began spinning and she put the fork down. "Would you please excuse me," she pushed her chair back.

Tim restrained her with his hand. "Dr. White, Felix, wants to talk to you. He feels you should discuss some of the paranoia you've been having."

"Paranoia?" She heard her voice sounding shrill, tension and anger exploding. "Why don't you ask your guest about that. She can give you full details."

"Darling, we understand what you've been through, and see you're not ready to accept your mistake, however the paranoia started before. Your last few articles about technology, the diatribes on mind control, the fear of programmed babies.... We aren't the enemy, Jenny. The Whites were kind enough to come here to talk to you. They can help."

"Help? You're setting me up!" She exploded. "Why can't you be direct instead of all this innuendo? I have to sit here on this island trapped till you figure out what to do with me. Don't you think I can see what is happening?"

"No, I think you're not understanding. All we want to do is communicate with you, and you're setting up barriers," said Dr. White softly.

"No you're not. You're evaluating me."

175

"That isn't true, Jenny," Jan was using her soothing doctor's voice.

Jenny pushed her chair back. "None of you want to talk to me. You're here to make judgments behind your dark glasses. The selection team."

"Jenny," said Dr. White, his face bright red, there is no selection going on. We're here to see if there is anything we can do to help you make this transition easier. That's the extent of any kind of conspiracy you may think we have planned."

"Maybe." Jenny pushed her chair back further and stood up. Tim came up behind her trapping her in his arms with a hug. "Let's go sit on the verandah and have coffee."

She allowed him to lead her as they retired to the stone patio overlooking the ocean. A silent servant brought a tray of coffee and cognac and handed each one a separate smaller tray of sugar and cream and a nearly transparent slice of lemon.

White cleared his throat when the servant lefts, rubbing his hands together like a praying mantis. "It seems you've been having some difficulties lately."

"Yes, " said Jenny, "because of the present company. "But that's life - surmounting difficulties till a comfortable space can be created. Like school, we go to receive problems that have to be solved - in order to learn. Then we pass the answers and guidelines to help others. I think I may have taught Jan something. Isn't that right?"

Jan smiled without responding.

White lit his pipe. "You've certainly had your share of problems in your work lately."

"Not really." Jenny's head started reeling. What was his implied threat now?

"Weren't you given some warnings?"

She wanted to leave, his impertinence was upsetting. "I don't know what you're talking about. But I do know you're making me uncomfortable. If you'll excuse me..." She pushed herself out of the chair, spilling the coffee and, shaking with indignation, strode off rapidly.

The reed walls of her room had no real doors or windows. She sat down in the middle of the bed and drew the mosquito netting around her. Tim had not followed her. She laid back, her heart beating. She could feel all the heavy food weighing her down, and focused on the thumping in her chest. It grew louder as it took over her whole body. The thumping vibrations lifted her off the bed. She could feel herself flying. She knew she should not look down or be afraid. She would be taken care of.

She flew through white veils flapping gently around her. They stretched and she could sense it was very much like her bed's mosquito netting. She must be hallucinating, she told herself. The clouds weren't clouds and she wasn't flying. She made it all up. Her body came down with a thump. She started to get up but felt too weak and laid down again.

She sensed someone in the room and turned to look. The curtains were drawn back and Tim and the Whites were talking.

"Because of the rape, her vulnerability has degenerated to the point where she is most highly suggestible," said Jan.

Tim looked sickly but didn't say a word.

Jan continued. "Our next phase is to implant organizational ideals and philosophies in every area of her consciousness and sub-conscious till she is able to use her own sources of creativity to convey what we have put there scientifically."

White films of clouds began to envelop Jenny as dark clouds rolled in from the West. Gray green in color, they tumbled over each other obscuring her vision from the clear white light. She tried to will them away and bring back the whiteness but the clouds persisted.

"What am I doing wrong?" she heard herself call out.

"You're blocking," said the familiar voice.

"What?"

"Your energy flow. Take a deep breath and let it all go."

Her body was pulsating tensely so she did what she was told. Her muscles loosened and she was sure she could feel her blood flowing.

She opened her eyes. It was almost completely dark. An owl hooted loudly. She went to the doorway. There was a rustling in the palm fronds - the old Indian woman was beckoning to her. Unmindful of the sharp stickers reaching out to prick her, Jenny followed her to a cliff overlooking the sea. The old lady stepped aside and pointed to a round raised stone in the center of the water. Waves lapped at the bottom of the cliff, slapping against huge boulders. Jenny looked around. The cliff was bordered by very deep jungle. The old woman had vanished.

The huge bowl of bright stars encircling her twinkled invitingly. The captivating brilliance of the white slash of the Milky Way was trying to envelop her. Orion's star blinked brightly. Saying hello? The Milky Way got whiter and closer, sending out a pathway of light. She stepped on to it without hesitation, knowing the light was a path to support her.

She walked through a tunnel of light, powerful energy surging through her, no longer able to tell where her body began or where the light left off. All was merged with feelings of exaltation, a honeycomb of pulsating light opening and growing stronger within her.

Whispered commands to the back of her head told her to get off the beam of light and directed her toward another. She stripped off her clothes and stood perfectly still. Parting her legs, she arched her body and began to float upward. Jets of bright lights were shooting through her, up through her vagina, up her spinal cord and out through the top of her head. Once, twice the energy shot through her. She felt cleansed, purified, satisfied like she never had been. Her whole body vibrating with good feelings. She never wanted it to end. She spread her legs wider and opened her arms. She still floated, but now she was shrinking into a corpuscle that surged through her own bloodstream. Everything was red, burgundy, and plush red. She could actually feel it - it was soft and fuzzy, almost made her palms itch. She turned to the right. A porthole revealed a blue sky outside an orange and red paisley print frame. Clouds were floating by but she wasn't a part of them. She could feel a restraining strap across her lap, the warmth of humans close by, a strong motorized vibration. She looked the other way. Tim sat next to her. They were on a plane.

She touched Tim's arm, terror stricken. "What are we doing here? I don't remember. How did we get here?"

He patted her hand gently. "We'll be there in a little while. Don't worry, you'll be well taken care of." He turned his attention back to the book he was reading.

What did he mean? She didn't remember getting on the plane. Just the old woman and the sky and the incredible sensation. She tried to think harder. Recreate what logically could have happened. But she was on an airplane and Tim was sitting next to her.

"So soon?" she asked silently. "Why so soon?"

"Because we have to," she heard in her mind. She could feel Tim's impatience. She looked at him. He didn't seem impatient now. The impatience was a memory. A memory she only remembered. She closed her eyes and a buzzing in her head took her deep into dreaming.

CHAPTER FIFTEEN

The back of the seat jerked forward, seatbelts snapped into place, passenger noise level increased as the plane banked into a turn and started it's descent. Tim leaned over and checked Jenny's seat belt then patted her hand. "Have a good nap?"

She looked at his hand on hers and wondered why had he made such an intimate gesture. Did he really care? She had no easy answer.

She turned to watch the approaching landscape outside the windows. She hadn't been dreaming. She had been in a suspended state of flat nothingness. She looked at Tim, dreading the need inside her to test him. "How long have we been on this plane?"

"About six hours."

"How long have I been sleeping?" She asked, trying to calculate the amount of time between the last times she had been with Tim at the house with his friends, the Whites.

"Practically since you got on the plane. You've been exhausted darling. And no wonder. After what you've been through…"

He turned back to his book.

"What are you reading?" she asked, fishing for something that would make her understand this man that she loved just a little bit. How she wanted to trust him. How she loved him when all had been without stress. The beginnings of their courtship, their attraction for each other had just been so perfect she thought it would always last. And now, this horrible self-doubt. This constant monitoring, If only she could turn back time and go to the place where they had once been.

Tim smiled brightly and picked up the book. "It's a biography on Roosevelt and it's riveting. The writer shows how Roosevelt was one of the first mass media manipulators. How he understood the necessity of garnering the masses, how he was an expert in understanding group consciousness and knowing how to use it. The fireside radio chats with the population left behind during the war. The coziness of his persona and the reality of this sharp and penetrating intellect."

"You love the power of manipulating millions of people, don't you?" she asked.

"I wouldn't call it manipulation. I rather see it as having been privileged in my own right and being able to pass on a higher consciousness and sensibility to all the masses."

"Through restrictions and pre-planned boxed existences?" she asked. "Programmed lifestyles that will not cut into the freedom enjoyed by those who make those rules – the ruling class?"

"I see where you're taking this Jenny and you're wrong. Roosevelt's political decisions, platforms and actions were for the people. But sometimes they don't know what's good for them, and the image of an elderly scholar confined to a wheelchair is a comfort that precipitates support. "

"You're talking manipulation – good or bad. I have a problem with that. I also have a problem with knowing where we are and how long we've been here. I'm disoriented."

He didn't answer, but smiled. When she didn't return the smile with one of her own, the smile disappeared as a look of concern crept across his face. "We discussed White's interesting therapy and we thought it would be useful." He said.

She looked at him without answering. "We never discussed anything like that. It didn't happen." She watched him carefully. He was lying. She had been super conscious all the time she had been close to the Whites. Jan White was extremely dangerous and if she let down for a second that woman would scoop her up and swallow her for eternity.

His concern stayed painted on. "You don't remember our talk?" His words were clothed in the tone of a statement not a question.

She watched him carefully. He was a good actor, but what if he did mean it? She couldn't remember anything like that. "It didn't happen." She unbuckled the seat belt, to get away, to think clearly, away from Tim.

The loud speaker was advising the flight attendants to go to their seats. Tim held her arm. "Please darling. We're going to land. You can get hurt."

"Maybe I already am." The bottom had dropped out, she thought to herself. She wanted to trust him, keep their love intact, but now she would have to be duplicitous. She could no longer tell him the truth. She would go to the sanitarium and keep conscious and discover exactly what was going on.

The plane bumped down on the landing, the engines revving in order to stop. Waiting for the other passengers to deplane, Jenny with Tim's firm hand at her elbow made their way through the customs area. Leading her to a bench he motioned her to sit. "Stay here, I'm going to get you some water."

'He was probably going to put something in it," she told herself, making a note not to drink anything unless she had poured it herself. She was in an interesting situation and was glad she had made the decision to stay in charge of it and use it purposefully instead of fighting it. It was too big. This conspiracy she had touched upon was all-encompassing and she would have to play it by their rules till she got to the core of it, the actual people and their personal and public ideals. She didn't know what else to do.

Like the others who seemed to be players in this mass manipulation Tim had everything, money, backers with power, built in prestige.

She wished she could go through immigration right now so she could get to a pay phone and call Rudnik. But it was impossible. Tim was holding her passport, even her driver's license. . And of course she didn't want to leave Tim. If he were genuine she would learn it and could trust and love him again. If not, it was good she learn the truth before she married him and lived a life of horrific misery.

She thought about the many aspects of abused women she had written articles about - prisoners invisibly chained in invisible prisons. And now, the Whites and possibly Tim believed she was in a helpless and hopeless state as well. Chained with the invisible leash of violent memories and excruciating pain and fear.

They had no idea how powerful her independent state of mind was. How objectively she could watch and perceive things while seemingly in the throes of complicated emotional factors. She would never be fastened by an invisible collar of fear and close her eyes to her abilities and condition. She knew nothing about the place she was going other then it was run by a sadistic woman who lost the first round with her. Now she would put her in her private forte with a retinue of aids, biological and emotional with which to control Jenny. And Jenny knew in her heart that no matter what this woman tried to do to her, short of murdering her, it wouldn't affect her She had built an impervious stainless invisible wall.

Tim came back with a paper cup of water and a pill. "Take this, you'll feel better."

She drank the water but palmed the pill and put in her pocket. It might be useful to use as a weapon, she told herself.

The arrivals area appeared to be nearly emptied. Tim helped her up. She moved with him but felt a bit uneasy. The hospital was waiting. Was she up to the task she had set for herself?

"There isn't anything to say now," came a voice in her head. "You know what's happening."

She shook her head slightly, protesting.

"What's wrong darling?" Tim asked.

"Nothing," she smiled wanly, glad she had kept her tinted glasses on. He could read her thoughts fairly clearly and she did not want him to see what was in her eyes, unsure of how much she revealed there

The voice continued talking. "Everything you see and experience, anything outside yourself, is set up for your learning. Everything teaches. Your personal world is a reflection of everything. You'll learn from this experience and you'll get your story."

"Thank you," she told the thoughts to herself.

Their bags were some of the few left in the baggage claim. The customs inspector barely looked at their papers or at them. She wondered what would have happened to Tim's plan if she told the inspector Tim was smuggling. Then she would be able to tell him that she was being shipped off to a loony bin. But would he have believed her. The words "crazy" or "insane" are the most difficult reputation to get rid of. People tend to draw back from one so branded. For years one branded crazy remains suspect.

Tim led her outside. A long gray limousine waited. Upon seeing Tim, a tall lanky body supporting a faceless driver got out and put Jenny's bag in the trunk. She turned to Tim. "Are you coming with me?" she asked.

"Sorry darling, I can't. I've got to get back to work. The election is coming up sooner than you expect I hope you'll be joining me in just a few weeks."

"I do too," she said, thinking how innocent and sincere he appeared to be. Could he not be a part of this conspiracy? Was he being used as a pawn just as they are trying to manipulate her? Is Tim no higher on the rung then the man Jan White had enlisted to rape her? Had he been compromised and forced to aid the devil in her work?

Tim was holding her elbow and ushering her into the car. She couldn't be sure but she thought there had been a glimmer of a tear in his eye. They didn't kiss, didn't say good by. Their exit from each other had become a very silent movie.

The interior of the car was dark. The glass had been tinted dark gray and there was a solid barrier between her and the driver. She tried to open a window. It was locked. An air vent like one on a plane was directly above her, and she twisted it open. A rush of freshness covered her face.

Flashes of light streaked by the window. Red, green, yellow - like the ones in the Indian's hut! Maybe they would always accompany her consciously now! Kurt Vonnegut had written a short story called READY TO WEAR in which conscious beings tired of the strife on Earth fled and existed as little blobs of energy in the atmosphere above the planet. Is that what she was seeing? Did Vonnegut know about the little beings? Had he written about them? Or was he a blob who planted that story so she and others would know?

She pressed her nose tightly against the glass. The outlines of letters were barely visible beyond. She was seeing neon signs and traffic lights. There were no outer space forces accompanying her. She was picking up things from stories she read and believing them.

Fear started to fill her head. Her belief system had been reduced to an inner voice that rationalized everything into passive acceptance. Was it possible to live that way in modern society?

She opened her bag and looked for her notebook. It was gone. Her pens were missing. Even the book she had taken with her. Where was everything?

Betrayal hit like a physical blow. A scream bubbled from the tips of her toes but she held it back. Did she think she would NOT be tested? This was just the beginning. She had committed to going through with this and she could not panic and protest with the first sign that this was not going to be an easy ride.

***

Parker slammed down the phone. Boyle sauntered over to him. "Now what's wrong?"

"I can't find Jenny Webster. It's been two weeks since I talked to her. The paper said she was on temporary leave and her boyfriend's office said they were away on vacation in Mexico - some place with no phones - no means of communication. I don't know, it doesn't feel right."

"You and your feelings. You need facts, cop. You got to track down leads. Don't worry about that one. Look at the wild goose chase she sent you on to that deli looking for two people who probably don't exist. She's at some spa somewhere getting massaged and pampered to smooth out the edges from having a brush with real life."

Parker flushed, "I don't think she's like that." He was worried about Jenny. Although he had only met her for a short while, there was something about her, haunting him, keeping her in his mind almost constantly. He accepted some of it was attraction, but there was something else, something more important, a need to protect her and shield her from what was happening.

Something felt very wrong about this entire Sebastian investigation. When they had gone to Anson Laboratories to investigate her employers and co-workers, Boyle had been putty in the hands of the company's representatives. Everyone had been polite and helpful - opening Mannie's files and giving them full and complete answers. It was too polite, too polished. When he had mentioned that in the car, Boyle seemed surprised at Parker's "misplaced suspicion". The senior partner said he was satisfied with the investigation and believed that a search warrant for Anson wouldn't be necessary. "Don't make waves in the wrong places," he advised. Parker wondered why this brusque man was suddenly so accommodating.

"Have we got the chemical results from the autopsy?"

Boyle shook his head. Not yet. But we know how she died - hitting cement from a two hundred foot dive.

"What about the preliminary analysis. Was there alcohol, any other substances in her system?"

"No. No alcohol. No cocaine. No sleeping pills. Clean as a whistle."

"What about hallucinogens?

"Nope."

"You sure?"

Boyle bristled. "I told you already. No coke, grass, heroin, nothing like that. We'll have to wait for the later reports. What was left of her was cremated and packed in a tin and sent back to her family in Brazil. By the way, Detective, this emotional attachment you seem to have for the case is getting a bit hard to handle. You better get your priorities straight. You're a cop. And when you're investigating something like this, there's no room for personal feelings. Get my meaning?"

"No feelings. Yes. What about the fetus?"

"Dead."

***

Jenny closed her eyes and leaned back. She thought about brainwashing. Based on documents supplied by the Freedom of Information Act, Jenny discovered that the CIA had used LSD supplied by the Swiss pharmaceutical company, SANDOZ, to unsuspecting American pilots after World War II to see if they could simulate the suicidal mind set of Kamikaze pilots. Had she in some way become entrapped in some kind of CIA operation? Because the media was becoming so important world-wide did they want to use people like her - writers, journalists - just as they tried with American pilots in the Fifties and early Sixties?

Maybe the Technical Services Staff, (TSS), was still intact. T.S.S. was the medical research arm of the CIA. Founded in 1952, by Allen Dulles, head of the newly formed CIA, they recruited doctors of all disciplines willing to co-operate in any phase of research, no matter how revolutionary it might be. This meant human experimentation that could prove to be lethal. One of the experiments was called, "Operation Artichoke". Scientists and doctors found subjects they labeled, "dubious loyalty"; suspected double agents or plants, subjects known for deception - expendables - or otherwise homeless people who ultimately could be terminated. They used electroshock to make the person susceptible to suggestion. Producing amnesia for nonspecific periods of time, they would try to implant ideas into a subject's shocked mind. According to the papers Jenny found, it didn't work. The electroshock caused temporary and sometime permanent brain damage but the implanted ideas didn't stay in place.

She had seen pictures taken during some of the experimentation. There was very little difference from what she had seen in archive Nazi concentration camp film, than the more contemporary version from the C.I.A. Had Felix White been in TSS? He could have been, his age made it feasible.

According to texts Jenny read, thousands of micrograms of LSD were used by TSS, but no matter how much was used, it wouldn't significantly change human behavior. Contrary to reports they found from Dachau, Mescaline didn't work the way it had been reported either. As far as Jenny could find over fifty years later, there were still scientists and research units funded by government intelligence trying to find a way to get into peoples' minds. No matter how many experiments they did and how many subjects died from drugs or having their brains burned out with electricity, the answer to how the enemy – North Koreans, Japanese, and Russians -- successfully brainwashed remained elusive.

But now, with EEG expansion and the program Mannie developed for decoding brain scan impulses, Jenny felt certain that the goal was close to being realized. Goose bumps raised on her flesh. She put her head back on the seat. This reality was getting difficult.

How many subjects like herself did they have; high IQs, extensive education, sophisticated and independent social skills?

The car turned off the highway and through lush green countryside. She felt very vulnerable and scared.

CHAPTER SIXTEEN

Dr. White stood in the driveway waiting as the limousine pulled to a stop. His bald head was shining, his eyes glittering in the moonlight. "Hello Jenny, welcome."

"Said the spider to the fly." She didn't take his outstretched hand.

"Are you upset?"

Her breath caught in surprise at his question. "Of course I am."

"Why should you be?" He feigned surprised.

"Look where I am."

"Jenny dear," he smiled. "You said you wanted to come. Remember?"

"No."

"You must be tired. You've been traveling a long time. Come in and rest." He took her arm and guided her up the steps. "If you want to leave we'll discuss it in the morning. For the moment just relax and enjoy what you can."

They walked across a wide colonial-style verandah, crickets dissolving the pall of silence in the air.

A shadow moved from behind a pillar. Jan came and took her other arm. A jolt shot through Jenny. She pulled away. "We're glad you came," Jan said in soft dulcet tones. "How are you feeling?"

"I thought you knew everything." Jenny steeled her weakening body. She was tired - extremely tired. Was it the airplane journey, or the one in outer space? Could that really have happened or had she been dreaming?

Doubts! They were coming back. She hadn't wanted to question anything. She had felt so positive that what she experienced in Mexico had really happened. It had not mattered what she should or should not feel. If she gave up her beliefs, she'd be sentenced to compromise - a purgatory existence. But doubts were cropping up and she was starting to feel she was being ruled by fear. The key to her stability would be to try to keep objectivity.

"We have an instruction sheet on your bureau," Jan was saying. "We advise our guests to read it."

"Guests?" Jenny laughed.

Jan unlocked a brown door and stepped aside. "Guests," she lilted. "Most people who stay choose because it's best. The life forces of normality as we call civilization are suspended here. People are allowed the freedom of discovery, to discover themselves and the meaning of their reality. At times we are called upon to enhance that inner freedom."

"You mean drugs." Jenny cut in.

"Inner Freedom Enhancers," not drugs. Stop thinking in such a one dimensional way." Jan sharply answered. She took a deep breath and returned her voice to it's melodious crooning. "Our guests return to the urban embattlements we call home or work, or they can stay here indefinitely, for as long as it takes."

"As long as WHAT takes? And, who pays?" Jenny now believed that her instincts were correct. This place was some kind of covert operation. This was not a legitimate hospital or sanitarium. It was a lab, and she was to be one of the rabbits.

"If you are meant to be here," Jan was saying, "the finances are found to insure it."

"I'll bet they are." She couldn't believe Jan expected her to believe that. But she had to be careful. People like Jan, ones without original thoughts who followed rules without question, could be dangerous.

"I've done stories on places like this," she lied, throwing out a red herring. "How you liquidate assets in return for lifetime care." She wondered if the covert money used to finance this place was government or private. Government would be easier. If it were the latter it would be more dangerous. Private organizations with this kind of financial power were far more efficient than government sponsored.

"We don't have to operate that way."

"Then who funds you?" She asked with innocence.

Jan ignored the question.

Jenny pressed on, her mouth wouldn't stop, and something was making her speak. "If it's government, then you're political and therefore lethal. Missionary mentality. Get rid of freedom of thought, individual thinking. Is that what you're doing?"

Jan motioned her toward the bed. "You're excited over nothing. Your finances are taken care of. Tim arranged everything."

"I'll bet he did!" She had to escape from here.

"Don't worry." Jan crooned. "We want the best for you so you can go back into the world and do the work you're meant to do."

"Your work."

"It'll be yours. Your own motivation. We don't implant anything. We give alternatives - alternatives to accept or discard. In the end one person can never control another. You've proven that haven't you? Of course, one can be destroyed, but no one can be completely controlled yet, can they?"

"You don't believe a word you said. "You believe people can be controlled through physical force and technology. Dissent means death of one kind or another."

"That's your belief." Jan turned away.

"That's what I know, and what I fear." She felt a shiver and looked around. "There's something about this room that is familiar."

"What is it Jenny?"

"It reminds me of another place. Its not good for me to be here." She walked over to the single bed pushed up against the wall under the mesh-covered windows. With the exception of the mesh, it reminded her of Tim's room at Harvard. She had lost her virginity there. Would she lose another kind of virginity here as well?

A small carpet of indiscriminate color covered part of the wooden floor. Or was it Tim's floor? She felt so tired. She closed her eyes and sat down on the side of the bed. Memories of that first night with Tim began to grow within her.

She took a deep breath. Going to the room with Tim had felt natural to her. She had been a little nervous when he led her to the bed, but the wine from dinner championed her recklessness, convincing her that this moment was inevitable.

She wasn't sure she would have made the decision to go ahead, but as he kissed her and he touched her breast through her soft cashmere sweater her whole body tingled. As the kiss grew deeper, he put his hands beneath the sweater, unfastening her bra and touching her newly bared nipples. She quivered as she remembered the excitement - the churning - a feeling she had never before experienced. It fit with her body and quickly took over, releasing a dormant energy that was now fully activated.

She helped him slip the sweater over her head. She watched him take off her bra. He bent to kiss her breasts. Were they going too far? His lips on her breast made her dizzy. Her nipples grew hard. This feeling was very different, she was crossing the line. His mouth was on her bare skin, her whole body shaking. She couldn't control anything, between her legs she was creaming. He had to keep going. She couldn't stop him now. Even though she was scared - she had to - had to - now.

The door opened. Jan had probably left. It was all right; she was locked into memory, enjoying it for the moment as she previously had. She curled up on the bed and closed her eyes. She remembered how Tim had looked at her that night. She smiled at his face and waited for his kiss. His eyes were so kind and shining with what she believed was love. She remembered their eyes locking, his mouth gently covering hers - kissing her softly and gently, her eye lids, her hair, her neck, her cheek... In innocence she strained upward, toward him, his touch creating need.

Until that moment, no one had ever seen her naked. Even her old family doctor had averted his eyes when he had to move the paper examination gown that covered her body.

Tim was still fully dressed in his tweed jacket and crew neck sweater, as he sucked her nipples, slurping the imaginary milk her virgin breasts didn't have. He slid his hand up her skirt toward the wet throbbing place. Her hips moved higher, her thighs parted, as his hand reached the place where she was already very wet.

"You act like a professional," he whispered.

"I'm glad," she whispered back, feeling very sophisticated, not considering the implication.

Tim was pulling off his jacket as he caressed her and kissed her. The memory was so clear - happening right this instant. She was arching, driving her hips off the mattress, remembering her wet panties, how embarrassed she'd been. How tingly his bare skin was against hers, the hardness between his legs making her weak. Her legs parted. He rolled on top of her. How right it felt, how good. She wanted him inside of her. Longing, crushing, anxiously, his hands moved to the button of her skirt.

Surprise as his fingers moved beneath her panties. No one's hand had ever been there before. The gentle fingers made her very excited. They had reached the point of no return. She lifted her hips and he peeled off her panties. Her heart still pounded with that incredible memory.

She lay on her back, feeling the ripples of the bedspread, eyes closed, rooting from the mental bleachers for her old courageous self.

His tongue was caressing as she moaned with every stroke. She had forgotten her morals, the standards she had lived by, and lifted her legs and spread them very wide. He kissed her and licked her, her legs a necklace around his head, his tongue deep inside her stroking virgin territory. He lifted her legs from his neck and climbed on top of her, thrusting himself into her for her very first time.

He felt cool and hard as he entered inside of her. Her body, her awareness experienced immediate change. New chemicals released throughout her body as she cried out in pain and incomparable pleasure with the burning, the semen, the blood, and the loss of her innocence.

Jenny opened her eyes. Jan was standing and watching. She thought Jan had left, she sat up abruptly, defensive. "This room is upsetting."

"Then brighten it. Use your perception."

"That's ridiculous." Chills ran through her, her hands were freezing.

"You know how to create what you need," Jan continued. "Make this place beautiful by seeing it's perfection." She headed for the door.

Anxiety clutched Jenny. She wasn't sure she wanted to be alone.

"Rest well," Jan suggested. She motioned toward the bedside table, then smiled and bowed before closing the door. The latch clicked shut, but it didn't sound as if it was bolted. Jenny assumed that it was, but she was afraid to test it, afraid to know if she was locked in.

On the small table next to the bed was a tray with milk and cookies. She sat down on the edge of the bed and bit into one, washing it down with the cold milk. She leaned up against the wall, munching the cookie.

CHAPTER SEVENTEEN

On the top floor of the UCLA Bio-med library, Detective Parker sat huddled behind books in a deserted corner. He made messy calculations on a yellow pad, while a man in a white lab coat, Dr. Edward Verruno searched through a book filled with formulas.

"Ketamine with Epinephrine, that'll do it," Verruno said.

Parker looked perplexed. "What's that?"

Ketamine is a drug that is sometimes used in operating rooms, veterinarians use it as well. It separates the conscious mind from the physical body so operations can be performed on patients while they're fully awake. It's especially good on accident victims who have full stomachs from eating. The problem with the drug is that it can cause severe hallucinations. It was used as a recreation drug but the side effects are very dangerous.

Parker was riveted. Maybe this was how Mannie was impregnated. "Could someone drive a car with it?"

"Not really, unless they want to cause an accident."

Parker held his breath; the implications of what this man was saying riveted him.

"My guess is they used Ketamine on the victim," Verruno continued. When it hit her system it divorced her from all physical proceedings while letting her stay conscious. They mixed it with Epinephrine which makes the fast acting drug last longer. They miscalculated. She never knew what hit her. Ketamine works almost instantaneously.

"So, it completely disassociated her from reality."

Verruno nodded. "And reality killed her."

Parker jumped up, excited. "We've got the murder weapon!"

The doctor in the lab coat shook his head. "Try and prove it."

***

Jenny woke up with a start. She reached for her pen. It wasn't there. Nor was this her bedside table, or her bed. She was in a strange room. Where was she?

Cookies! She remembered the cookies before she went to sleep. The rest was fuzzy. What was the significance of what she had just dreamed? She knew who Detective Parker was. Maybe it hadn't been a dream.

The cookies - hospital - airplane flight - Drs. Felix and Jan White. It was Jan who had left the cookies. Something in them - where's the tray? Gone! Someone removed it. Maybe it hadn't really been there. Maybe... Disorientation was becoming panic. She had to fight it away.

Mesh covered the windows. She tried the door. It was locked. They weren't going to release her. She was locked inside. Locked! They were going to brainwash her, kill her. Why? What had she done? For what? Could it be for thinking too deeply? For having information she wanted to put out?

A bell rang in the distance. Sounds of doors opening and people walking drifted in through the walls. She didn't move, didn't know what to do. She pulled the warmth of the blanket close to her.

The latch clicked in the lock. A fair young woman, blonde haircut bluntly around her chin like a Dutch boy, opened the door. She peeked around the edge, bright eyes shining, and a big smile on her face. "Hi Jenny," Her voice was light. "I'm Elizabeth. I heard you came in late last night. Thought you might like someone to show you the ropes."

"How did you know?" Jenny felt comforted. Something about this girl was familiar and appealing.

"I'm reading your thoughts," Elizabeth said teasingly as she stepped inside and closed the door. She wore acid washed jeans, a white cotton tee shirt, and a blue cardigan sweater tied around her waist. On top of her head were small round tortoise shell eyeglasses, which she pulled down and stared through at Jenny. "You're pretty."

Thanks, so are you. But I feel like hell."

"Well, you don't look it, you look great. Must have had a good rest. Did you eat the cookies?"

"Yes."

Elizabeth nodded wisely. "There's something in them. I don't know what, but there's an ingredient that makes you feel good. I'm sure its more then carbohydrates. But it doesn't matter, they're good. Don't worry. You'll learn to override them."

Jenny shuddered and hugged herself tightly.

"Why don't you get dressed?" Elizabeth suggested.

When Jenny came out of the bathroom she saw the girl sitting cross-legged on the bed, her eyes closed in meditation. She tiptoed toward the dresser. Elizabeth opened her eyes and smiled. "You're fast. Thought I'd get a couple extra minutes in." She grinned widely.

Jenny smiled back. She liked her.

Have you had your stabilizers yet?"

"My what?"

"Your centering rods. Inner enhancers - We have all kinds of expressions for these. Here. They make everything look better." She handed Jenny two oblong orange pills and she swallowed them. "They have lots of vitamin B and C to keep you in balance so you can appreciate the movie."

"What movie?" Jenny felt apprehensive about taking the pills.

"The life movie you're making while you're living on this planet. Once you step over and go into the next stage of transition, the movie gets replayed, so you can see what you've done with it."

"Step over?"

"Die, drop your body, change reality."

"That's putting it lightly," Jenny smiled, surprised at her irreverence. "Life as a movie. I like it."

"That's right," said Elizabeth. You're the producer, writer, director, and star, and when it ends you get to be the critic. The movie studio is what we perceive as Planet Earth," she made a flourish, "it's a training center for the gods!" Elizabeth literally twinkled. Jenny was spellbound. It all made so much sense. "The ground rules of the Planet Earth Game are: that Earth was, is, and always shall be in chaos; it's a testing place for the gods. Those who can rise above it never have to come back --unless, of course, you want to help -- but there's danger in getting caught here again. Life on Earth is a constant cycle of lessons, which grow more complex and intricate each time. The danger is you can forget your past lessons once you're caught in the new ones. It's the big trick in the game."

She drew Jenny closer, drawing diagrams in Jenny's notebook that looked like Tibetan Mandalas. "Look, once we're on Planet Earth we have to go through this multifaceted experience called life; the highs and lows, negatives and positives. And that high and low is all in your perspective.

"I'm confused."

"No you're not. Let's go get morning refreshments. The hospital movie is just beginning. I'm the narrator. Try to be more of a spectator than a star. Stardom is a vanity trip. Vanity will never keep you happy."

In the hallway people shuffled in the same direction. Some wore robes, most jeans or sweats. The building and the people had the ambiance of a college dormitory. Many were preoccupied and almost all were young.

Sunlight bounced off the yellow walls of the dining room. Chairs scraped on the wooden floors, dishes clattered, as everyone seemed to come in at exactly the same moment. Few people were talking.

Elizabeth led Jenny to a table and they sat down. A white shirted man brought over a tray and put down plates of scrambled eggs, bacon and toast. A pot of coffee and a pitcher of orange juice stood in the center of the long family-style table. Elizabeth poured a glass of juice for Jenny and one for herself. Jenny started to drink, then stopped. She had almost forgotten she was going to train herself not to eat anymore.

"Slowly," said the voice in her head. "Start slowly. You can drink juices, eat lightly, and start cutting whole things out. But keep your energy. Raw fruit and vegetables are good for that." Jenny lowered her eyes and brought back the soft moist green Mexican island where she had been taught this.

She drained the juice in the glass. It was delicious. Golden energy surged through her spirit. She poured another, ignoring the heavier food on her plate.

When she looked up, Elizabeth was gone. Jenny hadn't noticed her leave. Most everyone else had left. The man in the white shirt was picking up plates from the empty tables. He came over.

"Where is everybody?" Jenny asked him.

"In their rooms."

'Do you know which room the girl I sat next to is in?"

He shrugged. "Looked like you were sitting alone to me. I didn't see anyone."

Her name's Elizabeth. She has straight blonde chin-length hair, smiles a lot. You must know who she is, she's been here awhile."

He shrugged and picked up the dishes and started to walk away.

"Wait!" She called to him. "Where are Felix and Jan White's offices?"

He shrugged impatiently, his hands filled with dirty plates. "I don't know who you're talking about. You'll have to ask someone else. Go back to your room and wait."

"What shall I wait for? She asked.

The attendant didn't answer and went on his lumbering way. Probably an old mental patient, she thought, as she started toward the door. She stopped; she didn't know which way to go. She hadn't watched when she came here with Elizabeth. Taking a deep breath she put one hand against the wall to steady her and started walking.

The hall was deserted, stretching endlessly beyond closed doors on either side - a tunnel toward infinity. Slowly she crept against the wall, fearful she'd fall if she stepped into the center. She pushed a door open and saw her notebook on the dresser. She had found her room. Excited she bounced on the bed happily, till she caught herself in the mirror. She was acting crazy. Was that why she was here?

The thought slapped her across the face. Everyone thought she was crazy. Could they be right? What if the machines, the rape, were her imagination? What if it never happened? Even the girl called Elizabeth - what if she had made her up? The automatic writing! She could be nuts!

She banged her fist against the wall. They had put her away because she was crazy. Everything she saw, all she believed, were figments of a crazy imagination, a set of visions gone astray - beyond the boundaries of normal reality. She pounded her fist once more. No one believed her! Everything had been unreal! How could it have been unreal when it seemed so real?

She pushed off the bed and went to the window. People strolled along the garden path or sat on benches in the sun. She went to the door and opened it. Tentatively, testing, she stepped carefully into the center of the deserted hall, heading in the opposite direction of the dining hall. She found a door and opened it to the glorious morning sunshine.

The heaviness lifted. She stepped back inside. The heaviness came back. She stepped outside - light. Inside - dark. In - heavy. Out - light. In, out, in, out, - When she was inside she yearned to return to her room; outside she just wanted to be in the light. Inside the energy was gripping. Outside - light.

She chose the light and followed a path till she got to a fence running along the edge of the estate. An electrified humming came from it. She doubted anyone could get over it, it was too high.

Dr. White had said she could leave today, and she had gotten so involved with the external stimuli, she'd forgotten! But what if she was crazy, and she shouldn't be on her own. What should she do? She began pacing, emotion taking her over. She made her decision; this place was making her crazy. She headed toward the house to find White and get signed out.

As she reached the border of the house a chill dropped down on her. The hair on her arms bristled with electricity. There was an electric or static force encircling her, compelling her back inside.

She could see grids of electronic rays covering the house and spreading over the lawns and gardens. When she crossed the periphery she got wrapped up in beams. The entire area was covered, horizontally and vertically, a forest of charges vibrating through everything.

The greatest concentration surrounded the building. She stepped closer, squinted, and put her hand out into it and felt a subtle energy drawing her to the right toward her room. She tried the other hand and that pulled to the left. She squatted down close to the ground and felt lighter, less depressed. They had to be using microwaves for behavior modification. That was why she had feared she was crazy. They had weakened her so she would feel self-doubt.

She looked at the people sitting on the benches or walking around the lush grounds like extras in a movie. Off to the right, a large gray building was hidden between artfully planted trees. She started toward it, but the minute she heard screams coming from it she stopped. The building seemed to be rumbling with intense discomfort. She squinted, and noted it had a higher density of beams.

She sat down and took a breath, vowing to maintain her equilibrium. There was misery here, carried along a maze of electronic beams. Had Mannie been involved with this? Is that why she was killed? What would happen now? How would they use her - why did they want her?

Fuzziness started taking over her brain. As hard as she tried, she couldn't think straight. Maybe she should have had more to eat than juice this morning. Quickly she turned toward the central building. Others seemed to get the same message; silent automatons in an exodus from the grounds to their respective buildings.

Two more orange tablets sat on top of her bureau, a glass of water besides them. She picked them up and weighed them in her hand, then started to throw them out. But the pills vibrated as if they were alive. Alive like the little pink spots she had once found in fields that were baby mice. She hadn't known what to do with them. So she left them in the sun, probably to die. A sinking feeling came over her. Guilty of murder! A dozen infant mice. Because she had decided upon the meaningless, the non-importance of their lives.

"They had purpose. So do the pills.," the voice said.

"Why?" she asked with anguish. The voice was giving her the wrong message

"Dimensions."

"Hallucinogens?" she asked.

"No, brain cleaners, relaxants, open channels to view truth and reason."

"All right." She swallowed the pills then laid down to rest. She thought about Al, the newspaper, had anyone noticed she wasn't there? She tried to think of something else, but only anxiety wanted her attention.

A hand touched her shoulder. A tall, thin woman, her hair pulled back tightly like Jan's, shook her again. Her white moon-like face was framed by a black, turtleneck long-sleeve dress, making her pale face and deep-set eyes look haunted. She was one of those people who were such a perfect type they don't seem to be for real. But this woman was real, she was no joke. She either had one part of her head in another stratosphere or she didn't have another side at all, Jennie thought.

"Come," said the woman, "come with me." Her look was mesmerizing. Jenny silently followed her. They passed a large room and Jenny managed to look inside. More than a dozen beds were lined up in the half-light, every patient hooked to intravenous. A few patients in pajamas and robes walked or sat in chairs with helmets covering their heads and their faces. A steady murmur of recorded voices covered the room like a sound blanket, no one else spoke, no other sounds except the recording. It was unworldly. Jenny prayed she wouldn't be put there. It looked like hell. "What is that? She asked her ghoulish guide. What are they doing?"

The Moon faced woman didn't answer and continued her silent journey through the corridors. By the time they reached the back of the building. Jenny's heart was pounding. She didn't like what she was seeing and hated the feelings. It was too silent. Is this where they bury the corpses, she asked herself? Following blindly was not one of Jenny's favorite disciplines. But she had no choice. The people in the helmets had unnerved her. She didn't want to have any problem, show any resistance till she knew the punishments.

They entered a small room in which a large black box the shape of an Egyptian sarcophagus filled it. A convex door was in one end, next to it a stall shower. Somber Moon face handed her two towels. "Wash, including your hair. You will repeat this when you emerge from the chamber. This is a sense deprivation tank.

Jenny nodded. John Lilly, a scientist who wanted to see what happens to the mind when it's totally deprived from outside stimulus, had developed it.

"What kind of medication did you give me so you can control my thinking?" Jenny asked the woman.

"That isn't possible."

"You people are trying to do it with medication, aren't you?" Jenny asked.

"Keep quiet," said the voice in her head. "You can transmute any energy that tries to control you. Go beyond it into the power that is your self. That's the main lesson you want here. Use it."

She agreed with her own voice in her head. She would use everything that happened to her here as an experience to enhance her power and ability.

"You can think whatever you want inside or outside the tank. That's a choice you make. Said the voice in her head. "Use the energy of your emotions to discipline your perspective and your reason."

Keeping her back turned toward the woman, Jenny took off her clothes and stepped into the shower. The water was freezing. She was about to get out when it got warmer. She could feel the woman watching her and rushed to finish. Rinsing off, she went from the shower straight into the tank, closing the door behind her. The absolute blackness hit her with a touch of panic. Her eyes were opened wide, but she couldn't see. Anything She closed them and it was exactly the same. She couldn't tell if they were open or shut. She laid back. A cut on her finger stung. She knew the tank contained 800 pounds of salt in 10 inches of water so one would float in perfect weightlessness. She settled back and let her body relax, her head falling back, the water just stopping at her hairline like a halo.

Breath rushed through her ears like a pump, an engine a great power attached to the life force of her body. She watched the rushing sound of air travel through her till she felt she could jump on and sail along with it. Pressure circulated in the center of her forehead. Her jaw tightened, she willed it to relax. Breath came hissing up through her throat, filling the chamber. She no longer felt the water because somehow it had become air. She floated gently on top of it, her palms upward in meditation. The energy rose and took her over, a warm wave-like spell. No longer was she inside her body. She was a speck in the darkness alone.

"Do you feel it?" the voice asked.

"Yes."

"If you use this properly, you'll never have to eat or sleep again. You live off it, you are one with it."

"Is there anything else?"

"When you've mastered that, you'll know all."

A shudder went through her and she became aware of the water. It felt sticky and slimy. She heard the hiss of her breath and faint lights blinked on and off. She thought she could see the stars in the universe, maybe she was out there with them, but she wasn't sure. She could hear music in the distance, like the kind on airplane flights - the kind you're never sure you're hearing till it starts to grow louder like it was doing now. She reached out for the door, but she couldn't find it. She was trapped in the blackness. Suffocation grabbed hold of her. She sat up. There was headroom. The door! Reaching up she pushed outward. The light of the room spilled over her. The rush of relief was excruciatingly gorgeous.

The door opened and the Moon Face looked in. Jenny hurriedly dried herself. She paused in the mirror. She felt more at peace and the woman didn't seem as severe. "I'll take you to your room," she whispered huskily. "You should rest."

Jenny agreed. She wanted that, needed it. She felt a bit confused and wanted to write it down so it could become clearer. She went straight to her notebook and tried to recreate the feelings into words. She paused, focusing on her breath, trying to simulate those moments in the tank - but it wasn't the same, and she couldn't.

A knock - "Dinner!" It was dark outside. The lights had been turned on. She hadn't noticed. Hunger rumbled in her stomach. She joined others in the rush to the dining room. Everyone seemed to be hungry. Those who had arrived were already eating, isolated and impervious to the chaos so near them. Her stomach rolled with queasiness, but subsided when she sat down and smelled the aromic sweetness of meatloaf. She stuck her fork in and took a bite. Grease spurted and covered the roof of her mouth while the rest of the meatloaf chugged its way to her stomach. The bright canned green beans and mounds of stark white mashed potatoes waited, plastic replicas of the true vegetables they represented.

Elizabeth sat down next to her. Jenny looked up, happy and surprised. "Hi" she said, feeling a flood of relief. "I missed you today."

"I did too."

"Where were you?" asked Jenny. But the girl didn't answer. She was busily eating all the meat loaf on her plate. Jenny watched then looked at her own. The grease still coated the roof of her mouth. She couldn't eat it. Another woman looked her way and smiled. Jenny smiled back. A man at the far end caught her eye. She smiled. He winked. She winked back. A man sitting at the next table caught her eye. He stared straight ahead, one of the few ignoring the food, watching with disdain the way people were eating.

Someone touched her arm. "Don't get involved." The pressure on her arm kept her from turning. "Don't worry about anyone. He's doing what you were just instructed to do. He's your mirror."

"You need fuel and energy.," said Elizabeth, pointing to Jenny's uneaten food. Her eyes pierced Jenny with brightness.

"I've been instructed on other ways to get it."

"Good. Then I won't have to eat this junk too."

"Are you my mirror?" a tinge of fear grasping her.

"Everything is. We're all a projection of our own beliefs and thoughts. You should learn from everything. Keep your movie going. You're doing a good job." She winked and pushed her plate away.

CHAPTER EIGHTEEN

Snow! Jenny was shocked as she stopped at the window. It was May. How could snow be falling? She rushed to her room and took out her diary. "May 22". It was her last entry. But that had been yesterday, hadn't it? Ripples of dread started. She hadn't noticed what the weather was like when she had left the tank or on her way to dinner. Could she have lost time?

The room was cold. Winter clothes were hanging in the closet. Wool sweaters replaced T-shirts in the drawers. Even her washed silk nightgown had been replaced with a flannel nightshirt on the back of the door. How many months had she been there? She went to the window. This wasn't a trick -it was definitely winter. The room began to spin, frames of reference whirling. She thought she had been in the sense depravation tank for only a few minutes. But probably they had taken her out and put her in the "SLEEP ROOM"! Oh God. She didn't remember anything - anything! She was one of those Zombie-like bodies hooked up to intravenous, bombarded with sounds and visuals. She could see shapes now of ghost-like men and women struggling against nurses holding them down as they wheeled them into treatment rooms. She could feel again the visible and almost touchable tension, the uneasiness, the pervasive fear. She remembered hearing her own voice saying the same thing over and over, but she couldn't remember what it had been. There was the GRID ROOM, starkly beautiful in a geometric way, lines drawn across a wall, a hard ladder-backed chair placed in front of it. At the opposite end of the room was a concealed hole, large enough for the lens of a camera. The person sitting in the chair would be measured in order to record how much energy output they used when they were moving

Somehow the technical aspects of the experiments were clear and although she remembered the emotions anger and fear, she had worked at the time to stay objective and apart from them. She had tried to master an important aspect of herself, her emotions.

She let her mind wander to the ISOLATION CHAMBER. A twinge of the terror newly reminded her that she couldn't control her emotions all the time. It had been like a prison cell with heavy double thick doors and padded walls. She had been in there - isolated and disoriented. She could have been in there weeks, months, even years, till they thought she was ready to say what they wanted. PSYCHIC DRIVERS - ceiling microphones with disembodied voices booming from nowhere. They did the same thing with speakers inside the helmets as well as disembodied voices coming through pillow speakers, virtual reality goggles. She hadn't been allowed to think or see anything other than what had been programmed.

She didn't remember wearing a helmet, but for some reason she knew that patients had worn them for up to twenty-four hours. Jenny had focused on screening out recorded voices, by knowing the difference in her feelings, which couldn't be technically altered. The purity of truth came through with her feelings.

The door opened and Tim walked in. He wore a bathing suit, his bare chest tanned and glistening. She was astonished, breathless. He approached her, smiling.

"Good morning." He sounded tentative.

"Hello." She tried to sound normal but she was visibly trembling.

"Did you rest well?" He looked tan and fit. He didn't seem to notice her terror.

"Aren't you cold?" she asked, hugging herself.

"No. Are you?" He put on a look of concern.

"The way you're dressed. It's snowing."

He laughed. "You're dreaming. The sun is shining and it's perfectly beautiful. I took a swim before breakfast."

"Oh." She couldn't speak any more.

"Dr. White and Jan send their best. They hope you feel better." He wore his professional voice.

She lifted her head. "Where are they?"

They left a while ago."

"They were here?"

"They stayed the night."

She raised herself up and took her eyes off Tim. The sight made her head swim. The gray brown walls of the hospital were now the soft golden tones of the Mexican hacienda's natural reed walls. Filmy white mosquito netting fluttered around a bed no longer made of iron. Surf was crashing. "How long have I been sleeping?"

"Hours. You slept through the night."

She looked down at her clothes. She wore the white linen slacks she had on when she walked in the jungle. They were wrinkled and dirty. A dull ache in her head warned of a headache.

Tim sat beside her and rubbed her neck. It felt better. He used to do that before everything deteriorated.

Reality had become so confusing. Was any of this real? Was he really this loving, her head on his lap and she feeling happy? Panic reared it's head once again. Which was reality?

What about Elizabeth, was she flesh and blood like Tim? Were they both real, or one of them merely a product of her imagination? Maybe Tim existed only at times like this, and Elizabeth was a reality when she'd be with her later.

Doubt fed her panic. She wasn't sure. Maybe this was a dream - but then again, this was the way her life had become - living events before they happened, regression to past ones. Could she continue this sort of discombobulated existence?

Tim rubbed her temples and the nape of her neck, calming her. Oh how she wished she could trust him, trust this moment as fact. But it didn't feel real - it was too good to be true. Tears of regret for these lost moments they had together that would never return.

He kissed her forehead. "Feel better?"

"Yes." He had never done that. It was so bizarre. She thought she had all these insights into what he had become but now he was comforting, contradicting her new impressions. "I had a vivid dream," she decided to tell him. "So vivid I can't believe it didn't happen. Unless that was the reality and you are the dream."

"Maybe I am," he grinned.

"Maybe." A shiver ran through her, she didn't share his smile. "I thought I was in a sanitarium. You had taken me there. I had a friend, Elizabeth who was starting to show me strange things - like she could

215

fly. I know that sounds strange, crazy perhaps, but I think I can see the future and have been shown certain truths. It was all so vivid, yet this is too." She sat up suddenly. "My notebooks. Where are they?"

"There," he gestured toward the desk.

She got out of bed. Her legs felt shaky, as though she had not walked in days. She opened the first page of her red notebook. SOLID STATE CONSPIRACY was printed in caps. She brought it to Tim and pointed, "have I told you about this?"

"You speak of nothing else. That's part of your whole conspiracy theory."

"Yes, in part, not completely. It's more involved than that."

He crossed his arms and waited patiently - too patiently, for her to continue.

She leaned against the bureau, grasping the notebook, holding on to herself. "Technology has taken over - it's almost out of our hands, the hands that created it."

Tim looked amused. "We still have the on-off switch."

"For now."

"Have you seen a rerun of Kubrik's '2001' lately? Has Hal the computer influenced you?" He said it as a joke, underneath he was dead serious.

"No, but that's what I'm talking about... The population is expanding and we're running out of food, and need I repeat what's happened to our water." She drew him to her, softly. "Whales are being slaughtered because they're the largest mammals that require large bodies of water.

It's very possible their huge brains carry the history of the universe. If we could learn to communicate with them, then maybe we won't repeat past mistakes. So what are we doing? We're destroying them! In the next century there may not be enough water for whales to survive. Don't you think it's possible that the powers who wish to take control of this planet don't want us to decode the whales?"

"Sure, Jenny. I hear what you're saying." Tim started to pull away, but she held on to him tightly.

"With the population growing and people living longer, where is everyone going to live? We're filling in the oceans and lakes and diverting rivers. For what? Better environments for technology because it thrives in arid, dry climates.

Tim put his hand on her arm. "Jenny, all you say is true but the context in which you're putting it is ridiculous."

She gently moved her arm away. "Tim, you know we're abusing the land, that soon we won't have fertile soil to grow food. There's almost none left. If this keeps up, I saw a vision of this planet without animals or plants. Technology pollutes and creates deserts. It all fits. As a planet, we're either slowly committing suicide or being consciously suffocated."

"Jenny, your argument is convoluted. With technology we are creating better lives, healthier environments and more nutritious foods to consume."

"On one hand, yes. But what is going to happen when there are too many people with nothing to eat and no place to live? It's the plan of the Solid State Conspiracy to get humans to kill each other. That's what happens when people are hungry and don't have shelter. Society reverts to a primitive level. Pure survival - survival of the fittest."

"Is that what you're dreaming?"

"It's not a dream, it's reality. It's happening as we're speaking."

He tried not to smile. "How do you know?"

"I told you, I've seen the future."

"Really, how?"

"If I tell you, you won't believe it."

"Try me."

"By a higher intelligence."

"Right." He turned away.

She started to follow him. "I know it sounds crazy and if the situation was reversed I might have problems if you were saying these things. But I know in every part of myself that this planet is headed toward destruction."

"Sweetheart, next you'll wear a placard and walk up and down Times Square saying THE END IS COMING." He took her hand gently, patting it. "You're having vivid dreams that are creating an alien world because of personal problems you're having. You can't impose this kind of paranoia on rational minds. It isn't acceptable. I love you and I'm honest with you, so I'm going to tell you straight. You sound crazy. Can you understand that?"

She just looked at him as he continued. "I don't know what to do. At breakfast I told you we were expecting important company and you disappeared. You return from the jungle wrinkled, spaced out, messy, and totally surprised we have guests here. Then you leave in the middle of lunch. Now you talk about an alien form of life parading in the guise of technology that is taking over our lives. That's schizophrenia."

"It may sound crazy but I know it isn't. For some reason I've been able to tap into the future and see the global mistakes that need reversal."

"Jenny, you're going to destroy your life long before this planet destructs. You've got to stop this."

"And you? What about the group that is grooming you for the Presidency?

"What group darling?" He smiled at her in his most charming and photogenic way. "Your conspiracy theories sound straight from the Sixties."

She forced herself to stay calm. "I'm a problem, right? When we were younger my views were charming, but they're not now. I either have to be re-programmed, or gotten rid of. Dissidents don't work in American politics. Remember what happened to Martha Mitchell, Attorney General, John Mitchell's wife? She called lots of reporters to expose what was going on. She died suddenly. Was her death a result of having a big mouth? Dissension is allowed only when it is popular and can attract voters."

"Well," he shook his head, his hand covering his mouth. "Your behavior has become a problem - especially for you."

Jenny ignored that. "I'd like to think you're being controlled by some thing other than your own ambition. I say that because I love you and would like to give you the benefit of the doubt."

His face was turning white. He drew her close. "Darling, I love you, but you're not making sense. No one will believe you. It's nonsense." He kissed her.

She turned her head. She wanted to believe him, but something told her not to. His kiss didn't feel right, it felt angry. As she turned to him words tumbled out of her, "I'm being guided to counteract you. You and the people you're involved with."

"Why not?" He got off the bed, his face a portrait of contained anger.

"I mean it Tim."

"I know you do. That's what is so upsetting. Your delusions are getting worse. It's frightening. I just can't think you really believe this. Perhaps it was the rape - if that really happened - but you need psychiatric treatment."

"If that really happened," she repeated slowly. "You doubt that. Maybe you should doubt my existence. Maybe I'm not really here. Then you won't have to sell me out and send me to that hospital."

He stopped, surprised, and looked at her.

"I've been there," she answered his look. "I've already lived that part of the future."

He paused another moment, then walked away. A hole appeared in her stomach and started to spread. She turned and buried her head in the pillow, crying.

The air suddenly changed. It felt thinner and colder. Her pillow case was cold. She looked up and wasn't surprised to see the gray brown walls of the hospital, snow falling. Yet she knew what had just happened with Tim had been for real. It wasn't a dream - she knew it as well as she knew the pillow was wet from her tears. Do people cry in their sleep? She was going through some kind of time warp. That had to be the answer.

She rolled over and stared at the ceiling, her face wet with tears. What should she do? She could be in two different places at the same time. Suddenly a ripple of energy rolled through her. She rolled over to the side, then saw her body lying face up beneath her. Then she was outside the building and over the lawn, looking at the few people bundled up and sitting on benches. She swooped down like a bird, but nobody seemed to notice. She was flying outside of her body. Did this mean she was dying?

She was back in her room. Her body still lying quietly face up on the bed. She felt a connection with it. Next instant she was in it. She touched her arm. It was solid. Her cheeks were cold and still wet with her tears. But she was feeling light and liberated, more at peace than she had ever been. Joy was beginning to fill her with a new sense of power. She wasn't sure where her body was supposed to be, in this room or in Mexico with Tim, but she knew it didn't matter. She could be anywhere in the past, present or future.

"You need more training," a voice whispered.

"You mean I can't always do this?" She felt a twinge.

The door opened and Elizabeth poked her head in, she was floating. Jenny's body soared weightless off the bed and followed Elizabeth as she turned toward the open doorway.

Slashes of light slipped through the doors of the darkened hall. She followed her friend lightly and easily. The girl stopped and turned to her, her finger to her lips, and opened it slightly. Jenny looked in.

There was a modern lobby. It looked familiar. As she thought about going in, something started to pull her. At the same time something in the opposite direction pulled at her waist. A tug of war ensued with Jenny in the middle - Elizabeth pulling her back, and a force trying to pull her inside. Without hesitation she willed herself over to Elizabeth. The pulling stopped. They both tumbled backward with the impact.

221

"Let's go." Elizabeth gasped, worn out with the exertion. She looked scared. "That was a close one."

"What was that?" Jenny yelled, flying after her down the hall.

"THE CITY OF MATERIAL DESIRES." Once you go in it's hard to get out. Don't ever go near there again if you're alone. Its pulls are very strong and you can get lost without someone else watching."

She touched her friend sailing down the corridor in front of her. "What is all this?" she asked. "How is this happening?"

"You're learning to go back and forth in time, to different realities and experience them without fear or comparison. Nothing is holding you back. You want to fly, you do it. You're getting the technique and it's becoming natural for you."

All this information was making Jenny dizzy. She didn't want to be rude, but asked, "what do I do to go back?"

"Ask."

"That's it?"

"Yep. Watch."

Jenny found herself back on the bed staring up at the ceiling. Her friend had vanished. Outside the sky was dark with just a few stars sparkling. The snow had stopped falling. The moon was making its slow way up into the sky, it's thin crescent cutting through the clouds surrounding it. Far in the distance a dog was barking. She wondered if it was Christmas time. She had no idea.

She decided to visit Tim again and laid down to will herself back to him. But she stayed where she was on the top of the bed. She tried again. She didn't budge. A hand on her shoulder started shaking her. She tried to push it off, but it persisted. A vibration was buzzing. The hand shook again. She opened her eyes. A young woman in a blue suit and white shirt looked down on her.

"We're coming in for a landing. Would you please raise up your seat and fasten your seat belt."

Not again! She was back on the plane again. Why? She pushed the button for the seat back that jerked her into a vertical position and felt under the blanket on her lap. Her seat belt was buckled. Tim sat across the aisle, engrossed in a book. She looked through the window. Clouds floated past. The flight attendant moved away. She touched her arm. It felt real. She was in human form. She reached out and touched Tim's sleeve. He turned and smiled. "You've had quite a long sleep."

"You seem to be saying that to me a lot lately."

"Well, you've been out of it for a long time. Are you feeling better?'

"Am I sick?"

"Don't you remember? You've had Jungle Fever. You collapsed when Dr. White and Jan were over. He gave you some medication and you slept through the rest of our vacation." He smiled easily. "It's been good for both of us, very restful." He turned a bit more serious. "Don't you remember getting up this morning and saying you were feeling better? That's why we were able to leave."

"No, I don't." She bit a hangnail on her cuticle. She could feel the sensation. "Did I walk?"

"Yes. You really don't remember?

She shook her head. The plane started to shake as it lost altitude. Everything was quiet. Jenny leaned over and looked out the window. She could see her reflection in the glass staring back. She watched herself as the reflection bit her nails. It shook its head no and she saw it take out the finger. Simultaneously she felt her hand rest in her lap. Her finger was wet.

Her legs were shaky as Tim put his hand on her arm and walked her off the plane and through customs; bright lights, rushing people, baggage revolving on islands of silver, echoing voices coming through the air.

"We've already done this," she told him.

"No, we haven't."

"Yes. I've been here. There's a long gray limousine waiting to take me to a sanitarium. You're not going because it isn't a sanitarium, it's a training center. The illness you said I had was an excuse to knock me out for a while so you could get me here. I'm weakened from drugs and too much sleep, not Jungle Fever. That was a lie to get me to go with no resistance. I know what's happening, and I was hoping it wasn't true."

Tim grabbed her arm tighter and stared at her.

"How do I know?" She asked his surprised face. I told you, I've been here before. Been through everything. I'm a graduate. You're going to load me into the back of that car and stand and watch it go off and I'm going to feel sorry for you because you look sad and lonely."

He faltered a bit. "Jenny, I feel like hell this is happening. But it's for your own good."

A sinking feeling of anger and betrayal flashed through her. He was trying to turn this into her need instead of his own, the ultimate tool to instill weakness and self-doubt.

"Darling," he led her toward a bench and they sat down. "You're having disassociation problems. You need help. You've agreed to it. Your realities are getting mixed up with your imagination. And your imagination is very powerful."

She didn't answer. He was not going to talk her into being crazy.

"There is no conspiracy or desire to change you," he went on. "We want you healthy and strong. You seem to have lost all sense of time and become extremely paranoid."

She felt like throwing up all over him. Over his clean white pants and his immaculate white shirt. Over his strong tanned jaw and his deep-set eyes. He'd be horrified! She started to giggle. Mr. Immaculate with vomit all over him. She hooted with laughter. A smile touched his lips, he was about to laugh with her when something caught his attention. He straightened and stood up. Jenny's laughter stopped.

The gray limousine had pulled up to the curb. Tim led her to the inevitable. She wanted to scream and cry for help, but this was the past and future as well as the present. There was no changing it.

Tim helped her into the car. He quickly closed the door and stepped back on the curb. The big car pulled away. Jenny saw the replay of the scene she had been in before. Which was real? Or were they both real?

The sad lonely man standing on the edge of the curb, his coat collar turned up against the cold, his shoulders hunched, watching her go. Same events, different tone. Why? She settled back waiting for the inevitable.

She found herself back on her bed in the sanitarium. "You're going back and forth in space and time now." The words were so loud Jenny jumped. "You were definitely there. You just saw aspects you hadn't seen before, but you were definitely there. Didn't it feel like it?"

"Yes," she whispered aloud. "What if I want to go back to the experience now?"

The back seat of the limo was empty. The smoked gray Plexiglas divider between her and the driver was securely closed. She would not again try opening the window and turning on the light. She knew they wouldn't work. She knew she was being made to stay in darkness and silence on this long trip to the hospital . This time it was the same, but it was also very different. This time she knew. Truth and awareness were her tools.

CHAPTER NINETEEN

"Tell him Detective Parker has called for the third time and I want him to return my call as soon as possible," Parker slammed the phone down, hard. The officer at the next desk turned, surprised. Parker took a deep breath. He had a sinking feeling about Jenny Webster. Something was happening, and it didn't feel right.

Boyle sauntered up. "What's the problem? You on edge?"

"I can't figure why Jenny Webster is in that sanitarium. She had been upset after her friend Mannie's death, but she seemed to be in control. What did we miss?"

"Nothing. Look Detective," Boyle snapped, "The Sebastiane case is closed. It's for the insurance companies now. It was murder/suicide. End of story."

Parker turned his hand away from Boyle's labored breath. He couldn't accept the official decision. Why did they want to wrap the case so quickly? It was the kind of case they usually liked to draw out - it was flashy, it would create lots of publicity. Someone wanted it closed before there was sufficient evidence and it could be linked to Anson Industries.

"Come on," Boyle clapped him on the shoulder. "We have to see the Captain."

Parker relaxed his clenched jaw. "Sure," he exhaled.

***

Jenny thought that it might be cold in the Captain's office when she saw Parker shiver, or maybe he was anxious. Then she remembered that sometimes she made people shiver with her unseen presence, so she tried to stay very still.

The Captain was taking a long time loading his pipe. Jenny smiled at the irony of the large red and white No Smoking sign displayed prominently on the desk in front of him.

"We have a compromised police officer in this precinct," the Captain was saying, tapping the tobacco down into the pipe's bowl with a small silver trowel. "Weapons and drugs. The brass want him before the media finds out. We don't want negative publicity, it's a matter of pride, we don't want this precinct tainted." He struck a match and sucked on the stem of the pipe deeply. "It's touchy Boyle, that's why we want you on this." He looked over at Parker for the first time. "You'll learn a lot." Boyle rolled his eyes to the ceiling.

Jenny peered at the three men. Something was askew. Smoke was starting to seep from Boyle's skin, leaking through his pores. The dark, bottomless pools of his eyes turned toward her and pierced her with understanding. In that instant she could hear his thoughts, feel his contempt, and see his devious plans. The suspect the Captain was describing, was Boyle himself. She knew that as well as she knew Parker would be in danger. But how could she tell him? Maybe Rudnik? He always said he could read her mind.

She thought of Rudnick's rumpled white shirt, his loose tie, the ever-present cigarette in the corner of his mouth as the newspaper office came slithering into a wavy net of quasi-substance. But Rudnik wasn't at his desk and the air was clear of cigarette smoke. With the exception of a few writers and copy editors, the office was empty. She didn't know why Rudnik wasn't there. But then she wasn't sure of the day or time, or really, even the year. It could be the past, it could be the future. She wouldn't know till she got into it.

"Focus on the person, not the place," said the voice before she could think anymore. "Deal with his essence."

Jenny went into Rudnick's office and sat down in his chair. She tried picking up a pen to write a note, but her fingers kept going through it. Then she realized that her fingers were not attached to her hand at all, in fact, she had no hand. At the moment all parts of her body were just extensions of her creative memory and didn't have three dimensions at all. She couldn't pick up a pen to write Rudnik about Boyle or Parker. She would have to get through to him subtly, through his feelings and intuition.

She focused on his feelings and began to get a sense of anxiety and frustrating insecurity. He wanted to do the right thing, but he had to be practical, he had a family to support and he needed to keep working. His emotions started to take her over, binding and wrapping her inside of them and becoming one with her own.

Suddenly she found herself in the passenger seat of a car in which Rudnik was driving. She recognized the mountains heading toward Clifton Sanitarium. "Al?" she whispered. There was no answer. She doubted he would hear her even had she been there in the flesh with a frown as deep as the one he had frozen across his face. Rudnik hated driving and he was forcing himself to concentrate on the winding road in front of him.

"Al?" she tried again and touched his shoulder. He shivered and turned the radio on, but there was a lot of static. He pulled out a Henry Mancini compilation of favorite hits and put it in the tape deck, but forgot to push the START button as the road became more twisted and narrow. They passed farmland and forests as the car climbed higher, but Rudnik wasn't sightseeing, he was trying to stay on the road.

She looked at her hand - it was shimmering, light spilling from it. She loved this feeling and the absolute irony; here she was an invisible passenger traveling through space, defying the laws of three dimensions and gravity, driving to see herself with her managing editor.

Rudnik picked up his portable phone and pressed the automatic dial to his office. "AMY, What's happening?"

"Nothing unusual. Detective Parker called three times. Said it was important. Everything else seems to be under control. Do you want Parker's number or shall I give him yours?"

"Not now, I'm trying to stay on this damn road."

"Okey dokey !" she answered.

"Did you get in touch with Clifton and tell them I'm arriving?"

"Not yet. I tried calling and sending a fax but their phone lines are down. I'll keep trying."

"I'll get there before you get through to them."

"I hope not."

"Me too." He hung up, stared into space, then swerved into his next turn. Jenny held her breath, then realized she had none to hold.

Rudnik picked up a memo sheet with the phone number and directions to Clifton Sanitarium. Balancing driving and making the call, he managed to dial the number on the car phone. There was no ring, nothing. He pressed O for the operator and got a busy signal.

"Damn." He pushed the on button to his tape deck and settled back to Henry Mancini.

Jenny felt her transparent body leaning against the car door - practically through it.

Suddenly Rudnik hit the brakes, threw the car into reverse, and turned into a driveway leading up to a large iron fence. An intercom was embedded in the concrete fence poles. He got out of the car, lifted the receiver and pushed the button marked: RECEPTION.

"Yes?" answered a metallic voice sounding not entirely human.

The voice made Al pause a moment before talking. "This is Al Rudnik, Los Angeles News," he spoke gruffly. "You have Jenny Webster here. I want to see her."

"Do you have an appointment?"

"Yes. The arrangements were made yesterday. It was confirmed by fax." His face was starting to puff, Al Rudnik was growing impatient.

"I'm sorry, you're not on the list and there is no one available."

"Look, I'm managing editor of the Los Angeles News. This was arranged before I left. My office called to re-confirm and your phone lines are down. Let me talk to someone in charge."

"I'm sorry. No one is available. You'll have to call back tomorrow for an appointment."

"What are you, some kind of robot? I just said I have an appointment. Look at your list and open this gate."

"You'll have to call for an appointment and specify whom it is you

231

would like to speak with." The operator sounded more and more like a recording.

"I don't believe this !" The line went dead and Rudnik slammed the receiver down. He picked it up again and tried pushing every number on the board but there was no further response. Like a child at the zoo he grabbed the iron bars of the gate and peered in. The long winding road did not offer a view of any buildings. Only a single lane dividing the edge of the forest and meadow. Rudnik noted the multitudes of wires leading into the interior, the landscaping designed to both expose and conceal. Sophisticated surveillance was in effect. There were not any criminally insane here. This was all very sophisticated for a sanitarium that was supposed to be for depressives, substance abusers, and garden-variety psychotics.

A four-wheel drive vehicle came charging up to the gate in a cloud of dust from the interior of the grounds. Two hulking giants barely seemed to fit inside. One of them peeled himself out, his hand resting lightly on the gun at his hip. "Got a problem?"

"Yes. I have a scheduled meeting with one of your patients here. I made the necessary arrangements and now I can't get in. Would you please open this gate."

"You need permission from the attending doctor or supervising physician."

"I have it."

"May we see it please?"

"It was on the phone, damn it. My office faxed a confirmation. Call someone and tell them to look for it."

The taller of the two hulking giants came up close to the bars. His round little eyes did not reveal a higher intelligence, however his bulk and well developed muscles proved a kind of compensation. "You need a letter from the head Doc here, otherwise we can't let you in."

"That's ridiculous."

"It's the rules."

Shaking with anger, Rudnik pulled out a card and gave it to the giant. "Give this to your head guy. I'll wait."

"It could take days."

"Then I'll call damn it."

Jenny watched sadly as he went back to the car and slammed the door. A swirl of dust rose up and enveloped her as he peeled away. She wanted to be in the car with him, talk to him, but somehow she couldn't. She was caught in a milky white thickness and could no longer see. `

CHAPTER TWENTY

Tim paced in his office. He opened a small refrigerator in the wet bar, but slammed it shut. He tried to read the contents of a folder, then aimlessly wiped off its dust. He picked up a "Law Review", swatted an imaginary fly, then threw it across the room toward a chair, letting it stay on the floor where it landed. He picked up a picture of Jenny, sighed heavily, and put it face down. Suddenly his fist banged down on top of it, he withdrew it accusingly as if it had moved on it's own.

Grabbing a small overnight bag out of the closet, he changed into a pair of Levi's, a wool Pendleton shirt, and canvas hiking boots. He pushed a button and spoke into a recorder "Roxanne, I'm going to the cabin for a few days. No one is to know where I am except Jenny." He started to leave then went back to the button and pushed it again. "When I get back, you and I need to have a talk. Schedule it." He hung up.

Revving the engine of his black Astin Martin, Tim caressed the steering wheel like it was a woman's shoulders. He leaned back, grabbed the knob of the stick shift and pushed it forward. The car jumped to his command.

The machine showed its stuff on the empty country roads; 105, 110, 115 mph. He raced past horse farms and mountain passes till he got off the highway on to a steep and winding road. The sudden shock of clean fresh mountain air enveloped him when he stopped for gas.

In seconds his face was stung red by the cold, filling his dry lungs like a spring of fresh water.

He kept getting a busy signal when he used his cellular, so while his car was being serviced Tim went inside to use the public telephone. He dialed Jenny's hospital, but the circuits were busy. "Damn." He put his head down and sprinted back through the cold to his car.

***

Roxanne played Tim's message on the tape then erased it and put it into a large bag filled with other tapes and videocassettes. She picked up the phone and dialed a number. "He's going to Winrock, the cabin in the mountains."

***

Jenny's hand had dropped off the bed and was touching the floor. She had just awakened and felt so relaxed she didn't want to move. Her body started to vibrate, but she merely lay quietly and watched what was happening. She didn't want to go out of body - she wanted to rest.

***

It was dark and very cold by the time Tim got to the cabin. He stacked the few remaining logs from the cord of wood into the fireplace and tucked some old newspapers beneath, but the matches were damp and refused to light anything. Starting the first fire in the fireplace had always been a race so he and Jenny could cuddle, get warm and relax. This time was different. Jenny wasn't here, the wood was wet, there didn't seem to be any other matches, and the butane fire starter was out of butane. Annoyance grabbed him. Why does the simple act of lighting a fire have to be so difficult? he threw the lighter across the room. Tears of frustration cropped up in him. He never allowed any emotional display - not since he was in diapers. His father wouldn't allow it. Almost from the first he knew his father was right about that. Tim accepted everything his father demanded of him because he knew that his strict discipline would help him achieve what they both wanted, the Presidency of the United States. But why, after years of such strict discipline was he suddenly having uncontrolled emotion?

"Where in the hell is the butane refill?" he yelled, and hit his hip against the side of the stove. "Where are the god damn matches? Where did she keep the god damn matches?" He turned the gas jets on the stove - at least they worked, and tried to go outside to find some dry wood. But the door was stuck. He pulled and banged, but he couldn't get out. He looked for the ax, but couldn't find that either. He tried opening a window to climb out, but the windows were jammed shut. He stood still, trying to shrug off the cold fear shooting through him. Why was the door shut? Why couldn't he open it? He didn't notice the flame on the gas jets had gone out.

He crouched in front of the fireplace, tears in his eyes. "Jenny" he heard himself calling to her. The tears of frustration turned to cold hacking sobs, it was an epiphany, a release from a lifetime of repression.

He grabbed a piece of charcoal and scribbled on the wood floor:

Jenny, I tried taking the short cut. I destroyed what we had. Forgive me. I love you. -- Tim

A portrait of remorse and despair, he collapsed in front of the fireplace.

***

Something bumpy hit Jenny's hand as it went through the floor and continued to grow, growing down into the room beneath her. She asked her hand to return and it came back easily, it's outline glowing phosphorescently.

Toward the corner of the room a gray cloud gathered. It started to fill out and Jenny was filled with curiosity. What was it? The form materialized. She was amazed. It was Tim! But something told her not to go near him or touch him. Coldness was emanating from him and she sensed great fear. "Tim," she called to him.

"I don't know what's happening," he said. "I don't know what to do."

His terror grabbed and paralyzed her.

"They want me dead," he whispered strangely. "I'm scared."

"Don't be darling." She wanted to run to him. All the anger, all the resentment she had been feeling had evaporated. He was so vulnerable, she wanted to put her arms around him, take care of him and comfort him. But something was warning her not to off-set his precarious balance. She waited. Whatever was happening to Tim was something he had to go through and she couldn't help him. On the contrary, she had to stay clear. "I love you," started going through her mind - wanting to connect with him. "I love you," she called out soundlessly. He didn't seem to hear.

"They've trapped me," he called out desperately. The tone of his words matching his unworldly ethereal shape. "I don't know what is happening," he called out with shattering terror. "Am I dying, or am I dead? I'm in two places. I can see myself on the floor of our cabin, but I see you with me in some bedroom as well. How is that possible?"

"It's what I've been trying to tell you," she said through her thoughts. "We're on another plane, another level, no longer in Earth's reality." We're what is called spirit now, or you can think of it as pure energy."

"Does that mean we're dead?" He didn't wait for her answer. "They locked the doors and won't let me out. From the moment I left the office I realized how much I needed you and wanted you. I treated you

237

badly. Can you ever forgive me?"

"I always forgive you my darling because I love you. Don't be frightened. You'll be all right."

He started to turn into a gray cloudy form hovering at the door of her hospital room. She could still hear his thoughts. "I needed to be alone to think," he was saying. "You were right about everything. I wanted to call you and tell you, but I couldn't get through. They did that too. They kept me from contacting you and now they've trapped me. They followed me and they won't let me out of here alive."

"That isn't important anymore. You're with me now. You're still thinking, they haven't taken that have they? Please darling, stay calm, stay centered and let's see if we can get you through this." Her voice was very quiet, very calming, almost hypnotic.

"I don't understand this. It's like they're pulling me away from my body. I can see myself on the floor near the fireplace. But I also see you in your hospital room...." His voice went up in panic.

He started to freeze in midway position, attached to Earth - to life, yet out of his body and unable to get back to it. This was how ghosts were formed. Souls attached to Earth and can't leave the atmosphere, bodies or homes they loved.

Jenny knew Tim couldn't willingly give up his body, and she wanted to save him, free him from being trapped in this ghostly place, help him return to his body and living. But he didn't know what to do and she wasn't sure how to guide him. She called for her voices to help.

"If Tim returns in this panic," the voice said, "he might have physical or psychological problems. You are trained how to consciously leave and return again," the voice continued. "Tim isn't."

Jenny put her arms out to him. He shrank away. "Please darling, let's go back to Winrock together so you can get back in your body. Join me."

He recoiled in terror from her.

"Please," she called to him. "Let me help you."

The puff of gray matter was growing fainter and fainter. Fear was not letting him release his pre-conceptions.

"You must give up your attachment to having Tim on the planet, the voice said inside her. "Help to guide him to the place where true freedom awaits him."

"You mean kill him."

"Give up your physical attachment to him. For his soul's sake, you must guide him and then release him."

She closed her eyes and tried to picture Winrock. She could make out Tim lying on the stone floor next to the fireplace. The scene was desolate and cold. She pulled up and away from it and felt herself settling into a soft white cocoon that could have been a cloud. "Tim," she called out to him. "Feel yourself out here," she advised. "Visualize me surrounded by soft white. Come to me. Don't be afraid. You don't need your body. You're energy, pure consciousness. Energy can't be destroyed."

He whined like a pitiful puppy. "I'm afraid."

Her heart went out to him. She could feel his grayness trying to merge with her. Then she became a pulsation of movement, a sexual, sensual ripple like passion. A squall of warmth and wet thrusting energy exploded into her as Tim came and merged with her. They shook and vibrated in a series of love so explosive they forced themselves to separate.

She vibrated as if he were still in her as she floated toward her body lying on top of the bed. It looked smaller than it felt when she wore it, smaller and more vulnerable. She flew into it and hugged herself to it as she assimilated and assumed her shape.

Suddenly the realization of what just happened, struck her. OH GOD ! Tim was going to die ! Fear and panic seized her. She ran to the door. She didn't want him dead. Why hadn't she helped him get back to his body? Was she responsible if he died? Did she kill him?

She charged through the empty hallway of closed doors and dimmed lights to the brighter light of the guards' area. Leo, the night guard sat reading a magazine. The lone cone of light above his head set off the brilliance of his white shirt and pants. The large feet propped up on the desk quickly came down when she called to him, "Please...."

He had lost his composure and angrily pulled it back.

"You've got to call the police," she cried.

"Sure" he smiled sarcastically. "And after that I'll call the Queen."

"I mean it, Leo." She drew shreds of her former dignity around herself. She lost all veracity when she had become a patient here. Her choices were backfiring. Was she crazy? Was it all imagination? Scanlon had been right. She must get out of here.

"You're my first 'call the police' request tonight."

"I'm not crazy, you don't understand," she yelled, hysteria growing with the horrible reality. "You have to call the police. My fiancée is dying. He's unconscious and can't get back to his body."

The guard's mouth twitched with laughter. His eyes were cold.

"Look, I know what you're thinking, but you've got to understand." She grabbed his hand, pleading. He pulled it away. "I can see the future, see things that are happening far from here. My fiancée, Tim is in a cabin alone. The doors and windows are locked. He can't get out. He can see himself unconscious on the floor and he's panicked. It's horrible and cruel. Please, you can save him."

The burly man pushed himself out of the chair. He towered over Jenny in her thin nightdress. "Please," She shivered from fear, and emotion. "He can't get back to his body. He doesn't know how. He needs someone there to save him. Otherwise he's gone."

The man yawned. His breath smelled sour. Muscles rippled in his shoulders and throat. "Want a tranquilizer?" He picked up a clipboard and flipped through the charts. "You're scheduled to have one if needed."

"Please, I know what you think. But you have nothing to lose. If it's true you will have saved someone, if not, I'm crazy. But if it's true and you do nothing, then you're partially responsible."

"O.K. Jenny. I'm responsible. I'm a dirty rat. Now go back to bed." He took her strongly by the arm and led her to her room. She was helpless with rage.

Leading her roughly to the bed he shoved a small pill and paper cup of water at her and demanded, "Take it."

She took the pill quietly and placed it in her mouth, then took a swallow of water. As she started to hand the paper cup back he swatted it out of her hand. It flew across the bed, water splashing her. He grabbed her by the hair, pulled her head back, and stuck his fat tobacco stained finger in her mouth. He found the pill and shoved it to the back of her throat. She choked but he kept her head back till she

241

swallowed. Then he let go and lumbered out of the room. The door locked behind him.

"You're not thinking clearly," came the familiar bell-like voice. "You're caught up emotionally." Soothing breath pumped through her body. Every pulse, every movement becoming strong. "Go to him now," the voice said. "Guide him."

Jenny started to concentrate on the center of her forehead. Shudders came up through her toes, the familiar pulse in her genitals, the quickening excitement in her body before she was going to take off. "Tim," she concentrated strongly. She wanted to go to Tim. She could remember the feel of his skin, his hands on her, the sense of his smell.

She felt the weight before she saw his shape cradled in her arms in front of the fireplace. She stroked his face softly.

"I set you up," he whispered, tears falling softly down his cheeks. They mixed with her own.

"It's all right. You did what you had to."

"I've caused you great suffering."

"It's brought me great strength. I've discovered inner peace. I bless you for it."

"They think you're crazy."

"Only for now."

"No one will listen to you." His voice was plaintive.

"They will," she said, I have powers that go beyond anything that can be used against me."

"Not possible..." his voice started to fade.

"Everything is possible - beyond your imagination. Tim I can leave my body. That's why I'm here with you now. Can you understand? You're more than just body. You're pure energy, spirit." She sounded distant, drifting.

"Are we both dead? You as well?"

"Not yet. But I think it's too late for you, you've been out of your body too long. I think you're supposed to leave." She felt him shudder with terror.

"What will happen?" He sounded so distant, so scared. He was so unprepared.

She called to him. "Your mind will rule. You can create any place you want to be. Even with me right now if you trust."

"Where are you?" he called out in the very far distance.

"At Winrock, with you."

"Will you find me?" His voice was growing more and more faint.

"Of course I will. I'll always find you." She would also find the cause of his murder, find out who was killing everyone who might be in their way. She had lost her best friend and now her love, the man who would have been her husband. She vowed on Tim's expiring life she would find the core and expose what has happened.

Tim suddenly appeared close to her. He seemed whole again. They held each other and he seemed to be calm. He lifted his head close to hers and they kissed lightly, gently, full of love. "Good bye." His eyes closed.

She felt his head on her lap, his limp body heavy in her arms, heavy and empty of the essence that was Tim. It was then she became aware of the gas. So many sensations had been bombarding her she hadn't noticed till then. She tried to lift Tim, but he was inert and heavy. She tried connecting with him but there was no longer any part of Tim inside his body nor in the atmosphere around them. He had gone off far away. There was going to be an explosion, a big one, but she wasn't sure how it would affect her.

"Don't get caught in it." said the voice in her mind. Fatigue was closing. She bent and held Tim in her arms one last time and kissed his flesh, the only part left of him, then asked to go back to her body. His weight disappeared and her body lay twisted in a semi-fetal position on the bed. A headache hammered. The medication the attendant had given her fought for attention. It wanted her to sleep. She gave in to its persistence, closed her eyes and drifted.

CHAPTER TWENTY-ONE

Dr. White walked somberly into the dining room and headed towards Jenny. His eyes cast down, his shoulders drawn together. Jenny fought the tears that had suddenly come. White cleared his throat and sat down beside her.

She tried to collect herself. She had been hoping it was only a vivid dream. But White's face and posture broadcast that it had all been very real. Tim was dead. He would never walk on this Earth again. She would never feel his touch. They would no longer laugh or have their serious talks. Her trusted friend, another one, gone. Grief crashed in on her in a breath-taking wave. It had become too familiar, would it never go away?

She pulled herself up, she would not reveal her true feelings - it could weaken her further. "Re-focus" she heard something say. She sat up straighter and measured White carefully. His furtive eyes gave him away. He resented her probing. Knew she was aware of his insecurities. She picked up her unused fork and turned to him, innocence and openness her weapons. He must not know what she is feeling.

"Good morning, Dr. White. Joining the inmates for breakfast? You can have mine if you'd like. You know I don't eat and this isn't quite cold yet." She pushed the plate of scrambled eggs in front of him.

White twisted and turned, uncomfortable with his body as he tried pulling himself into a semblance of power. She smiled at his discomfort.

"How are you this morning?" he focused on the sugar dispenser, pouring globs of it into his coffee.

"Doesn't white sugar cause schizophrenia?" she asked sweetly.

He put the sugar dispenser down and jutted his head like a brontosaurus. "I want to speak with you in my office."

"About Tim?" A strange euphoria was building, like she was about to float out of body.

"You know," he uttered both questioning and answering.

"Didn't the attendant tell you what happened last night?"

He looked at her evenly. "You woke up in the middle of the night and required tranquilization. I immediately receive reports of uneven behavior."

"Uneven behavior." She worked to keep the bile down.

His lip curled, "A patient gets up in the middle of the night agitated, requests the attendant to contact police to investigate somebody who might be dying because he can't get back to his body. We videotape everything, otherwise I would have thought the attendant was having hallucinations." he shifted uncomfortably.

"Dr. White, in all your years of research and study, you must know something about out of body experiences."

"There are books recording near-death experiences in which people believe they are out of body. But there are many explanations for that."

"Yes, and there are many that have almost the exact visual and emotional experience - whether it's an eight year old child on one side of the planet, or an eighty year old person on the other."

"Well you obviously have read books on the subject."

"Not really."

They looked at each other. She didn't want to say another word, but the voices were talking for her. "Dr. White, research in the manipulation of human behavior is considered by many to be professionally unethical."

"I agree." He looked straight at her.

She tried to control the building anger. "It isn't legal either."

"What are you saying?" He was getting aggressive.

"You're putting peoples' rights in jeopardy."

"Jenny," White was slow and precise. "You came here for therapy. You signed yourself in. Your rights aren't jeopardized."

"Few people sign themselves in here, although on paper it says they do."

He didn't move a muscle. "You can't prove anything, Jenny."

"Maybe." she shrugged and looked at him innocently.

White shook his head grimly and poured himself another cup of coffee using the rest of the sugar. "Jenny, we know you have a vivid imagination, but save it. We don't fit your manufactured fantasies. We're trying to help you live a better more fulfilling life. You get too agitated."

Jenny pulled back. "I don't know for sure what you've done to me, but you haven't succeeded in changing the way I think. You don't know me, can't even see me most of the time." Jenny shrank from his reaction. She had better change the subject. "Why did you keep my editor, Al Rudnik from coming in here?"

"When was he here Jenny? I wasn't informed."

"Of course you were. He called before he came here, and was told he could get in, but once he arrived he was denied entrance."

He looked at her steadily. "He wasn't here. He never came. It's your imagination."

"Want to tell me Tim is my imagination? That nothing has happened to him?"

He ignored that. "Al Rudnik never sent me any correspondence. I'm sorry Jenny. I'm sure you would have liked him to do that for you."

She looked at him steadily. "All you managed to do is make Rudnik angry. He has probably set a huge investigating team in motion by now. You're going to have major problems if anything happens to me. Destruction of the mind is worse then death. There are people who know what you're doing and are ready if anything happens to me to expose you. I made sure of that."

He was calm, almost passive. "Jenny, you had a nervous breakdown when your friend Mannie Sebastiane died."

"Did I?" Her tone was incredulous.

"Jenny dear, you're very upset."

She looked at him wide eyed. "Am I?"

"Yes, I think you are. Maybe you should have another tranquilizer."

"Don't you dare."

He paused a moment, considering. "You've reached the wrong conclusions because you're upset." He wasn't smiling.

She shook her head. "All your chemicals and technology are not working with me. I've connected with something stronger and that is protecting me."

White bent toward her, sinister, speaking softly, a low monotone. "As long as you believe the fantasy, that's fine. It's a nice positive attitude. Better than despondent. Anything that keeps you comfortable while you're recovering."

She drew back. "That's destructive Doctor White. You can't make me insecure with drivel like that. You've got to do better."

"We will. That's why you're here."

Fear shot up her back. She could handle him, but she wasn't sure how she would stand up to more treatments than she already had. What if she lost her ability to go out of body? What if there was no conspiracy? What if everything she believed wasn't possible? She shivered. There had been travelers that had taken her similar path, and they expressed their journeys in art, music and literature. Most importantly, those mediums told her she wasn't crazy, she wasn't alone.

White shifted in his chair and pushed it back. He was about to leave.

"Just because some see the world differently, does not mean they're crazy Dr. White. It's useless to destroy anything that is different from your own perception."

"I understand how upset you must feel," he was saying. "We expected this when we learned about Tim."

"Upset?" She fought to hold her temper. "You called my reaction to seeing him out of his body and unable to get back in it 'UNEASY BEHAVIOR!'"

"How did you see that Jenny?"

"I was out of my body as well, Dr. White. It isn't schizophrenia, it isn't a hallucination, it's fact. There are those of us able to do what you're trying to do chemically. I know all about that."

White sat impassive, unresponsive. She tried to keep her voice low and contained, not let him see her shaking. "Tim died. It didn't have to happen. Or was it planned because you lost control of him? Was he feeling remorse? Was it the second thoughts you didn't think he could handle?"

White visibly hardened. "If you were there with him, why didn't you save him if you have such extraordinary powers."

"That doesn't mean I can overturn destiny." She gazed at him steadily. "Why the explosion? It was primitive and unnecessary, Tim was dead already."

White smiled sadistically. "Accidents happen."

"That was no accident. I'm not sure how you killed him, but my guess is you used a drug that attacks the nervous system. That's why he was so panicked. He had lost his body and had only his mind."

White tried to keep his expression even, but his seething anger looked ready to explode.

Jenny decided to take a chance. "The police and press have information about Mannie's research. Your people were sloppy and left some behind. You and Jan should co-operate now, it might reduce your prison sentences."

He ran his finger across unsmiling lips. "Unlikely." he smoothed his bristly scalp, and scraped his chair back loudly. "Come see me after breakfast. Let's talk about your discharge."

"Sure," she pushed the scrambled eggs around on the plate. The mushy bright yellow glop looked like soft cardboard. She couldn't touch it. She hadn't eaten in days, or was it months?

CHAPTER TWENTY-TWO

Jenny reached White's office before he got into it. He didn't see her, she was invisible. He flicked the switch on the intercom. "Jan, come in here." He drummed his fingers, turned his head. "We have a problem."

Jan came in from the interior office, immediately concerned when she saw his face. "What's wrong?"

"Tim Jenkins is dead. There was a gas explosion at his mountain cabin. Everything was destroyed - pulverized." He looked at her steadily. She didn't react. "Jenny Webster says it was murder. She says Tim was separated from his body by some artificial means and he couldn't get back to it. She said he was dead before the explosion." He took a deep breath, his face contorted with worry. "Can the coroner determine that?"

"I suppose so." Jan reasoned calmly. "If there was enough left of the body."

He shook his head. "I don't know." He exhaled deeply. "Jenny said explicitly, he was out of body !" He took another deep breath. He was having some trouble breathing. "Could she know what we did to him?" He held tightly to the edge of the desk and leaned toward her. "I don't know, but she practically said she did. The way she looked at me -" he shivered convulsively. "I think she knows everything."

Jan shrugged. "So what? What can she do? She's crazy. I don't know why you're so upset. It's good this happened now before we went further with either one of them. We need perfect specimens. He was flawed. Sentiment was overtaking him."

"You're in denial. You're not hearing what I'm saying. Jenny may have been with him out of her body. She says she was and knows how to do it! Everything we've done to her has turned to her advantage. It's all gone wrong." He was wringing his hands, his face white as stone. "What about the coroner's report?"

"Stop worrying. Nothing is going to happen. We can take care of that, it's Sid Smith. If nothing has happened so far, it isn't going to happen."

He looked at the wall beyond her. "We made a mistake. Her reports didn't compute well enough. She should have been re-programmed by now. Do you realize what we've given her? How much more can she take? You wouldn't have believed our conversation just now. She is completely even - barely reacting to Tim's death. Had time to grieve already because she was there when it happened."

"Will you stop!" Jan banged her hand on the desk. White jumped and looked at her in amazement. She hadn't shown that much passion in all the years they'd been together. "None of that is important. What's important is to decide if we should keep her or kill her."

"We can't keep her much longer, that's for sure. Her army of lawyers want her out." He paused then pointed his finger for emphasis. "Make sure her admissions sheet is signed and says voluntary commitment due to job stress, do not mention anything about a rape."

Jenny listened. These people were truly scum.

"We must determine the extent of her powers before we release her," White emphasized.

253

"Yes," Jan agreed with him.

"She can cause problems."

Jan shook her head. "No she can't." Her voice was soft, calm, soothing. "She's in a mental hospital. What is she going to say? We kept her here against her will? We did things to her mind? That's paranoia. You're not looking at this logically. Anything she says will make her sound crazier."

White didn't respond to that. "I can't accept she hasn't been affected by what we've done to her. Those who have gone as far out as she has, usually don't come back. The few that have, are no longer able to communicate. She can. You should have heard her at breakfast just now."

"Was she eating?"

"No, she wasn't. It's been more than three months and she still looks healthy. Maybe healthier. I don't like it."

"Hmmm - " Jan was pensive, not liking it either.

Jenny watched from the corner, afraid to move, she didn't want her energy to rustle anything. A movement might cause detection. They couldn't see her, but there was a chance they could feel her presence. Some other times when she traveled out of body, especially around the hospital, she noticed a few people seemed to experience her presence with a chill. Did the Whites know those signs? What would they do if they recognized it?

White looked harassed. "Do you think it's possible she has the power to do naturally what we're trying to create artificially?"

"Not really. She may have dreamed something was happening.

The time bending we have been working on is a chemical reaction. I don't see how it can occur naturally."

White looked out the window then back at Jan. "You know that she alerted the attendant about Tim."

"No, I didn't."

"It was that stupid idiot, Leo. Have him fired."

Jan patted him on the hand and tried to soothe him. "Calm down. If we fire him it might cause suspicion."

"Quite the contrary. We accept prescient vision. One of us should have been consulted."

"It was the middle of the night."

"I don't care."

"You're being unreasonable."

"I'm being cautious."

"All right," she sighed. "Maybe we should just kill her."

He shook his head disbelieving. "We may finally have someone with the ability to go out of body and return to it consciously. The problem is that we haven't conditioned her sufficiently. It would be a terrible waste to kill her ! We have to step up the programming - change her way of thinking, create vulnerability and dependence, then we can use her !"

Rebuked, Jan cast her eyes down. "You're right."

"If we can harness her she's an incredible tool. I think we should try stronger doses of chemicals in conjunction with hypnosis."

Jenny went behind White and sat down next to him. He didn't seem to notice. "What we have to do," he said, "is make her feel safe and comfortable. Complacency is a powerful tool. But I also think we need someone to go out of body with her, to control her."

Jan looked at him evenly. "Give me the preparation, I can do it."

"You haven't been trained or tested. Forget it. No one's done it except those transients and illegals we brought in here. Need I remind you what happened to them?"

"Yes," she sounded impatient. "But we did consider keeping some of them when they came back. The chemicals work. Look, Jenny is beginning to trust me. You read her psychological profile. She wants to trust. She's already started."

White shook his head. "There have been too many failures. You forget the amount of sacrifices."

"Consider the genetic types." Jan shifted in her chair, re-crossed her legs. She seemed to be losing patience. "Am I hearing remorse?"

"Not at all. I'm talking about the independence factor that can't be controlled. There is something out there that empowers people. Makes them more than what they were. That's why we have problems if they return. It happened with some of the astronauts. And you know how disciplined they are."

"You're displaying remorse." Her eyes narrowed, "It's time to let me go. Then we'll know everything first hand. My allegiance is to you and everything we're doing."

White wouldn't look at her. He was angry with her accusation.

"It's my choice, " she continued. "You need me out there. I know the consequences and I'm not afraid. You know how dedicated and devoted I am. This project is my life and I'm one of the few you can trust. We are going to have to use someone from the group and it may as well be me."

White weighed her words.

Jan sat closer and crossed her legs. She smiled and leaned in closer. "I keep my loyalties. I should have been the first of us to go out of body."

He rubbed her knee. She smiled at him. He pulled away. "Too many things can go wrong," he said, "look what happened to Tim.

"He wasn't strong enough." Jan put his hand back, high on her thigh. "We've done enough experiments with the Disposables, the only thing that ever goes wrong is personality control. And you know mine." She smiled and brought his hand a little closer up her thigh. She watched the last vestiges of his resentment melt as his fingers moved up between her legs. As he started to play there, she pulled away. "Let me try to go out of body with our chemicals. Only for a few minutes. You can regulate it. It's necessary."

He pulled his hand out from under her skirt and picked up a chart on the desk, making a pretext of looking at it, sneaking a whiff of his hand. "Do you notice anything strange in here?" he suddenly asked. "Something has been bothering me since I came in." He took a black rod from his desk and pointed it around the room. Jenny leaned so far into the wall she was halfway through it. He looked around, then opened the door and shut it. "Funny. I just had a strange feeling we're not alone. We're not bugged. That's for sure. There is no way anyone can get through these defenses."

Jan remained still, waiting for White's decision.

"I guess you're right," he conceded. "You're the one I can trust. Let's do it."

Jan smiled relieved, excited. "Now."

He nodded.

They went through an inner door of the office into a small laboratory. The woman went straight to the white metal table at the end of the room and sat upon it. White prepared an injection with a clear fluid. He rubbed her arm with alcohol. "We'll start with three minutes." He leaned down and kissed her on the cheek. "Thanks." He injected her with the shot. She immediately sledded into unconsciousness. He helped her lie down, then checked her pulse, the time, and recorded it.

Jenny stood by the table where Jan lay. She stood ready to meet her when she emerged from the physical. But Jan didn't come out. She merely lay there, trapped in her body. She checked the woman's aura. It was gaining in brightness, growing and spreading, leaking out of her. Jenny watched in amazement, everything was out of control. Jan's ethereal body was separating and taking off without her.

Jenny tried to intervene, to send a message to be aware. But she knew she was throwing her energy into the void. Jan's disappearing light was streaking into the cosmos. Jenny knew without asking her inner voice that she must not follow. There was no coming back from the realm the woman was going.

Jenny went over to White and tried to get his attention. He was watching Jan from a stool, checking his watch, making notes on a pad. He couldn't see that the light was almost gone from her body.

Jenny threw all of her energy against him. He seemed to shiver a bit then got up and went over to the prone figure. He checked her pulse. She had none. He pulled back her lids. Her fixed eyes stared straight ahead. He put his ear to her chest, then started artificial respiration pushing and using his whole body for power. He stopped. His hands trembling, he rushed to the medicine cabinet and prepared a hypodermic. On the way back he punched the intercom and yelled for help. He injected the syringe directly into the woman's heart. There was no response. He started to push on her diaphragm desperately, then breathed into her mouth. Nothing. She didn't respond.

Jenny watched as the last remnants of light leaked from Jan's body. She knew she was completely gone, gone so far she had skipped the fourth dimension where most people go when they first leave their bodies. Jenny willed herself back to her physical body and found she had put her head down on the table in the dining room as if she had been napping.

All the people and breakfast dishes were gone. She got up and started down the hall. A few nurses and orderlies rushed past her. She knew where they were going.

Jenny went back to her room and sat cross legged in the middle of the bed, closed her eyes, resting her hands palms up on her knees, and asked her voice for guidance.

Al Rudnik came into her thoughts. "Can he be trusted?

"Not really," said the voice inside her. "He's too frightened to think clearly. Go to Detective Parker. He's sensitive and a clear thinker. If you keep your thoughts simple and pure, they'll flood him with inspiration. Just stay where you are and focus on him."

Jenny hoped she could remember Parker well enough. There was a quickening inside when she thought about his crooked smile. But his face wasn't too clear to her. She remembered red hair, a thin face and penetrating eyes. So penetrating she started feeling tingling and a warming within. She was having strong stirrings - not the usual out of body ones, but physical and maybe a little bit sexy.

Parker was very appealing in a sensitive, intelligent way. She had always preferred smart men, there was better communication with them.

She smiled when she thought of Parker's freckles, the way he looked that made her tingle. She remembered when he had smiled at her the first time, when her life was in turmoil, how everything he said and did made her feel so much better.

She felt herself being drawn through a vortex, soaring through the air like a bird. She looked down and she was north of Hollywood Boulevard just above the Hollywood Bowl. She "landed" in an apartment that was essentially the opposite of her own. This one was dingy and covered with simulated wood paneling, furnished with ancient overstuffed armchairs and a sofa bed with a cover from decades ago. In the center of the threadbare sofa bed sat Detective James Parker. She could read his mind and he was thinking about her !

Red and blue lights flickered from the neon sign outside the window, creating a multicolored warrior's mask onto his thin, pale face. He looked weary.

"Nothing is going right with the Webster case," he was thinking. "Why are they stalling the investigation? If they want to indict her, why haven't they brought it to the Grand Jury? Something isn't right. There is foot dragging. What is happening?

There were notes scribbled on a pad next to him. "Cover-up" was scrawled on the pad. "Set up? Who? Why?" had been written.

"I like what she's made of ..." Parker was thinking. If Jenny had a face at this point she would have been grinning. She liked being able to eaves drop on him, but the irony didn't escape her. What she feared and tried to expose, was exactly what she was doing. She vowed never to take advantage of this extraordinary privilege.

She almost turned away as Parker absent-mindedly started to stroke himself through his seersucker pajamas. He was grateful for holidays and birthdays because his mother always sent him underwear or pajamas that he would forget to buy for himself. These blue and white seersucker pajamas were Mother's gift from Easter. This was the first time he had them on. They felt scratchy and not particularly comfortable. He wouldn't wear these with Jenny.

She giggled, embarrassed. She shouldn't be listening.

What would I wear with her, he mused. Silk? Boxer shorts? A robe? Nothing? Where would he wear nothing with Jenny? He stroked his penis as he saw her in his mind, fantasizing that she walked toward him wearing only a smile. Her hair was shining, she was laughing - beckoning... But he's dressed. He can't take off his clothes. He can't be nude with Jenny. Not even while he's dreaming.

He continued to stroke himself. He was growing larger and getting harder. He opened the drawstring and took out his penis. God, how he would love to have Jenny's mouth on him.

Jenny was enjoying herself, even getting excited. But she couldn't touch him, couldn't go near him, not out of her body.

He fantasized her face coming closer, smiling with desire. He was standing straight up, his penis quivering, growing larger. All he could think about and see was Jenny as semen squirted over his hand and onto the green covers. He stroked himself rapidly, moaning her name, licking his lips, coming and coming.

Jenny kept watching, she couldn't stop smiling.

CHAPTER TWENTY-THREE

Grainy lines forming a head squeezed out of the fax machine at Santa Monica Police Headquarters. Rolling out was a picture of Timothy Jenkins, followed by his curriculum vitae and all available information.

Parker studied the aristocratic face. There was no softness in the handsome portrait. The eyes were cold and calculating, the lips turned down in a familiar yet distant sneer. Some women liked that type. Jenny obviously did. Parker caught himself. Why was he making these judgments? He never met the man and now he was dead.

There were no leads and not much had been left of Jenkins body except a few charred bones. Finding the exact cause of death would be impossible. He had to find out if it really was an accident. Two fiery deaths like Jenkins and Sebastiane's couldn't be coincidence. If they were linked, then they pointed to Jenny. She could be the next victim. A death staged as a murder or suicide in a mental institution would be easy. He could think of a hundred scenarios that would do it. Parker had learned in philosophy class that the obvious was always the most difficult, and he had an unsettling feeling he was overlooking the obvious.

Boyle sauntered over to him. "I've got a surprise for you college boy," his grin borrowed from a Cheshire cat.

"What is it?" Parker asked.

Boyle bent down and whispered in his ear, "We're doing a sting tonight." Parker leaned away from him.

"That cop's getting a pay off. We're not sure who he is, but our informant will be there with the connection. Ready for it college boy?"

Parker was excited. Except for the short time he had been a uniformed policeman he hadn't seen much action. The Sebastiane and Jenkins cases required detailed research and investigation but it was mostly paperwork and conversation. Tonight he'd be in the trenches, a foot soldier once again, adrenaline pumping, mind and body sharpened. "When does it happen?"

"We gotta talk to the Captain first." Boyle clapped him on the back as they headed for the Captain's office.

***

Jenny heard pounding and roused herself from her dream. Or was it a dream? Unsettled she rose shakily to the door but didn't make it all the way before Dr. White came barging in. "Happy now?" He was seething. "You got rid of both of them."

"What are you talking about?" she asked, groggy from sleep.

"Your boyfriend and my wife," yelled White, nearly out of control.

Jenny started to answer, but before she could speak reason stopped her. White was irrational. She wouldn't join in his dance.

"You're being investigated for both murders."

She could barely make his words coherent. "It isn't possible. Jan just died. How could I be a suspect?"

"You don't remember much do you?" White's lips twisted in anger.

"Remember?" Panic joined dismay. Was she going to sink?

"You've been sleeping," he spit the words at her, "a month," he added sadistically.

She sat down on the bed, shock threatening to collapse her chest. She couldn't breathe, she could only whisper, "Bastard."

"You were hysterical. It was for your own good."

She tried to calm herself. "Before or after Jan died?

"After."

Her lips played with an ironic bitter smile. "Because she died?"

He looked at her steadily. "Yes."

Jenny was angrily cautious. "Why am I under suspicion?"

"There is evidence someone changed the labels on the drugs. Jan was having a seizure. When I injected her, it was with the wrong drug. She died. But of course, you know that."

"How could I?"

"You always say you can go out of body. It's a metaphor for being able to get in and out of places like a cat burglar."

"How could you …"

White's eyes glowed. A chill ran through her. She remembered her last meeting with Scanlon - how he had begged her to leave. How much time had passed since she had been with him? Everything was so jumbled. She had lost all sense of time and place. She knew the events, but not their sequence. She dreaded the next question, but needed an answer. "Was I in the sleep room?"

"Yes."

"Bastard." She would have liked to strike him. "How long?"

"Since you changed the labels on the bottles. You were hysterical and it was all we could do."

A scream of anguish was bubbling in her chest, but she forced it to stay down. she had to know the rest. "Did you give me electroshocks?"

"You signed the consent."

"Liar," she screamed, unable to hold back.

"You blocked Jan's re-entry." He stared at her.

"You're crazy." She screamed. She was shaking badly, didn't know how much time she had lost, how much memory. She thought she remembered most of her out of body states, but when had they happened? How much had she been suspended? Scanlon had been right. They were going to try to take everything away from her. They hadn't yet. She could still use deductive reasoning.

"You killed her," White kept saying.

Didn't you inject her, Dr. White? Maybe an overdose?

The wrong dosage .

On purpose."

"I want you out of here." His anger shook everything.

"Do I walk, or on a slab?"

"We're not going to kill you. We already own your brain."

"Do you?" she tried to keep from shaking. He was bluffing. If he had been successful she couldn't think clearly. But what if she wasn't always self-aware? Could her mind have been grabbed then? Were her out of body experiences created by others and only put in her head? Had she been immersed in a virtual reality machine while White and his staff twisted her dials? What if she had underestimated his power, his destructiveness, and his evil? Was her inability to accept the extreme cruelty of others to be the cause of her downfall?

Doubts continued to pour through her head. If she was wrong about the out of body, maybe the rape didn't occur either. But she had felt the bruises, the contusions on her skin. She knew they had tried using chemical hallucinogens with her and they had the technical ability to project three-dimensional programmed dramas into her eyes and ears. It was growing more and more possible that her own beliefs and truths could not be her own but were implants with the use of virtual and chemical reality.

"The police want to talk to you."

"First I talk to my attorney. May I use the phone."

"The lines are down"

She knew he was lying.

"I want to know how Jan died," he was saying. Tell me what you saw."

She shook her head. His lip curled. "Tell me what you saw." He was on a platform he wouldn't step off.

"What makes you so sure I saw anything?" she asked evenly. Calm on the surface she felt split in half. Half filled with dread that she may have said something when they drugged her, half hopeful her higher resources would keep her from trouble.

White paced the room, a crumbled, discolored fish out of water. "Leave. There's nothing more we can do for you."

"Thank you doctor." She hadn't expected this.

He jumped to attention and started to speak, then changed his mind and walked out, slamming the door behind him.

Almost as quickly Elizabeth walked through the door without opening it. "You keep making me manifest myself when you have these stupid doubts. You've got to trust your higher self and know what you're about. It's good you're open to others, but you must learn to listen to yourself."

"Did they do anything to me? Program me?"

"They tried."

"Did they succeed?"

"Only you know the answer to that. You're the student and you're also the teacher. Mix all your information with your intuition - it will come out right."

Jenny adored this girl. Love poured off her like a fountain.

Elizabeth continued. "Don't you want to get off this planet? It's the pits. It's always in chaos, there's always a commotion. I'm getting tired of coming here. This Urban blight and bad air is lousy for my aura. I've got to do a major cleansing whenever I leave here."

Jenny laughed, shaking her head. "Are you for real?"

"Are you?"

"That's part of my current crisis. I'm not sure if I'm making you up. You could be a dream, which would be a lot easier. Or maybe I'm manifesting you for myself which makes me certifiably crazy."

Elizabeth hugged her. "How do I feel?"

The girl's energy was electrifying. "Good." Jenny's fears were arrested.

"You're on the right track with Detective Parker," declared Elizabeth. "He'll get you out of this mess. Keep him in the positive and perceive him as working with you. That's important."

Although Jenny wasn't sure if Elizabeth was a figment of her imagination or a spirit from another world, she was such a positive, reinforcing energy, it no longer mattered. "You make it sound so easy."

"It is. That's the fun of it. Remember when you were a baby, you had no concept of time or space? Your needs were pure and you could summon your changes; food, dry clothes, heat, cold, by crying or screaming? You're doing that again, but in another way. Only this time your demands are more complex and the way you ask more devious and sophisticated. Then, to complicate everything, the minute you learn something, you want to run and blab it all over to save the world. But the world doesn't always want to get saved, or see the future. Change is frightening, especially with unseen forces."

Elizabeth sat down on the bed next to Jenny. It bounced with her weight. Jenny wanted to hug her, but restrained herself and waited.

"Think you should call your lawyer? Get signed out of here?"

"YES!"

"Then come on, time to go. Lets get this show on the road. Follow me."

They flew through the half way house and entered a small office in the back of the administration building. The room was empty except for a desk with a telephone.

"Is this for real?" she asked Elizabeth.

"Call Scanlon. You'll see."

Scanlon was surprised with her call. "Jenny, hello !"

"Thank you for accepting the charges. And thank you for helping me see. I want to get out of here Uncle James. You were right. I need to be physically free."

"Get a release from White this instant. Go to his office, and get out today if possible."

"Will you call him?"

"Yes, of course I will. Jenny, are you frightened?" Scanlon sounded concerned.

"A little. White told me he wanted me out of here," she said, "But I want to walk out and not be carried horizontally. He said I was responsible for his wife's death, that the labels on her medication were switched. I wouldn't know what to switch, the accusation is ridiculous. But so much of this is. First I'm potentially harmful to myself so I'm put away, and now I'm accused of murdering two people. Uncle James, you've been so right. I desperately need your help."

"Don't worry, we're doing everything for you. You'll be exonerated."

"I only watched." She started crying.

"Watched what?" He sounded alarmed.

"I saw White give Jan the injection that killed her. It was an experimental drug they were working on that would propel people out of body. They know I can do that and they wanted to counteract me. But her death wasn't my fault. I only watched. I didn't do anything."

There was a long pause. "Did White see you?"

"He couldn't. I wasn't in my body."

An intake of breath as Scanlon hesitated.

"I know you think I'm being delusional Uncle James, but you have to believe me. Out of body phenomenon can happen. It's been proven. I'll try to show you one day, I promise." She liked calling him Uncle James, it made her feel comfortable, herself again.

"Jenny, listen to me. Don't say another word about that. If you say you can leave you body, they won't let you out of there."

Elizabeth snickered. Jenny motioned for her to keep quiet, but she laughed out loud making Jenny giggle. The attorney's silence continued.

"Look, I know what you think," Jenny managed, "but it's true. If there had been an autopsy, it would be proven."

"There was an autopsy, and there was evidence of a strong tranquilizer that is used for hyperkinetic children and nerve spasms. It wasn't enough to kill her."

"What if it was mixed with something undetectable, and the two together were toxic?"

"Possible. We have a lab working on it."

"Will you call White and get me out of here?"

"Yes, and I'll send someone from my staff to get you."

"I adore you ! I promise I'm going to start living again."

She hung up the telephone and hugged Elizabeth.

CHAPTER TWENTY-FOUR

The moon was low, the street very dark, as Boyle and Parker waited in their car at the top of a block dead-ending in a wall of warehouses. A single street lamp at the far end painted a glossy sheen of light across the bricks of the buildings, splashes of red and green graffiti the only color in the chiaroscuro setting. The air was thick with deathly stillness, the total desolation of the urban canyon. Even though Parker knew SWAT teams were posted on rooftops and inside vans and doorways, he wiped his hand again to keep his heavy gun from slipping.

A shadowy figure emerged from between two buildings. Parker was sure Boyle could hear his heart beating. He looked over at him. Boyle seemed to be smiling.

"Ready?" Boyle asked him.

Parker took a breath. "Yes," he exhaled as he put his hand on the door. "But there's only one. Shouldn't we wait for..." He didn't finish. Boyle was already out the door, hissing over his shoulder, "come on..."

Boyle walked down the middle of the street, his gun drawn, toward the figure in the shadows.

Parker lunged for the car door, but something stopped him. He couldn't see Jenny blocking his way, using every amount of thought and force she possessed to keep him from getting out. He could only watch as the shadowy figure whirled, gun raised, and pulled the trigger.

Boyle hesitated, then slowly, in slow motion crumbled to the ground, a spray of blood beginning to dot the belt buckle engraved C.O.P.

Bright lights, screams: "DON'T SHOOT ! "FREEZE, DROP YOUR GUN..." stopped Parker before he could fire. He ran to his fallen partner and tried to find a pulse. But his heart sank immediately by the look in Boyle's eyes. They were vacant. Someone took Parker's arm and led him away. "Sorry," said another as a crowd of policemen closed rank around the fallen figure.

Unthinking, unfeeling Parker turned and went over to the prone suspect handcuffed with his arms behind him. He looked like a transient. Parker stood over him, holding his gun, wanting to pull the trigger, but keeping it down. A hand patted his shoulder. It was the Captain. "Come on," the hand tightened as he led him away, "there's nothing we can do here. Let's have some coffee and talk till they book him."

The smell of disinfectant in the small coffee shop made Parker nauseous. He waited while the Captain lit a cigarette and stirred cream into his coffee. "Why did Boyle get out of the car?" he finally asked him. "You had orders to wait till there were two suspects."

Parker shook his head. "I don't know. Boyle asked me if I was ready, and I said yes, but then I told him I didn't see the other suspect. He said he was there as he was getting out of the car, before I had a chance to do anything. I don't know what I should have done..." He started to choke up.

"You did the right thing. You followed orders."

"Parker shook his head in despair. "It was all wrong. I knew it while it was happening, it was like," he paused for a moment, started to pick up his coffee cup, then decided against it. He looked straight at the Captain. "It was like he did it on purpose. I don't understand why he did that..."

"I had the same feeling. Do you think you should have counseling?" asked the Captain.

"No, I'm all right, really. Captain, let me interrogate the suspect. I'll get the truth out of him."

The Captain shook his head. "I said counseling, not therapy. We can't afford rough stuff. We go by the book on this one. I want the guy convicted. Murder One - Special Circumstances. I want him receiving a lethal injection, compliments of the State of California."

"I wouldn't use force, it's not my style," said Parker. "Not physical force. I was a psych major before I went into jurisprudence."

The Captain took a long drag of his cigarette and blew out a perfect smoke ring. "I watched you when you went over to the suspect. I knew what you were thinking. I would have too. You showed good discipline." He appraised Parker through the smoke. "We want this guy to talk. I don't think I could handle it if it had been my partner."

"With all respect Captain, I think I can."

The Captain gave him another long appraisal. "All right, we'll try. I'll put Jimmy Grady on with you. He's a good cop, level headed. But remember, the minute you start to lose it, you're off. Clear?"

"Yes sir," Parker answered, anxious to get back to the station.

***

Tracey Seebert, a slick young lawyer from Scanlon's retinue, was noticeably tense, her fine wool crepe shoulders drawn up around the shiny gold Paloma Picasso x's pierced through her ears. She sat rubbing her fingers together as she hunched on a chair, watching Jenny pack. She had been sent to pick Jenny up and expedite her departure. But she didn't feel comfortable here and wanted to get out as soon as possible. A few miles away a private plane waited to lift them away. Jenny shut the suitcase and the lock clicked with finality. Now she had to find Elizabeth, she wanted to make sure she would see her again. She loved her so much - felt such gratitude for what she had taught her.

"I love you too." grinned Elizabeth as she materialized and took Jenny's arm in hers. "Congratulations, you're getting out of here."

"How do you know?"

"Do I really have to answer that?"

They giggled. Traccy turned and smiled at the laughter but couldn't scc Elizabeth. "We've got to get going," she said with an apologetic smile. "We can't keep the plane waiting." Her tone didn't match her smile.

"Why don't you take a walk on the grounds while I finish up here," suggested Jenny. "It's pretty." She wanted to be alone with Elizabeth, and she couldn't talk to her with Tracey in the room, she would think she was crazy.

"Is it safe?" asked the young attorney.

"Don't worry, the ghouls and real crazies are let out after sunset."

Tracey's eyes went wide with calculation as she went over Jenny's words and processed them. She decided the smiling Jenny was joking and she shouldn't take her seriously. However, she didn't want to get caught outside in the dark, so she hurried.

Jenny and Elizabeth laughed when Tracey was out of sight. They had read her mind. Jenny felt a twinge of guilt. She hoped she wasn't abusing her newfound powers. At the same time, Elizabeth thought the same. They looked at each other and erupted with laughter. Jenny scolded herself not to behave like this, Elizabeth shook her finger at her, while Jenny tried to pull herself together. Feelings of love kept swelling inside her. "I'm going to miss you." Jenny wiped one of the tears that escaped from her eye.

"You don't have to." Elizabeth hugged her. "I can always be with you. Don't forget that." Her shining smile was enchanting, lines of golden energy surrounded her and stretched into a radiant halo that outlined her body. "Our relationship is special," she said, continuing to comfort Jenny. "We're soul sisters. We can always be together."

"But what about when I'm gone from here?"

"I'm not gone forever." She bounced down on the bed nearly toppling Jenny. "Look, I can always be with you, I'm a time traveler. All you have do is call me and we'll be together - whatever, no matter."

"But what if I forget?"

Elizabeth frowned. "That's a problem." She seemed to turn pale as she thought about it. "You will be entering major interferences. You're going to have to live life like an Earthling - a regular. If you talk about me or the things that you've learned here, most won't understand it and they'll get scared and call you crazy. You'll have to be careful because if that happens, then nothing you say will be believed or taken seriously."

"It'll be lonely out there," said Jenny with sudden misgivings.

"Perhaps - and maybe frightening." Elizabeth got up and walked toward the window. "I hate to lose you for now, but I don't want to compromise your time here either. When you were asked in the other world why you wanted to return to Earth, you said you had work to do and you must continue. You must find ways to do it. But remember, always stay with truth and that will make it easier."

"Can I work at the newspaper and use what I've learned? Go out of body? See the future? What a way to investigate stories !"

"Dangerous. Too much visibility. There are people who need what they believe is control, and if they think you have more power than they do, they'll throw everything they have at you and try to annihilate you. You'd be a threat and they'll do anything to silence you. You've had a taste of that already - that's why you're in this hospital. You are going to have to use the utmost of discretion to accomplish your mission."

Jenny shrugged. "I can't worry about anything personal. When my time's up, I'm ready."

"No fear?"

"Why? I know what's waiting and it's beautiful. I just don't want to have to go through another hell like the one wrapped around this learning experience. God, it was awful."

Elizabeth shook her head, a tiny frown of worry creasing her forehead. "Maybe, but you used it positively and learned a lot from it. Jenny, there are no guarantees. But don't leave your body completely till you've accomplished what you set out to do. Always go back to it. Otherwise, your life and all you've learned will have been wasted. You know what you must do and you'll join with others to accomplish it." She reached over and gave Jenny a hug and kissed her on the cheek. "And hurry up. I don't want to have to keep returning to Earth for you. This time should be enough." She started to leave, then paused. "Remember, even if you forget me, I'll always be there for you - in some way that knowledge shall be your security and your foundation." She blew a kiss and swooped through the window where she began stirring up wind around Tracey.

Jenny laughed, tears streaming down her face.

***

Parker looked around, then shoved the filthy man up against the wall. "Son of a bitch..." He drew his fist back to hit him but Detective Grady grabbed his arm.

"Don't."

"Dirty Bastard. Let me at him. Boyle was going to retire soon - son of a bitch - I want to kill him."

"You almost did," said the other officer, holding Parker back as he flexed and strained against the officer's hands.

"I'll make you a deal," the filthy man said.

"What? Take a bath?" Grady yelled at the prisoner. "You stink like shit."

"No lawyers. No trial. I plead guilty - second degree - do time, and that's it. No publicity."

"Second degree - you got to be kidding. If I don't kill you with my hands I'll personally inject you." Parker feinted an attempt to go for him again.

"Cool it - he might have something to tell us." Detective Grady took Parker out of the prisoner's hearing. "Good show, but back off a little. He's scared. That smell is coming from his pants."

Parker walked over to the man and motioned him toward a chair. The man backed away and sat down immediately. Parker opened a window and the door. "You stink. How can you stand yourself?"

"Close the door if you want information." The man had lost his cower, his trembling voice, his persona sophisticated and solid beneath the stench and rags. "I was paid to do that job. I did you guys a favor. Boyle was dirty. He was going to pin it on someone - probably you," he gestured toward Parker. "He's been on the take for years and my employees were afraid he was getting too hot."

"That's bullshit," yelled Parker, about to jump up and go for him.

The man kept talking. Parker settled down. "Think about some of your partner's actions. You're lucky you're alive Detective. That man was dirty. Greedy. Did you ever wonder why he overlooked details? About the way he sucked up to powerful people? Ring a bell? Huh?"

Parker didn't answer but stared, his fists closed, his jaw clenched.

"He was going to be investigated - drugs, arms - you name it. He was in a lot of people's back pocket. He was stockpiling money for retirement. This is one cop whose family won't need a benefit. They're very well taken care of - if they know the number of the Swiss bank account."

"You're full of shit - literally," said Parker.

"Keep going," said Grady.

"Look, you got me. I have nothing to gain from this besides helping you guys. Your partner would have been a big embarrassment to the department, and he could have dragged you down with him. You're lucky."

"Cut the crap. You have something real to tell us?" Parker said to him.

"I work for a group who like to have things their way. They say

279

they're non violent, and they guard their privacy. If you cross them, their punishment is fast and lethal"

"Why are you telling us this?" asked Grady.

"Because the minute they find out I'm arrested, I won't get life insurance. And I don't want to be tortured before I die."

"What do you want?"

"I give you solid gold information, make you look real good, and you protect me: new I.D., second degree charge so I don't get the death sentence, and I get lost in the prison system for a few years, nothing more."

"No promises. Give us a preview. We're going to record it." Parker nodded at Grady who turned the tape recorder on.

"It'll help me write my memoirs," a smile played at the corner of his lips. It ended with Parker's look. "Remember the television newscaster who killed himself on the 6:00 evening news?"

Parker nodded, "Go on."

"That wasn't suicide. It was induced by hypnotic suggestion and a new drug in development. Very suggestible drug. Works good, huh? The suicide served two purposes. He was a field test and my employers thought it would be good for their ratings - vested interest - but I don't want to get into that. That's not what this is about."

"Get to what it's about," said Parker, practically on the edge of his seat.

"Not long ago some girl, a scientist or something drove off a cliff in Santa Monica on to rush hour traffic. Neat huh?"

Parker froze. The other detective snatched a look at him and motioned the man to continue.

"No one expected the bitch to take so many with her. She got shot up with a version of that same drug and we were going to pull her into a van. But a cop car came along and I had to let her go. She got into her car and I guess you know the rest." He paused and looked at the other detective then quickly at Parker before he continued. "They had factored in a time provision for an unforeseen event and figured the worst that could happen was that if she ended up driving she'd hit another car or a post or something. The chemicals were too hot. They should have taken longer to kick in. They were supposed to be timed to take fifteen minutes but..." he shrugged and grinned. "Someone fucked up."

Parker made a note that the man had incriminated himself with the word, "I". Grady saw the note and gave him a sign he too had picked it up. "Anything more?"

The man shrugged and shook his head.

"We sent your prints to DC They're being put through the main frame now. You may as well tell us your name, it's just a matter of time."

"You won't find anything. I don't leave prints around. They can be changed - don't you know that? We're professionals - not common slobs like you guys."

A flush worked its way up Parker's neck. He used his discipline to keep from exploding. "Want to give us something to call you besides dead man?"

"John."

"Like in Doe?"

"That's right."

"You're pushing me..." said Parker, half out of his chair, ready to go for him again for real this time.

"You got the first two - guarantee me protection, second degree charge with parole, and put out a press release that I was killed. Then let me get lost in the system.

Parker would have liked to smash the man's arrogance, wipe out his face, but said to him instead, "We need names, more than what you've given us."

"You'll have them. It's all tied up with the group I work for. They have interesting plans on the drawing board for your futures. The clock is ticking."

"Sure, John. A conspiracy now? How about a global one, just like in the movies." chuckled Grady. "That's always a good one."

Parker pushed his chair back, his fists clenched tight. Since the filthy man mentioned Mannie, Parker wanted to grab him and pry every bit of information out of him. He knew he would be able to link Tim's death with this guy. It was almost the same MO as Mannie's. This guy might have information about Jenny too. What a strange piece of luck.

The man smiled and Parker leaped over to him and grabbed the front of his shirt, ripping it more than it already was as he leaned back to turn off the tape recorder. "Don't you even think of smiling, dead man. Understand? Just tell us what you know." He turned the tape recorder back on.

"You got the introduction. I don't give the rest till the deal is done."

"We can't promise you anything, cop killer, you know that. You're on videotape killing a cop. That's MURDER ONE with special circumstances. Santa Monica has eighteen more murders with your name on them now that you cleared Manuela Sebastiane."

"What do you mean?"

"You admitted you injected her. It's on our tape. You used her as a weapon. Very special circumstances."

The man stayed silent. He wasn't about to say anything else.

"You don't have a glimmer of hope until you give us enough information that could bring down the Pope."

"I have some Vatican scam material - but nothing about the Pope. He was on vacation," quipped the man. Parker pushed back his chair but before he could get out of it the prisoner held up his hands, "just kidding ! I'm talking about the government and the garbage that surrounds it."

"Yeah, you and every other two bit criminal." Parker didn't mean it. The guy might have something. He had mentioned two sensational deaths that looked like suicide. He would check out the coroner's report and see if there had been any evidence of drugs found in the newscaster. "What about Tim Jenkins?" Parker decided to ask. "Know anything about that?"

"Detective Parker. You want me to give away the jewels before the deal is negotiated. That isn't good business."

CHAPTER TWENTY-FIVE

Southern California had been having one of its infrequent thunderstorms as the private jet carrying Jenny bumped through the clouds covering the city. The flight had been incredible and she had discovered near the start of it that she was very hungry because she hadn't eaten for a very long time. Although she tried to be cautious and not over-do, the steward was delighted with her enthusiastic responses to his cooking and created a dinner that she said was "fit for a queen!" For the first time in what had to have been months, Jenny had a different feeling in her body, she felt re-attached to it now. The videocassette library of first-run films was remarkable, as was the audio book library of classics and current best sellers. The service far surpassed any she had ever had on a plane - commercial or private, and the flight passed so quickly she was disappointed when they started to land. It had been a fantasy, a floating carpet of elegance for the very, very, rich.

When she finally got to her apartment, Jenny was relieved that Clarita had come in and cleaned everything. She opened the Oriental window screens and fresh air entered the apartment. Everything seemed clean, sparkling, and fresh, yet there was still an undercurrent. Was it the memories?

She would have to move out of this apartment. She had originally taken it only for a short time from a writer going on foreign assignment. The apartment had been geographically centered between the newspaper office and Tim's home and could be used as a place to spend time when she wasn't with Tim. But then the writer decided to stay on the foreign desk and Tim had surprised her with tickets to Europe and they had turned it into a shopping spree for her new apartment. Some of her hopes and dreams died a little when she ended up with marble tables instead of his final commitment to set a date to finalize the ring on her finger. She had resented being considered part of his election plan. But that was all history and she had her future to deal with.

She put the chain lock on the door. This was it ! She was home. Her beloved desk, her computer - she could hardly wait to sit down and start to write - there was so much to say, so much to deliver. Yet a tiny speck nagged her - would she be allowed?

Jenny believed the warning about the destruction of this planet had been an invitation to add her voice to the growing concern that the Earth's resources were not being respected. At one time Jenny had studied the myths of Atlantis, a highly evolved society that was said to have inhabited Earth many thousands of years ago. This society was supposed to have been far superior to the present one in terms of sophisticated technology. Supposedly it had been able to harness crystals to the power of the sun. Allegedly this linkage led to a series of great explosions that caused earthquakes and volcanic eruptions among other disasters that ultimately destroyed not only Atlantis, but most life on this planet. If the myth was based in truth, then the fate of Atlantis could be a metaphor for our time, history could repeat itself. People could say she was crazy. Commerce would try to discredit her. And worst of all, she could get shut out of her public forum, her work, and the newspaper.   But she would try her best to write what she believed necessary. Clear thinking was adversarial to destructive behavior.

"Most people won't believe it," whispered the voice.

Defiantly Jenny ignored that and picked up the phone. She was going to call Rudnik and get back to work, but the phone was dead. It wasn't supposed to be turned off. What was wrong? She went into the kitchen to try the other one. It was dead as well. A cabinet door was partially opened. She looked inside. It was crammed with groceries. Who would have done that? She never ate at home.

Something wasn't right. Everything felt different. Perhaps it was she who had changed. But she couldn't be sure of that - not yet. Maybe this was just another hallucination or she was out of body again. Maybe this foray back to what is called reality wasn't real at all. Dread started to take over. "Get control," yelled the voice, "don't get scared, stay strong."

She took a deep breath and allowed the usually annoying sounds of her neighborhood - children yelling and horns blowing - to comfort her with their familiarity. At least something had remained the same. She started to feel better. The doorbell rang.

Slowly she went to the door, praying the nightmare she thought behind her had actually ended. Through the peephole Detective Parker, a smile on his face, stood with a bouquet of flowers that he handed to her as soon as she let him in. "This is probably against regulations, but, welcome back," he said.

"Thank you." The color rose in her cheeks and she was at a loss for words. She felt flustered, hadn't expected this. She motioned him to sit down, "These are beautiful. I'll put them in water. Can I get you anything?" and started toward the kitchen. "My kitchen is mysteriously filled with food. I've never had more choices to eat in my life."

It was Parker's turn to blush. He was glad she was in the kitchen. "Ah, the department, actually, I did that," he stammered.

"You did?" She popped back into the room pleasure and surprise beaming from her face.

"I thought it would be nice for you to come home and not worry

287

about shopping or having anything to eat. The manager let me in."

"That's so lovely, thank you." She came over to the sofa and sat down, overwhelmed. "I have to admit it scared me a bit when I saw everything in the kitchen. I couldn't imagine where it had come from."

"I'm sorry."

"No, I didn't mean it the way it sounded. I'm thrilled. It was only because I was having problems with time when I was in the hospital. I went from one reality to another. I'm still afraid I'm not really here, afraid I'm going to wake up and find myself back in that terrible hospital again. The things you've done could be a wonderful fantasy and if it is, I prefer not to wake up from it."

"You won't, this is real, I promise." Parker's smile was warm and gentle. It soothed Jenny's nervousness and embarrassment. "I can assure you, you're very much here." He started to put his hand out to touch hers but drew it back abruptly, cleared his voice and stood up. "This is actually an official visit. We would like you to come down to headquarters and look at a line-up. We have someone that we thought might have a connection with Mannie's accident. If you recognize anyone, perhaps it will strike some memory, some detail to connect with the last night you were with her. Think you're up to it?"

"Absolutely."

He went to the phone and picked it up. It was dead. Then he picked up the cord. It hadn't been plugged in. Tears of relief quickly sprang to Jenny's eyes. She was so grateful to him she almost couldn't stand it !

For the first time in her life she understood the meaning of topsy turvy. She was feeling that way and it was a terrific feeling.

Parker put down the receiver. "We have time for coffee, then they'll be ready. Okay?"

She shook her head affirmatively. She couldn't believe this was happening. She was scared, but happy, and also feeling hungry.

The bright lights and noisy din of the police station almost threw Jenny into a panic - the raw emotion and the contained violence reached out enveloping and attacking her sensibilities. It was only because of Parker that she felt any stability.

He held her tightly, guiding her through a maze of people: the victims, perpetrators, attorneys, and police; the stench of stale cigarettes and coffee, the sounds of ringing telephones, voices of anger, despair and grief.

They reached the sanctuary of a quiet, darkened room, it's haze of somberness changed with the flick of a switch. An interior window ran the length of one wall, separating it from another. The room on the other side had a raised platform Jenny figured was for the line-up. Although she knew the glass was one way as the six men filed in, she felt uncomfortable, almost conspicuous. They were all of similar height and weight - some scroungy - terribly so, and most looked like convicts. Jenny assumed most of them were policemen.

But there was one man, so disheveled and filthy it seemed she could smell him just from the way he looked. He also had a steady, quiet dignity that kept him aloof. Through the dirt he showed a strong discipline, and though he wore the ragged garb of the homeless, his demeanor belied his looks. Her eyes kept widening as she studied him, shuddering, disbelieving. Oh God. Can this be possible? Her blood ran cold. She knew who he was, she had recognized him almost instantly.

Parker snatched a look at her but she was still, unmoving. Jenny's head was locked to the window, the truth staring at her, waiting for

289

her to reveal him. Dare she face it? Could she turn to Parker and speak it? Could she tell Parker that on the other side of the glass was a horrible, filthy man who had seen her naked, stripped to her primal essence, who had entered her body and joined her in sex? She tried to take her eyes away from him and look at the others, but she couldn't. It was futile. She knew who he was and she had to tell the detective. She leaned toward Parker, her hands clammy, her body shivering and perspiring. "Is it possible to have number three put on dark glasses?" Her voice was thin and skittish.

Parker was placid professional, making no sign she had chosen the one they arrested. He lifted the receiver and made the request. Someone on the other side of the glass went over to the man at the place marked "3", and handed him a pair of dark tinted sunglasses.

The man who was in her apartment, who had approached her in bright daylight on the street and who had grabbed her in the garage, the one who blindly followed the orders of that doctor, was also her best friend's killer hours after he had tortured her. She felt like he could leap through the glass, revulsion and fear knocking her virtually speechless. She hadn't known the horrible truth till this very moment. The filthy man was her tormentor and rapist, and the blind man who killed Mannie. There was no mistaking him as she had before. He was both men, and she hadn't known it till now.

Questions piled on top of questions. How could she not have recognized him when she saw him in the deli? How could she not have known he had been her attacker? Had she been that rattled, that out of focus? Why had she never seen him, put the facts together when she had been out of body - if she really had been. How much had she missed, how much more had she misinterpreted? Pin pricks of dread stabbed through her whole being.

"Does he look like anyone you've seen?" Parker kept asking.

Jenny's head refused to move, shame and anger kept her rigid. She wanted to run, the man still scared her. What would he say - they had made love, her encouragement, did it matter? Anything said would defile and mortify her. She was skidding into denial, what could she be thinking? Tears no longer threatened, they streamed down freely.

Only a thin piece of glass kept her separated from the man who knew her naked, who had been inside her, who had rubbed his own naked skin against hers, who had felt her shudders, saw her pride, knew her pain tolerance. Sickness and conflict raged brutally inside her. Once again, he would mock her, once again expose her. She didn't want Parker to see this. Everything she had gained, she had lost. If she had recognized this monster earlier, she could have saved Mannie.

She shut down her thoughts, as a sigh came through her. She had to tell the detective the whole truth of what happened. What this man had done to her. She had to expose the extent of her exposure, reveal her dark places that had been opened. Did it matter that what happened had changed her forever? That stripped to the marrow and exposed as she was, her vulnerability was forever raw and open to terror. She lived with fear daily. She didn't want to tell him, she felt so ashamed.

Intellectually she understood that emotionally she was still his victim. Jan was no longer living, but this man continued to haunt her. She was so afraid to accuse him. Could she say only that he was the blind man in the deli? She turned still further away, mortified by her own thinking.

"Who is he?" insisted Parker.

"He's the blind man in the deli. I think he killed Mannie." She paused, then ... "He has other connections." She said quietly, then continued on quietly. "He wore dark glasses - had a red-tipped cane. He was the blind man that I told you who kept watching us and made me feel uncomfortable. I guess on some level I knew he could see us. I knew who he was. I had seen him before." Parker looked surprised. "Not at the time of course," she interjected quickly, "but now." She took a breath. "I know who he worked for and I know a name he used."

Parker was almost wide eyed with surprise at the extent of her knowledge. "What is it?"

"Larry Martin."

"How do you know that?"

Time stopped for a moment. She had to continue. "Because, he was used by ..." She opened her mouth but nothing came out. Parker waited.

"I know ..." she started, then stopped again, looking at Parker whose kind eyes were sympathetic and encouraging. Dizziness was overwhelming her, making her confession less concrete and easier. "He was a man who picked me up outside Anson Industries, kidnapped me and helped rape me in my home. He was under the control of Jan White, one of the supervising doctors at the psychiatric hospital where I had been hospitalized after the rape." She felt very light-headed, she wished she could pass out.

He looked at her steadily, then picked up the phone "Number 3." He smiled gently, "let's talk." They left the room and went to the coffee machines.

"Can I go home?"

"In a little while. I need some clarification on what you just told me. You dropped a bombshell you know. How about hot chocolate, it will make you feel better." She nodded and he pushed the hot chocolate button. "We want you to sign a paper with your positive identification. He paused and motioned her to sit next to him, handing her the paper cup. "Did you report the rape?"

"No," she answered. "But that was the reason they put me in the sanitarium. They said I attempted suicide, that 'my reality testing was impaired' - medical double talk for not behaving the way others thought I should act."

"Could that have happened?"

Jenny froze and looked at him, shivers of fear shaking her had stiffened in anger with his question. "I was set up," she said curtly, "I know what happened and why, but if I tell you, you might think I'm crazy. It's so outrageous, so insidious, that if I were on the outside maybe I would have trouble believing it." She turned away. She had thought it all was behind her and she no longer had to justify her behavior and feelings, but here was someone she thought she could trust, and now he too questioned her. Would she ever find peace? Did truth have to cost so much?

"Jenny," he said softly, leaning in to her, sounding comforting. "I know how terribly difficult this is for you. Your life these past months has been a nightmare. Keep yourself strong and you'll endure this. You're on the last lap now and it will soon be over. But I need you to tell me as much about that man as you know. It will help our case as well as your own sense of security. Trust me, I know it's difficult, but I'll try to lead you comfortably through this."

She wasn't sure she could believe him. She just wanted to get away, go home, and sleep till it was over.

"Your conspiracy theory is checking out, it's valid."

She looked up. Was she imagining this, was there a light shining around him? No, it had to be her imagination. It was the glare of the overhead fluorescence.

"The man you singled out is the one we have in custody. He's a hired gun," Parker told her. "We've got him on other charges. He shot and killed my partner."

"Oh no !" She shook her head, upset. "I'm sorry." Parker went on. "We might be able to get him for Mannie's murder as well as all the other's. Your testimony could help get him the death penalty. But first we want to know everything about who hired him."

"He was part of a team to make me psychologically vulnerable." she said.

"Rape as a political tool," he asked. When she nodded he wrote it down. His fair skin turned red and she noticed he gripped his pencil tightly, "Disgusting," he said, then he looked up. "The pieces are all coming together, making a lot of sense. I always thought some of these cases were linked." His blue eyes were deep and caring. "It will come together," he was saying. "But it won't be easy. We need your information, you've got to tell me everything."

"I'll try," she said.

***

The interrogation room was cramped and filled with a bad odor from the unwashed man. Some of the cops couldn't take it and left. Only Parker stayed close to him.

"O.K. Man of a Thousand Faces. We got a positive I.D. on you for kidnap, assault and rape with intent to kill. You admitted injecting Manuela Sebastiane moments before she died with some drug - we have you on tape with that. We also have you starring on videotape killing a cop. Now, Plastic Man, want to put on record what you carry in your mind? You're a dead man now, any way you look at it."

The filthy man stretched his legs out and pulled an empty chair toward himself with his foot. "Mind if I put my feet up? My circulation is killing me."

"Good." Parker kicked the empty chair away. "Then we can watch you die and save the taxpayers a lot of time and money."

"Hey," said the vagrant. "What did I do?"

Parker picked up a clipboard but didn't look at it. "I just told you. You're on tape killing a police officer, you're under suspicion in the death of Dr. Manuela Sebastiane and the resulting death of eighteen others, we have a victim who has fingered you for kidnap and rape - for starters."

The unwashed man threw his head back and winked. "Rape. They always call it rape - after. She loved it, asked me to come in her, got off on it, said I was terrific. Ask her. She had such a great time she couldn't stand it. You know how those broads are. Now she's angry and crying rape. Well at least she gave me a good time. Tell her thanks next time you see her." He ran his tongue over his filthy cracked lips.

Parker lunged for him and Grady pulled him back. The vagrant sat up, interested. "You seem to be emotionally involved, Detective. Perhaps you shouldn't be on this case. Conflict of interest here? Are you personally involved? Have you been bought like your partner? Have you fucked her? If she's who I think she is, she's very good..." He smiled, taunting...

Parker kept his anger internal, boiling, rushing. On the outside he was calm, his quiet menacing, his voice low so only the dirty man could hear him. "We're going to charge you with Murder One - special circumstances, kidnapping, attempted murder, extortion, everything we can possibly cram down your fucking throat. Do you hear me?"

The guy nodded. The smirk faded from his face.

"Are you going to tell us why you're taking the fall and for who? We want names. They can't get to you."

The man's mouth curled, his eyes narrowed. "The people I'm involved with can get to anyone - anywhere - any time. Believe me."

"Names," whispered Parker, coming closer. "Give me names and then you can go take a shower and get clean clothes; nice laundered and ironed prison issue so we can start feeding and housing you for the rest of your life." He came in closer. "Which might be shorter than you want." Parker walked a few steps away and turned back to him. "We'll keep you alive if you want to sing. If not," he shrugged, "it's going out you talked anyway. And if you're right about your friends, they'll get to you no matter where you are."

The unwashed man remained seemingly impassive, however, his eyes exposed busy calculation.

"You have five minutes. Then we put you out into the general prison population." Parker started to gather his things up. "How long you figure your chances of staying alive in there? Five minutes? Half an hour?" He checked his watch. "It's three o'clock now."

CHAPTER TWENTY-SIX

Three hours into the interrogation and the room smelled like an open sewer. Parker, and the two FBI agents had no intention of taking a break, and the defendant did not seem ready to crack. Parker changed his tack. "I gotta tell you JOHN, you'll be doing us all a favor if you give us names so you can get rid of those clothes and wash off that filth. I can't imagine how you must feel being that close to yourself... You'll be doing yourself a great favor." He looked at the two impeccable FBI men, looking as fresh as they had when they first entered the room. "Us too." Parker could have been cast as an insurance salesman in a Mutual of Omaha commercial. He couldn't have sounded more honest, more down home wholesome, more all-American.

The filthy man wasn't buying it. He knew Parker was as tough and cold and manipulative beneath that simple act as he was himself. "Give up my life for a bar of soap?" sneered the man. "Think I'm a Jew in Auschwitz?"

Parker thought for the umpteenth time he would lose it. He really wanted to wrap his fingers around the bastard's throat till his palms touched. The misery the man had caused, the human lives he had taken, the traumas he brought, the vast emotional destruction he represented! Yet Parker forced himself to stay calm. A lot could be riding on this man's information. He would have to do everything in his power to get him to talk. "I told you, as soon as you give us the names, we'll have the D.A. in here cutting you a deal." He turned to the Feds. "If that's all right with you gentlemen." The two federal agents blinked their assent, a look not wasted on the prisoner.

The man realized that if he didn't compromise soon, it was only a matter of time till the FBI men left the room and the monster would be unleashed from Parker. At least, that's what he would have done if their roles were reversed. Unexpected behavior overpowers an opponent by catching him off guard and thus weakened. "How long do I wait for the D.A.?"

"He's here."

"I wash first."

"You gotta be kidding," said Parker. He nodded toward the door and it opened almost immediately. Ed Wiseberger, a handsome politician who had recently been elected D.A. and was now starting his campaign for Governor elegantly sauntered in. He nodded to the two FBI men, started to say something but stopped as the onslaught of offensive stench permeating the room reached him. Pulling a monogrammed handkerchief out of his pocket, he held it to his nose and looked at Parker in surprise. Parker shrugged and suppressed a smile. Totally ignoring the prisoner he addressed himself to Parker. "Uh, is there any way we can take care of this uh, problem - before we talk?"

Parker shook his head no, very slowly. The D.A. read the warning in his eyes and girded himself, sitting down opposite the foul man. They sized each other up carefully - both costumed for their respective roles, both confident in their ability to outmaneuver and outsmart the other. Born con men - one taking the high road, the other - the lower.

"O.K. John Doe. What have you got for us?"

"You tell me what you have for me first," countered the prisoner.

"Life without parole," answered the D.A. smoothly.

"No good." The man's lips twisted in anger.

"Okay., it's Special Circumstances - death penalty in each case unless you talk to us." He pushed his chair back and started toward the door. A moment's pause, only the clock ticked, as everyone watched the D.A. reach for the handle.

"Congressman Leef," tossed out the prisoner. "Life sentence with chance for parole..."

"You've got to give us more." The D.A. took his hand away but didn't move from the door.

"Concurrent terms with chance of parole will give you corporate names as well as government," bargained the prisoner. "Look, I'm a professional, I'm hired to work for those guys. I don't give a shit for their politics. I take their money and do the job. That's it. But I don't want my competition hired to take me out. You give this case any kind of publicity at all, you won't have to fill the needle because I won't make it there alive."

"That's right," agreed Weisberger. "You don't give us names we hold you for murder-one - right in the middle of the general prison population."

"My life expectancy should be less than two hours."

The D.A. looked bored, shrugged.

The prisoner hesitated, but started talking the moment he saw Weisberger begin to move again. "Okay Mr. District Attorney, come back. Here are the keys to your political future. Remember me when you give your next acceptance speech, because your prize witness is about to rub out your competition. But first - I want to see your deal in writing - officially; You won't put me in the general prison population, I want to represent myself, writing privileges, private television set, access to books, telephone, four hours of exercise, no talk of the death penalty, eligibility for parole, and while you're having that typed up I want a shower."

"You get a shower WITH a bar of soap after you give us what you know. You can start singing after you sign." The D.A. mumbled something into the phone and within seconds an aide appeared with an official document. Weisberger scanned it a slow and agonizing time, handing it to Parker who was able to speed read it. "Well," said Weisberger. "Is it all right with you? I know it sticks in your gut, but..." He handed it to the two Federal agents who scanned it together.

Parker bit his lip, angry, then tossed his head. "Make the deal - it will be good to see him go stir crazy."

The agents nodded in agreement and handed the paper to the prisoner. The man scanned the paper, went back over it, weighing every word. The D.A. sat back comfortably, cracking his knuckles. Parker stayed poised on the edge of his chair. The two FBI men remained unflappable, their eyes darting from the prisoner to the D.A. to the detective. No one dared say a word. Were it not for the incidental noise of the street and the outside hallway, they would have been able to hear each other breathing.

The prisoner put the paper and pen down and stared at the D.A. The professional politician made a point of checking out the condition of his manicured nails. The man picked up the pen and Parker leaned toward him, willing him to sign. But once again, he threw the pen back down and picked up the paper to read another clause. "What about parole?" he asked.

"I put 'Best Efforts', that's all I can legally do," mumbled Weisberger, flicking a speck of nothing off his perfectly tailored lapel.

The man's face seemed to darken, his lips twisted, his fist opened and shut. Once again he picked up the pen, hesitated, then slowly - ever so slowly - signed a name to the document. The D.A. snatched the paper and left the room. An inaudible sigh of relief ran through the room.

Two policemen brought in a video recorder and tape recorder. They set it up quickly and quietly while everyone else filled their coffee cups, took off their jackets and settled in.

"I'll be glad when this is over so I can breathe again." Parker said then read the prisoner his Miranda rights for the camera. On video and audio-tape the man waived his right to an attorney.

"Shall we start with the television reporter who committed suicide on the evening news?"

The man leaned back and smiled, relishing the moment for the dramatic response it would elicit. "Seth MacDonald, Chairman and CEO of Larkin Communications," he said in loud deliberate tones. "He hired me for that hit when I was working for a company developing surveillance and," he couldn't contain a snicker, "other forms of technology. Good hit, huh? Looked like suicide."

Parker's eyes narrowed, his mouth twitched as he wrote the name down with three question marks after it. Even the two unflappable FBI agents looked around as unease rustled throughout the shocked room. Seth Macdonald one of the most powerful media moguls in the country had just been given one of the White House's greatest honors, the Presidential Service Award in a ceremony that was broadcast nationwide.

"What was the name of the company you worked for?" asked Parker.

"Anson Industries."

Parker's pencil nearly dropped. "Who was your immediate superior?"

"Robert Jordan."

A flush spread over Parker's face. "You went directly to the CEO?" He used discipline maintaining his composure.

"Yes."

"Will you directly state his position."

"Why? You already said it." He shrugged then looked directly into the camera lens. "Robert Jordan is Chief Executive Officer of Anson Industries."

"What kind of work were you doing?

He leaned back smiling, knowing he had dropped a bombshell. "I told you, security, surveillance..."

"Details, John Doe - your requests run high." Parker said through clenched teeth.

Although the room was hot and airless and the men inside had long since become accustomed to the putrid smell, they sat in rapt attention as the filthy man began to tell a similar and sordid tale of uncountable wealth, unaccountable greed, and lust for power that closely matched everything Jenny Webster had told Parker.

As the digital clock clicked to 4:30, streaks of dawn managed to filter through the smudged windows that peeked through a mountain of Styrofoam cups, soft drink cans and overflowing ashtrays. The prisoner's voice droned a tale of such immorality, that the men who listened could find it hardly recognizable. But nevertheless, they were spellbound in rapt attention as his story unfolded.

"Senators Brume and Hunt and Congressman Leef were at the last meeting," repeated the man, his tone impatient, his throat husky with fatigue, his voice heavy with the drama he was creating.

"Can anyone corroborate that?" asked Parker, his shirtsleeves rolled up, his usually pink face a color similar to the mess spilling out of the ashtrays. "Do you have video or audio tapes?"

"Yes, I have them. But I'm not sure they can be found unless my sentence is commuted."

"Not possible." Parker was quiet, patient. The FBI men gave him an approving nod.

The exhausted man stopped. He didn't want to continue, but the smell and the stress and the time was reaching unbearable proportions. "What the hell - it's my patriotic duty to pull the scum down." The video and tape recorders seemed to rumble and shake as he continued.

CHAPTER TWENTY-SEVEN

Dawn was quickly turning into daylight as Parker leaned on Jenny's bell. Announcing himself he then ran up the stairs two at a time to get to her door. Sleepily she opened it and invited him in.

"Here's some coffee." He opened a bag with two paper cups. "I want you to be awake to hear this." Jenny led him into the kitchen. "What is it?"

"The guy talked. He named Robert Jordan, Seth Macdonald, Senators Gerald Brume, Lloyd Hunt and Congressman Erik Leef. Do any of the names besides Jordan's mean anything to you personally?"

She nodded. "Well sure, besides being well known public figures I interviewed some executives from Larkin Communication, and then of course, you know I had interviewed Jordan the day that…"

"Yes," he interrupted before she'd have to explain. "But if Jordan ordered that, it doesn't seem likely he would let it happen on Anson property. Doesn't make sense."

"Exactly why it was chosen. reverse logic."

"Perhaps. Go on."

She hesitated. "I could tell you my suspicions about some of the people you mentioned, but it isn't evidence."

"Then tell me about Mannie."

Jenny took a deep breath. "Okay. I've done a lot of thinking and piecing things together. I have Mannie's external hard drive before any of this happened. She had mine. We exchanged them in case something happened to them. There was a diary, notes, correspondence - you know, private things. Anyway, with that help I put together this scenario: Mannie had alienated the other scientists in her lab because she wasn't a team player. So they decided to make her one."

He looked at her quizzically.

"They needed a human fetus to develop full term outside the body. Mannie objected, thought it was too soon. They could have merged any egg and sperm in a Petri dish, but they decided that Mannie might lighten up if she went though the beginnings of pregnancy - it started as a joke. So they drugged her and impregnated her using a vial of their collective sperm - they did that so no one would feel personally responsible."

Parker looked genuinely shocked. "That's disgusting."

She shrugged. "People have different perceptions of humor. Anyway, as soon as Mannie conceived, they were going to retrieve the fertilized egg and start the experiment. But something screwed up and they had to wait three and a half months before the artificial womb was ready. Meanwhile, Mannie was unaware anything was happening - except she felt miserable and didn't want anyone to know it. Including me."

Parker pulled the plastic cover off one of the cups and spilled coffee on the counter. Jenny got a paper towel and started to mop it up, but Parker took the towel from her and she continued talking as he took over the mopping. "When Mannie found out she was pregnant and what they planned to do, she wouldn't go along with them. They tried to pressure her saying she had reverted to stereotyped behavior and was turning her back on her scientific responsibilities, but she remained adamant. So they decided to give her an operating room drug that would knock her out so she wouldn't remember anything, but would leave her ambulatory. That way they'd get the fetus and would accuse her of having a false pregnancy when she realized she had lost the baby."

He shook his head. "It doesn't sound feasible, too amateur. Couldn't sophisticated scientists find better ways to conceive a baby? I'm sorry Jenny, but it sounds ridiculous."

"I know, but I'm pretty sure that's what happened. It was a mixture of arrogance and cruelty. That man you have in custody - Larry Martin or whatever his name is, worked for Anson and injected her with the drug that caused the accident."

"We know that, he confessed to it. We have it on tape."

"Good," her eyes teared up but she was able to control them. "They did it to retrieve the fetus from Mannie. I don't know what happened but for some reason after she was injected Mannie managed to drive away - and then you know what happened..." She shuddered, "a slaughter."

"That's pretty close to the prisoner's story. A police car had parked near them and he couldn't pull her into the van without arousing suspicion. So he let her go."

Jenny slowly shook her head. "Because I left her alone at the restaurant people were maimed and killed." Her eyes filled with tears as she stared into space.

"You can't blame yourself for that." He wanted to touch her, comfort her, but left her alone.

She let her breath out. "Why didn't they kill me for knowing what Mannie did? They must have known she told me."

Parker's eyes narrowed. "Maybe they didn't." He frowned. "You can't blame yourself for any of this -." He seemed to shiver a little. "It all seems unreal."

"Mannie tried to keep as much information from me as possible, but..." She closed her eyes, then opened them a moment later, hopeful. "Do you think her baby could still be alive?"

He smiled gently. "Jenny, I'm sorry. It never had a chance."

"I guess it was a dream then..."

"Mannie was four months pregnant," consoled Parker. It isn't possible a fetus could survive a trauma like that - nothing could. You have to be realistic and accept the worst."

Jenny reached for her coffee. "I'm sorry if I sound bitter and self pitying, but I think I have accepted the worst."

"I know you have, I'm sorry."

He looked so sweet, so sincere that Jenny felt like crying. "I'm sorry, I shouldn't have said that."

He took her hand gently, "We could be apologizing to each other for days like this. I know what you've gone through, believe me, and you handled it splendidly." He paused, "but Jenny, tell me, why the conspiracy? Why the elaborate technology? What's really happening?"

Her hand was tingling, warm from his contact. He was so kind, so caring. He had said all along that he wanted to get to the root of Mannie's accident. She was sure she had found an ally. She took a deep breath to steady herself. "Anson Industries," she hoped he would believe this, "is manufacturing human beings - flesh and blood designer humans."

A long pause - he searched her face, looking for a sign she was kidding. She wasn't. He tilted his head. "Are you sure?" He finally asked, whispering as if he didn't want anyone else to hear them.

Her eyes met his and she went on. "They're creating different types of humans - genetically, and they've set up a manufacturing process to create them."

"Humans? Flesh and blood?" He looked at her, then off to the side, across the room.

She nodded. "Have you ever read "Brave New World", a book by Aldous Huxley?"

He thought for a moment, "Yes, in high school."

"Well, Huxley foresaw a society that was divided into categories, workers with mental limitations but physical abilities to do menial work, managers who were a little brighter to tell them what to do, and the top of the pile - the ruling class."

"Yes, I remember..."

She sat back. "If you're **in** the wrong class, no matter how hard you try, your genes will never let you get higher - no matter what."

"Right, but that was fiction, science fiction."

She looked straight at him. "Detective Parker, remember the space shuttle and the space stations that Isaac Asimov wrote about?"

He looked like he hadn't but she went on anyway. "Asimov's fantasies are now very much reality. It is the same with Huxley's Brave New World. Except our society has not yet succumbed to that level of mass mind control. But believe me, the people at Anson and other places are working on it and they're not far from achieving it."

Parker stared at her. She looked so intelligent and she was speaking in such a clear and rational way, but the things she was saying... Perhaps the guys at the station were right. She might be a bit out of kilter, still traumatized by the things that had happened to her. He had better proceed with what he came here to talk about.

"Genetic engineering has made the manufacture of different types of humans possible," Jenny was saying. "It's been in development for years and is now ready for commercial application."

Parker leaned toward her, "Jenny, I'm not taping this because it sounds - well..."

"Unbelievable! But completely feasible if you look at it scientifically. Since genetic engineering we've had the power to create and manipulate different kinds of life. Our scientists are playing god. It's natural for them to want to take the science further. It's what Mary Shelley warned of in Frankenstein."

"Yes. Clifton's records say you were hospitalized for..."

"Schizophrenia. That's what they labeled me to discredit my attempts to expose what they were doing. It's an easy diagnosis with the things I was saying - mind reading machines, thought producing technology. That's classic Schizophrenia. And I told you about the transponder implants they're putting in fetal and babies' brains that first night when I told you about Mannie."

"Yes, but why would anyone need that clumsy technology if they were about to manufacture humans with predetermined abilities?"

asked Parker. "Why use implants if they can do it from the moment of conception?"

"Because it's going to take at least two or more generations to cover the planet with manufactured human creations. In the meantime they have to gain control of the existing populations. They're starting with the leaders and people in communications, that's why they tried to use me."

"Yes, I see your point. Good logic." His hand was shaking as he put his cup down. "Uh, Jenny, that brings me to..."

She interrupted. "Scientists can now add or delete certain pieces of genes that decide intelligence, physical and creative abilities. So now, instead of being born on the wrong side of the blanket or the tracks, a human being will have their destiny determined by the whim of a medical technician."

Parker looked at her somberly. "This is very big, you know. Explosive."

"Yes, I know."

"I knew it was bigger than I possibly imagined when we got that confession - but this goes beyond anything I envisioned. Jenny...." He seemed shaken, undecided. "Are you absolutely certain?"

"It's happening under the corporate guise of Research and Development." Jenny felt herself getting excited. He was trying to believe her, trying to accept what she was saying. If someone with his intelligence and sensitivity could help her, they could cut off the head of the organization. She was feeling happier, relieved, he was going to believe her. Tears started to come to her eyes again but this time they came because she felt grateful, vindicated.

Parker started to sit down, then changed his mind. He handed Jenny a napkin so she could wipe the tears from her eyes. "Uh, Jenny, I have to tell you something."

"Yes?" She looked at him, her eyes shining, her smile brighter and happier than he had ever seen her. And even though her face was wet with tears, they added a luminance, a glow and sparkle to it. He turned away and busied himself, wiping the edge of the counter top. "This is going to be very hard for you."

"Oh, these aren't unhappy tears, I'm very happy. I know the difficulties facing us. I'm a realist. But if we can get those people and prevent what they're doing, we could divert what would be one of the worst human disasters that has ever happened. I'm not sure anyone other than a few will ever know about it, but think of it's ramifications, think of how many millions of people we're saving. If I weren't so shy, I'd throw my arms around you and hug you."

Parker blushed. "Jenny, I understand how important this all is..."

"Important?" she interrupted. "It's monumental! Thank God for giving me the strength to survive and find somebody like you to help fight this." Jenny was radiant, practically floating with excitement. Parker felt uncomfortable.

Jenny became quiet. "I know this won't bring Tim or Mannie back, or maybe even my trust for a very long time. But at least incredible good has came from these sacrifices." Her voice cracked.

Parker choked up as well. "Jenny," he cleared his throat. "I don't want you to take this the wrong way. I believe you, but there are many people who won't."

"I know that. It's all right, I understand."

"Yes, except."

"Except what? You don't have doubts? You can't have them now."

"Well, of course I have doubts until I see proof. Doubts go on till the proof comes in. Look, I want to believe you and..." He could barely go on.

"And?" She smiled, waiting.

"Except, well... This is hard."

Her smile started to fade. "What is it? Come on."

"Jenny, you've given us a hell of a lot. You're like - a heroine! The heroine of this whole thing."

She giggled and touched his arm. "The heroine! You're a romantic! Do you know that?"

His face went bright red and he moved away from her. "You've uncovered something incredibly big, except." He stared at his feet. "I can't tell you how much we, I, appreciate what you've gone through..." His voice broke.

Uneasiness started creeping over her. What's he trying to say? Why is he so uncomfortable?

Parker finally looked her in the eye. "You've suffered more than anyone deserves, but..." He cleared his voice. "It may be more difficult for you."

"What do you mean?"

"Jenny, I know how you want to be a part of the investigation. But you can't, we can't let you. We'll have to be distanced, you can't be involved."

"What?" Disbelief shot through her. Who says I can't?" Her face began to cloud. "Why?"

"You're going to have to keep a very low profile. You should not cover this for the paper, go anywhere near it. In fact, I don't think you're going to be able to testify."

"What? What do you mean? I'm probably one of the only eyewitnesses you have. They've killed everyone else. I'm totally involved! You may not have a case without me."

He steeled himself. This was hard. "That's a chance we're taking. But we think it's better if you stay away. Believe me Jenny. I know what I'm saying."

"You know what you're saying? I have incredibly important information. I've lived this! I've seen so much - so many things, things that no one would possibly dream of having happened." Her face was turning pale, almost translucent. "I can't believe you're throwing me away like this, discarding me like some disposable nonentity. I can only think you don't want to solve this!"

"I'm sorry. It doesn't come from me."

She nearly lost her temper and fought to keep it down. She spoke softly, quietly. "Then where is it coming from?"

"They." He stopped.

"THEY what?" She demanded, her eyes burning.

He returned her gaze, his eyes soft and sad, a hint of tears in them. "They think you're crazy."

The words hit like a club - exploding in her face, breaking up, shattering into thousands of little pieces of matter and sound bites. "Crazy? She could barely speak. "You think I'm crazy?"

"Not me. I told you."

She could hardly hear him - pieces of the word were still falling through the air. "Who?" she managed. "Who thinks that?"

"The system. Law enforcement quarters are not secure with this kind of thing."

"What thing! Dealing with mad women - Like me? I know what you're saying."

"No, Jenny. You're taking this - well, yes, I can understand how you feel - but you have to understand that anything you say will discredit our findings."

Her breathing stopped. Water dripped from the faucet, the shine from it's metal almost hurt her eyes. The detective had gone out of focus, the floor was moving, undulating, imitating the waves of dizziness coursing through her body. Insanity's stain had already cost her almost a year of her life. She had really started to care about this man, and now he was acting like the rest. She had to fight back. "I could give you leads," she managed. "I know so much about this."

"I'm sorry. This was discussed at the highest levels."

"Highest levels - you've got to be kidding..."

"Jenny, we think it's for the best. That's why I came here. To tell you what was decided."

"Decided," she said. "You've decided, like Robert Jordan and his cronies deciding what is best for everybody. Is there any difference between you or Jordan's group wielding your power? Who says you're capable - or they are - or even if I am? You people say I'm crazy. What do you think I feel about you when you throw away valuable information? That isn't a sane or intelligent action."

"Look Jenny, I understand your anger."

"I'm not angry. I'm astounded. How can this happen? I've lived this case, lost, two people I loved very much because of it. But I never backed off till you guys found that man who can prove everything I said is happening. And you need me to testify against him."

"No, we're going to plea bargain him. Look, You have us wrong. Believe me."

"How can I? I know where the records are in the hospital, what has been done with all the experiments. Hell, they tried them on me. I remember them! All that pain, all that suffering and you have an eye witness you don't want to use! Incredible!"

Parker stood silently, shaking his head imperceptibly.

"Please," she was starting to cry. "I think you'd better leave."

"Look, Jenny we want your information, we need it. I didn't say that we didn't. All I said was you were going to have to stay low profile. You can't be involved. If we do it can cause problems."

"Problems because I know the truth born of insanity. I understand you want to use me expediently. It doesn't matter what I've done or can do - just take what you want when you want it. No different than

Larry Martin, except this time the rapists leave the clothes on."

Parker stood stiffly, clutching the counter. "No you have it entirely wrong. It's..."

"Sounds like I don't. Sounds like I'm a police department public relations problem. Please. I don't want to hear any more of this. Just leave my apartment."

He scraped his chair back. She didn't look up. Her heart pounded heavily with hurt and betrayal. She heard his footsteps leave the room, cross the living room, and the sound of the door as he opened it and went out. The door clicked shut.

After all she had been through, all she had learned, how could this possibly happen to her? She walked over to the counter and started to clean up. Parker had left the morning newspaper. She opened it up. Robert Jordan's picture stared out from the center of the top of the page. The headline read that his company Anson Industries had just bought one of the three major television networks, creating one of the largest communications conglomerates in the world. "WHAT NEXT?" said the headline and under it were listed all the different companies and interests the company had under it's umbrella; covering almost all the needs of modern civilization. Would this newspaper be next?

If she was kept away from the investigation and could only give them one-dimensional information, many could lose because of it. If the police department's public relations didn't want her to be seen, that was no problem. But she couldn't stay at home with the doors shut and not helping. She couldn't wait for the police to come when they hit a brick wall. No, they needed someone to go through those walls, clear the paths, show them the way. She was trained. This is what it had all been for.

She closed her eyes. A white light swirled in the middle of her forehead. She could feel a buzzing, a vibration in the top of her skull, whirling and lifting her up off her body, through the kitchen wall into the living room, past the front door and down to the sidewalk.

Parker was heading for a car parked a few feet past her apartment building. The shaking rippled up through her body. She could see him so clearly - as clearly as if she were next to him.

Parker checked out the street. There was stillness, yet he had an unsettling feeling. He reached the car and pulled out his key and put it in the lock. He stopped. A cold breeze had swept over him. He was tired. He needed a shower. Perhaps a half hour nap before he went back to the police station. He slid into the driver seat, not really seeing anything except the ignition. He stifled a yawn and buckled his seat belt.

"A nap's a good idea Detective Parker. Perhaps then you'll think clearly."

He looked up and grabbed for the door. He couldn't believe it. The voice came from Jenny. She sat in the passenger seat of his car.

"What! How did you get here?" He looked around desperately."

She smiled. "Believe me. I know how to help you. I can keep a very low profile, Detective Parker," she smiled at him dazzlingly. "An invisible one."

THE END

EPILOGUE

THOSE WHO SEE A VISION THAT IS WITHHELD FROM THOSE LACKING THE NECESSARY EQUIPMENT FOR IT'S COMPREHENSION, ARE REGARDED AS FANCIFUL AND UNRELIABLE.

WHEN MANY SEE THE VISION IT'S POSSIBILITY IS ADMITTED. BUT WHEN HUMANITY ITSELF HAS THE AWAKENED AND OPEN EYE THE VISION IS NO LONGER EMPHASIZED BUT A FACT IS STATED AND A LAW ENUNCIATED.

SUCH HAS BEEN THE HISTORY OF THE PAST AND SUCH WILL BE THE PROCESS IN THE FUTURE.

Printed in the United States
149835LV00003B/66/P